MOVING MEN

by karene horst

Flying Trees Publishing

Published by
Flying Trees Publishing
www.flyingtreespublishing.com
First Edition

Cover design by Ajax Zero

Identifiers: Library of Congress Control Number: 2021938644
ISBN-13: 978-1-955552-00-4 (e-book)
ISBN-13: 978-1-955552-01-1 (paperback)
ISBN-13: 978-1-955552-02-8 (hardcover)

to my fourth grade teacher, Mrs. Flanders

1

I found Johnny and Ellis on the ride home from WAL-MART that blistering hot summer afternoon.

Or maybe Johnny found me.

Any other day I would never have stopped. I wouldn't have given them more than half a look. I'm not that stupid. I don't need trouble from strangers pacing the side of the road even if plainly wrestling with a crippled engine or out of gas, emergency blinkers flashing. Someone else would throw them a rope. A woman driving with a child pulling over to pick up two hitchhikers? Two men? Hell no!

Except that was not just any other day for me. They could have been crooks or jailbirds; I didn't care as long as they could help me get the job done.

It seems long ago, but I guess not much time has passed as I remember everything clearly. I sweltered inside the truck cab while Mitchell snoozed. His head flopped back and forth with every bump in the asphalt, the rest of his body held snug by the seat belt straps.

The two figures shimmered in the distance like a mirage. Rootless. Drifters. No ties to a community.

I can still picture them to this day. Standing near some weeds along the highway, they had raised their fists when they saw my pickup in the distance. I didn't know their names at the time; they told me later on.

Johnny stood straight and tall as a walnut tree someone would chop down for a fancy veneer cabinet. Ellis, the skinny redhead, stuck out his thumb while he shoved his other hand underneath his T-shirt to scratch his belly. Johnny's light brown arm extended level with the pavement as his thumb pointed toward the cloudless sky.

By the time I drove near enough that they could peg me as a lone woman, they gave up. Johnny's arm lowered the slowest. A measured decline, one inch per second. Ellis kicked the gravel as he fiddled with the hem of his T-shirt.

Maybe they'll do.

I swallowed and the baseball lodged in my throat since the night before started to roll away.

Maybe they'll help me fix this. Maybe I will end up living happily ever after.

I eased my foot off the gas pedal as I blew by. I steered onto the shoulder several hundred feet farther south. Mitchell stayed asleep. Ellis skipped toward us in the rearview mirror. Then came Johnny.

Johnny's swift strides matched the rhythmic swing of his arms as he aimed for my truck. He reached the closed tailgate and hurdled over it. While jumping, he grasped the tailgate with both hands and launched himself in a sideways sort of leap so his feet would clear the metal barrier. He was big: more tall and lean than stout, but he looked as if he harnessed the power of a steam engine. Quite a sight, seeing a man that size move like that. The pickup bed rolled when his boots hit the metal surface. The cab shook but didn't wake Mitchell. His head just lolled in the opposite direction.

Johnny squatted after landing, resting on his haunches

but at the ready to hurl himself back the way he came if necessary. Only his eyes moved as they scanned the tops of the pin oaks scattered along the deserted fields of over-grazed fescue creeping up to the highway. He didn't peer into the cab at Mitchell or me. His unwavering gaze seemed to possess a purpose as if collecting vistas to file away for some future use. I latched onto Johnny, tucking him up my sleeve like an ace.

Ellis scurried toward the passenger side of the truck bed, climbing on the rear tire and crawling over the side into the back. He flung one scrawny leg at a time over the edge, then tripped and fell on his butt. He grimaced as he glared at the palms of his hands before flailing them in the air then patting them lightly against his T-shirt. The sun-baked metal of the truck bed must of scorched his hands some.

After he stopped fussing with his hands, Ellis struggled onto his feet and scampered across the ribbed truck bed to poke his scraggy face into my window. Blackish-red bristles erupted around his chin and along his jawline. Patches of freckles streaked across his skin, leading a wild trail from his face down his chest, then under his shirt sleeves to run up and down his arms. My Mitchell calls people with freckles "spotted."

Ellis panted and wheezed through his gaping mouth. A sour milk odor coursed through my nose and I winced.

"Hey, thanks for stopping for us. We been trying to flag a ride at least an hour. Been hoofing it the last half. Hotter than hell today, if you'd excuse the language, ma'am. Had a ride, but they would only cart us so far, let us off by ..."

He would have babbled on for another ten minutes or so if I hadn't cut him off. "Where you wanting to go?" I tossed my words at him over my left shoulder like salt for good luck.

"Could you drop us off near Carlton? Well, we're shooting for

Milesdale by tomorrow," he paused to gulp a lungful of air. "If you could get us to Carlton, I'm sure we could hitch from there to Milesdale real easy. And we would sure appreciate it, ma'am." He finished by flinging his head as if for emphasis, his fingers floundering between his pockets and his empty belt loops to his greasy bangs, which he swept off his sweaty forehead with a jolt.

He probably thought it a polite gesture to call me "ma'am." That always makes me feel old, someone addressing me as "ma'am." I'm only thirty-six, almost thirty-seven. I'm not a ma'am yet, am I? My grays don't show too badly, and I still wear my dirty blond hair long, same as when I was a teenager. And I figured he was about my age. You couldn't ignore the crow's feet stretching from the corners of his eyes and some gray strands of his own. So I didn't appreciate it all the more.

"I'll take you all the way, but first I need help with moving ..." My voice lost its footing and ended in a whisper. I cranked myself around as much as possible for a better view of Johnny. I scoured his eyes, praying for a ledge or a limb I could hang onto without slipping. For a second, the bricks on my chest shifted and my heart quit racing.

Ellis' reddish-blond eyebrows skyrocketed and his mouth sagged open as he gloated at Johnny.

Johnny's face registered a blank. Not dumb. Just nothing. No happiness, no sadness. No anger, no pity. No niceness, no emotion.

Ellis jerked his hands to his face, stuffing his hair behind his ears, and then plunged them toward his waist to smooth his T-shirt over his slight potbelly as he turned to me. He responded for the two of them as if he'd received some sign, some secret signal from Johnny issued by the tiny creases leading from his eyes or a twitch of his lips. If so, I'd missed it.

"You mean you'd drive us all the way to Milesdale? That would be great. Awesome! Indeed!" Ellis' eyes widened, his head pumping up and down as if I'd handed him a winning lottery ticket.

"Sure." I didn't share his enthusiasm.

"We can help you move whatever you got to move. And you'll take us to Milesdale. We just gotta be there by tomorrow at the latest, well, by tomorrow lunchtime would be OK. Tomorrow morning? My, my that would be very good. Yes, yes, very good indeed." Ellis went to town on the jumble of tangled shoulder-length hair he rearranged with both hands.

No way would I put them up for the night. "Tonight. I'll take you there as soon as we're done. It's only two o'clock," I said.

Hauling them to Milesdale meant at least four hours of driving. Each way.

Will my ancient truck make it? I can leave Mitchell with Sadie. Have to anyway to break free of this mess, no matter how many miles I gotta travel.

I eyeballed Johnny, crouched in the back of my fifteen-year-old Ford, the gooseneck hitch rusted out and the paint so sunburnt you could call it black or you could call it dark blue.

They made an odd pair. A tall, silent black man with no expression and a thin, bent, scrap of a man who needed to shower, shave, and brush his teeth or at least chew on something sweet-scented.

Once they sat in my truck bed within arm's reach of Mitchell and me, I shuddered.

What have I done?

The truck cab separated us and provided some protection. Sure they could have smashed through the glass window behind my neck. But if I gunned the engine, then slammed my foot on the brake and swerved the steering wheel left then right, the rocking motion could fling both of them away and just maybe catapult them out of the pickup bed into a crumpled, bloody mess on the side of the road.

I took a deep breath that cut through my chest like a sharp blade.

Calm yourself girl! Stop freaking out. These two mean no harm.

I wanted to believe that these strangers did not pose a threat. I had to. I was in danger all right, but not from Johnny or Ellis. And right then, they were all I had to protect me from worse.

Ellis plopped cross-legged, his back pressed against the rear window of the cab. He rapped his knuckles on the steel floor as if to say, "let's go." We sped off, steering away from the shoulder to the tune of tires crunching gravel and shattered shards of plastic and glass. The movement chucked Ellis sideways until he steadied himself with one hand clutching the edge of the pickup bed as he wedged his body into the corner. The tattered black straps of a dull kelly green backpack hung from his bony, rounded shoulder blades. A wad of clothes and a sorry collection of odds and ends tried to escape through an opening in the broken zipper.

Johnny carried nothing I could see. Maybe he had stashed something out of sight in the pockets of his jeans. Hunks of forearm busted out of his denim shirt below the rolled-up sleeves. His kinky hair close-cropped. His jeans and buttoned work shirt frayed and faded, yet he tucked his shirt into his pants and laced his boots all the way to the top through each eyelet, no cheating. Solid, that Johnny, like a huge boulder a raging river couldn't budge. A soothing sensation hinted I could count on Johnny. Between the three of us, we would muddle through. I seized this lifeline, maybe my last, my only chance to keep from sinking.

The sun roasted the air and my throat burned with every breath. A hotter than hot June. Hotter than June's supposed to be. Johnny didn't break a sweat. Maybe slightly near his hairline, although I couldn't detect it. The truck rumbled over the pavement, and the vibration shook the mirror so I could barely focus on him. He wasn't even gripping anything. He balanced himself in the middle of the truck bed, resting on his tailbone with his legs bent in front of him and feet planted firm, his elbows propped on his knees, his palms fused as if in prayer. The vehicle lurched, but he held fast as if carved in stone. He leaned into every bend in the road. He appeared quite at home in the back of a pickup.

Ellis clambered onto his knees, clung to the side of the bed with both fists, and stuck his head out past the cab. The wind peeled back his eyelids and whipped his hair about his face. A flea-bitten hound dog thrilled to tag along in his master's vehicle. I could not get my fill of studying the two of them, but I had to keep my eyes on the road or we would have wound up in the ditch. I settled for sneaking a peek through the rearview mirror now and then. A gust of the burnt-rubber stink of skunk poured through the windows; I sucked in a lungful through my mouth instead of my nose.

We coasted until I reached the gas station at the turnoff to Englewood. Then another four or so twisting miles to Willisburg where we live. Mitchell and I that is. A town of fewer than five hundred souls. I grew up here, but I won't be here much longer.

2

Our two-bedroom sits on about a half-acre of cedar trees and thornbush strangling each other quietly out back, while gobs of crabgrass and hard-packed dirt in front separate us by about twenty feet from Judge Weaver Lane. The street where we live's on the other side of Willisburg, so you have to drive down Main, past the brick post office, Larry's Tavern and Juke Joint, three gas stations, Hearts & Kisses Gift Shop/Flea Market, the one-story local branch of Central Savings & Loan, Willisburg's tin-roofed metal-sided sad excuse for a city hall, and several boarded vacant storefronts and such. If you try, you can spot the ivory-colored Butler buildings of the elementary, junior, and high school that sit back a couple blocks off Main. Now that they hauled off the charred shell of the diner that caught fire awhile back, you have a great view of the single-wides in Newton's Trailer Village, with its pit bulls and mutts in chainlink pens or tethered to stakes in the dirt yards, and laundry lines strung up between the roofs with underwear and stained T-shirts flapping.

Not many out that afternoon. Too hot. An old lady clasping her purse to her chest hobbled toward the senior center, located in the basement of the Sunshine Baptist Church off Main on Dogwood Court. Mary and her retarded daughter Lucy definitely would of hidden inside their trailer to dodge the heat. Most other days you could expect to find them walking single file along the main drag, Lucy plodding five to six feet behind her mother while clutching her rag doll and a bag of pretzels or marbles or crayons she showed off to anyone who tolerated her for two seconds of attention.

At the intersection where Velva's sold beer, bread, frozen stuff, and canned goods with only a few dents, I made a left on Briar Avenue, which narrows into a zigzagging, partially paved, mostly graveled road called Judge Weaver Lane. Decades back, they named our dead-end street after a state judge who grew up on a farm nearby. A couple years ago, they arrested him after discovering in his basement a box with photos of naked young boys. He spent one night in jail, then surprise, surprise, the charges got dropped.

I really can't wait to bail out of here.

We bumped along until I turned into our driveway of scattered gravel and weeds. Clouds of fine rock dust billowed and doused me, cementing with my sweat and leaving a gritty paste on my skin. I parked in front of the garage with its aluminum sliding door jammed halfway open, so you have to duck pretty low if you care to go in and out. But you can't. Years of clutter blockade the opening. Can't park in it because of the busted door and because the garage is full of junk. Crap I can't let go of. My whole damn life I've held onto shit I should have carted to the dump. Get off your ass and have a yard sale, I scolded myself as if I were just having another normal day, home from work or errands in Cliff City, planning what to heat up for Mitchell and me for dinner or what we could watch on TV before bedtime.

I switched off the engine, and the sudden silence and stillness must have woken Mitchell. He blinked as he lifted his head from the cushioned seat.

"How you doing, baby?"

I always say that whenever he wakes after napping during a drive, his brains rattled from tossing this way and that. We had zoomed away from the WAL-MART parking lot right before siesta time, that early afternoon lazy spell when I would gladly snooze myself if I could relax and quit thinking and worrying about everything for ten fricking minutes.

"We home?" Sleep coated his words in that tone that sends my heart spinning.

He coaxed his drooping eyes to open wider. He's a dear boy. Sweeter than milk chocolate Kiss candies. Slivers of green speckle his gray eyes. Sandy hair similar to mine. Skinny like I used to be. A sloping, turned-up nose. He gets that from his daddy. I don't know where he got those eyes. They don't run in my family. I only remember his daddy's eyes as dark and angry, swimming in liquor.

I unhooked his seat belt. He can do it himself, but I baby him sometimes, especially after he's just woke up. His hands fumbled with the strap as he freed his shoulder. He reached for the handle and prodded the door ajar with the tip of his sneakers. My breath snagged in my throat as I glimpsed a miniature-sized man strutting about in his seven-year-old body.

Ellis scrambled out of the truck bed and trotted over to the driver's side window. He jabbed his head forward and back like a chicken pecking at a corncob. He shoved a fist in one pocket and smacked his chest with the other as he concentrated his blood-shot, watered-down blue eyes at me, his eyebrows dancing a silly jig above.

"Let me introduce myself and my esteemed partner. Name's Ellis, and this here's Johnny." He delivered his speech while pivoting from side to side as if speaking to an audience of more than me. Johnny didn't stir even when Ellis barked his name. Johnny squatted in the pickup, his gaze glued on something I couldn't see.

I signaled with my hand for Ellis to move away so I could climb out of the truck. He skittered backward in a jarring manner. I scooted out of the driver's seat, and as my feet landed on the gravel, a pointy rock gouged against the sole of my right flip-flop. I leaned onto my other foot as my eyes flitted over him before I told him my name. I tipped my head toward Mitchell while saying his. Smart to stick with first names.

"What are you having us move?" Ellis' question sprung from his lips in a giddy tone despite his attempts to sound business-like about my proposal. As if he couldn't take anything serious. He yo-yoed from one foot to the other. He jiggled like a human bobblehead. He swung his limbs backward and forward like a toy soldier. If Momma were alive, she would have murmured, "That boy's got ants in his pants." He squirmed or shuffled or strummed his spindly fingers through a wad of greasy red hair matted to his scalp. His hands traveled continually: to his pockets, to his bangs, to his forehead to scratch an itch. He'd clap his palms against his hips before hooking his thumbs through his belt loops, unhooking them and then cramming his hands into the pockets of his jeans. After he finally found a spot where he could commit them for two seconds, he started tapping his toes in rhythm with the throbbing screeches of the thirteen-year cicadas that had crawled out of the dirt with the unseasonable heatwave. Millions of bugs with nothing to do but fuck and die.

"We're moving today?" Mitchell asked. He yawned while glancing sideways at Ellis, who pulled out his hand to examine his fingernails before proceeding to chew on one with his crooked, tobacco-tinted teeth.

"No, sweetie. Hop inside," I said. It's my sitcom mom routine. You know, the one where the TV mother parades through her tidy, designer-decorated home ready to bake cookies or dish out witty advice that inspires her adorable children to roll their eyes as the studio audience laughs stupidly.

Doubts began surging from my gut and wedging in my throat. I had to trust these two unfamiliar men. Completely.

What the hell was I thinking picking them up, bringing them to my home?

But they seemed so perfect. That crazy lady locked in my skull shrieked, "They're nobodies! They're not from around here. After you ditch them in Milesdale, you'll never see them again." Her less batty buddy repeated what I'd comforted myself with for the past fifteen months. "You're leaving soon. Splitting for Colorado to start fresh. Tammy has a one-bedroom apartment and can help you find work. Hang on!"

I met Tammy loading and unloading machines at a Cliff City dry cleaner ages and ages ago. She's earning a steady paycheck. She says Mitchell and I can stay a while with her. Says she's got a pullout couch in her living room where Mitchell and I can bunk until I nab a job and a pad of our own. Mitchell's almost excited about it, although he has his reservations he keeps to himself. He's a lot like me. I'm so glad he's nothing like Mike.

Ellis coupled his jittery movements with a refrain he delivered in a high-pitched voice that quickly grazed my last unjangled nerve. "So what are we moving, where we got to move it, where's it at, where's it at?" He clasped his hands behind his back. He rose onto the balls of his feet, then rocked back onto his heels over and over again, while repeating his jingle in time with his rhythmic swaying. His seemingly innocent questions boomeranged around my skull until I could of started screaming.

I wrestled with a sudden urge to swat him as I would a gnat. "It's in the garage." I snapped. I'd known Ellis less time than required to eat your lunch, and I'd already found him way too annoying.

Ellis jolted to a stop while he gawked at the garage. His mouth slumped. His body rigid for almost two seconds. Then he resumed his strange performance, this time jogging in place while rolling up an edge of his T-shirt with his fingers.

“All that stuff? Well, that’ll take forever!” Ellis whined, disappointment wrenching his face into something even uglier.

“No, just one thing. The freezer.” I gulped, trying to ignore the thumping in my temples.

“A freezer? Shoot, that’ll be heavy. Where do we have to move it? We got to move it somewhere else? Or move it inside? Up those stairs? Where you wanting it moved? Well, we could use your truck. You got a dolly or something, maybe some extra boards to roll it into the truck or up the stairs? How far you needing it moved?” His words poured out like cornflakes from a cereal box.

“Would you shut up one minute! I’m trying to think, damn it! I don’t know where. I’m thinking on that,” I said without thinking.

Mitchell’s eyes widened as he edged away, remembering it best not to mess with Mom when she cusses. He turned and dipped his head, hoping I couldn’t tell what he was up to. I knew just what he was up to.

“Don’t pick your nose,” I muttered for the ten-hundredth time. Mitchell lowered his hand but kept his back to me while he inspected the tip of his finger in private.

Ellis’ face broke into a you-gotta-be-kidding look, and he shoved his fists back into his pockets, pulled them out again, and rubbed the back of his neck. He paced and kneaded his back as if he’d already strained it from just the prospect of relocating my freezer. Then he swiped his brow with his wrists and investigated the sweat he’d corralled before wiping his arms on his yellowed T-shirt that sported a once-fire-engine red racing car flashing past a graying checkered flag.

Johnny raised himself upright from the pickup bed and surveyed my garage and what little he could see stored within. Mounds of wilting cardboard boxes, a lawnmower that only blows smoke before it dies, and a headless broom handle clogged the opening. Mitchell's tricycle with the bent wheel buried under boxes of Momma's moldy curtains that I swore to her on her deathbed I would hang in my own home someday. I just can't make myself throw out those floor-to-ceiling drapes she slaved and saved to buy, but Father refused to hang.

"Well where the heck is it? We gonna have to dig all this junk out to get to it. I ain't sure about this." Ellis strutted across the driveway, swelling his chest, playing like the man in charge.

He wasn't. We all knew who was in charge. Ellis just had to put on his show. I ignored him so he couldn't goad me further.

Johnny still stood straight and tall in the truck bed. A calm draped across my shoulders like a shawl. One more deep, pain-free breath and my shoulders relaxed.

The door to the garage faces the side entry to my house. The freezer rested next to the door inside the garage. We could drag the freezer outside, make a sharp left between the garage and the concrete steps that lead to my house, then out to my pickup. I could back in, parking the tailgate closer. That alone would spare us a few yards of backbreaking labor.

"Over here." I waved toward the side door.

Ellis followed me. Johnny remained in the back of the pickup and watched. I dug out a single key from my front pocket, jiggled it into the ancient keyhole, and wrangled with the corroded metal knob as I tugged on the wooden door.

Ellis cupped his palm to his mouth and snickered, "What's we got here? She's locked the door!" His shoulders shuddered and shrugged with a phony, noiseless laugh. "That'll fool them tricky burglars!"

Johnny relayed no sign he even heard Ellis.

Since earlier that morning, that locked door had provided me the tiniest peace of mind by erecting one more hurdle for prying eyes. Tons of crap barricaded the yawning entryway, preventing anyone from tinkering with the freezer. The only thing standing between the freezer and the outside world was that scarred door that barely hung on its hinges and wheezed when its warped wooden edges grated against the door jamb while I joggled it loose. Before that night, I'd always left it unlocked and a tad ajar as the door tended to stick when latched. I usually propped a shoe-sized rock alongside to block the door from swinging wildly in a fierce wind.

I tugged the door open. Ellis fluttered about as he sidestepped me, making a production of hoisting his arms high so as not to touch anything and steering around me before poking his chin through the entry for a peek.

I bought the freezer at a used appliance shop maybe five years before, and it was pretty old to start. Once upon a time, I'm sure it had been a brand-spanking-new white. On that particular summer afternoon, it looked like someone had spilled sour buttermilk over the top and let it drip down the sides. Chipped paint, dents, and scuffs from its drama-filled past smudged the exterior surfaces. The freezer had a tarnished chrome-plated latch smack-dab in the center to seal the lid. A sticker once pasted on the front then torn away had left behind streaks of dirt-encrusted glue and jagged strips of discolored paper. It was a mid-size chest freezer. Four feet long, three feet high, two-and-a-half feet deep. I scored it after cooking up big plans of planting a vegetable garden and storing tomatoes, beans, and strawberries. It ended up stocked with pizzas I bought during Velva's two-for-the-price-of-one sales or days-old bread, frozen vegetables and such from the food pantry when I mustered the patience to stand in that line.

Surely two strong men could move the freezer.

Ellis stretched his neck to gawk at all I'd socked away. His roving eyes scouted for something worth sneaking to a pawnshop, I bet. I marched through the door to the freezer. I reached out my arm to begin removing the near-empty cans and containers I'd stacked on the lid the night before. I stopped, my hand arrested in midair.

"We can haul it in the truck. We just need to load it up and ..."

I'd no idea how to finish. They didn't seem to care what I had to say anyway. By then, Johnny stood directly behind me. He had moved so silently I hadn't heard him coming. Hadn't heard him climbing out of the pickup. No crunching of gravel under his boots. I hadn't heard him utter a sound since I picked them up from the side of the road. Not one peep.

After leaving the truck, Mitchell had sprawled on his back and basked in the sliver of shade from a pin oak that leaned against the shingle roof of our rental house. Once Johnny reached the garage, Mitchell bolted up onto his knees as he observed Johnny's huge frame blocking his view of the doorway.

Even with his low-key ways, Johnny projected a presence that inhaled all the spaces surrounding us. Despite his fidgeting and fussing, Ellis almost disappeared. Johnny examined the freezer, nothing else, but he noted everything. He nodded.

Then it hit me like a blast from an ice-cold draft. I had found the right man! All the crying and fretting through my sleepless night, and now here it was, The Answer to my prayers! No more nightmare. He would take command. I had a certainty of this so intense I could taste it, roll it on my tongue and swallow it whole if I wanted.

All of a sudden, I felt dizzy. Woozy. The blazing midday heat congregating inside my garage smothered me with its damp woolen blanket, and I closed my eyes.

Then a blurred image of Mitchell hovered inches above me. His mop of hair dangled toward me as it framed his face. His lips twitched. Tears threatened to fall as his wide-open eyes darted around mine. The sun-drenched sky behind him formed a halo. I giggled and told him I mistook him for an angel. He clenched his fright a couple moments longer before a smile tiptoed across his lips.

"I thought you was dead," he said in a loud murmur. His breath wetting my cheek whispered the scent of the salty potato chips he'd munched for a snack an hour earlier.

What? Why does he think that?

I floated somewhere else, someplace where my worries and problems could not track me.

"She fainted, she just fainted, that's all. I'm ready to faint too. It's so hot! Do you have anything nice and cold to drink?" Ellis asked as he dawdled on the porch with his fist grabbing the handle to my screen door, swiveling it in both directions without pulling it open.

Kneeling at my side, Mitchell shielded me from stray shafts of sun that pierced through the branches overhead, his hands clinging to my arm. Then he tilted his head upward at Johnny. "Sir, would you help my mom up?"

Odd how Mitchell called Johnny "sir." I didn't even know he had that word in his little boy's vocabulary. I never heard him call anyone "sir" before, not that we mix with any guys who deserve the title. They had barely even met, yet Mitchell instantly demonstrated a respect for Johnny. He didn't appear anxious about this stranger. He knew Johnny for who he was: someone we could trust. How did Mitchell figure out that?

My mind drifted in a daze. I'd no idea what had hit me: why the ground rested beneath my back rather than under my feet. Withered dandelion stems tickled my neck, bare arms, and legs, as someone had placed my body on a grassy patch beneath the sweltering canopy of the massive sycamore, the only grand tree that survives in this yard. Ellis must have guessed correctly. I didn't recall how I wound up there, so I probably fainted. I didn't want to get up.

Johnny knelt beside me opposite Mitchell. He must have broken my fall or picked me up and carried me from the door of the garage and out of the sun, protecting me from the burning heat of the afternoon glare. His eyes greeted mine. Such beautiful eyes. A rich brown. Dark chocolate with sprinkles of a paler color same as chopped nuts surrounded by vanilla ice cream. They said nothing. I could have been gazing into a hot fudge sundae.

Johnny extended his hand. Large, calloused, rippling with muscles. I grasped it. Energy surged through his fingertips as he lifted me to my feet, supporting my back with a light though firm nudge.

Thankfully I'm not the type to have worn a dress. I brushed bits of grass from my cutoffs and collected myself. I'd lost a piece of time, and I glanced around while I smoothed my T-shirt with my palms. Maybe I could find it again, like a barrette that's fallen out of your hair. Fainting's not like sleeping. You have no warning. All of a sudden you're down, then you're somewhere else when you come to. Maybe fainting is like dying, but you don't come to. And you do end up somewhere else. I have never fainted before or since. I don't recommend it.

Then the clanging of an alarm quickly cleared my head and sharpened everything into focus. Ellis had walked into my home.

“Stop! Wait one minute!” I wailed as if my cries could force him to retrace his steps.

Mitchell sailed up the stairs and caught the screen door before it banged shut. Johnny lingered by my side. I no longer gripped his hand, although I sensed I could reach for him if the urge struck me. Mitchell, my perfect gentleman, held the door for us.

Ellis had already opened the refrigerator, and I found him rooting through our food. I dashed into the house with a who-the-heck-do-you-think-you-are face. He straightened, displaying his palms to prove they were empty.

“Hey, I’m trying to locate me something to drink is all. A tall glass of lemonade maybe? We can all use something. Water would suit me fine. Too hot to be without something cold to sip. Johnny and me been in the sun for the worst part of the day. Sorry, sorry. My throat hurts like I’ve eaten a bucket of sand.” He thrust his chest forward and didn’t strike me as the least bit sorry, lecturing me as if I had no right to confront him even in my own home.

I shook my head as if I could unfetter my brainwaves. Was I the one stepping out of line? I wasn’t sure about anything except I needed Johnny and Ellis. I needed them badly.

“Sorry.” I stared at the floor.

Ellis veered back to the refrigerator, acting miffed but satisfied he’d made his point and won that bout. He swung the door on its hinges as he studied the budget-brand containers of food I’d shoved into every available space. “Nothing but TV dinners and, what's this, ice cream? Why ain't the ice cream in the freezer?" With his pinching fingers, he plucked up a thawing plastic package of peas, once hardened into a clump.

"The freezer's full," Mitchell said as he eyeballed Ellis, placing his tiny fists on his slim hips.

"You mean the freezer out there we're suppose to move?" Ellis scanned the shelves, plopping the limp and dripping sack of peas on a mound of partially frozen food cartons.

"Nope. Mom moved that in here last night from the garage freezer. She filled this freezer in here and then put the rest in the fridge." Mitchell only repeated what I told him earlier that morning when he opened the refrigerator for milk to soak his Cocoa Puffs, unleashing an avalanche of bags and boxes of once-frozen chicken pot pies and vegetables.

"Then what's in the freezer outside?" Ellis directed his question toward the ceiling as if only God would know. He no longer directed his questions toward me. I must have pissed him off, and that was fine by me if he conducted his conversations with the wall, the kitchen cabinets, a shriveled potted plant even. I'm not friendly to strangers, and I'd decided I didn't like Ellis at all. It's amazing how we can sum up a person in a matter of minutes. And how that person can tell exactly what we consider them worth.

Ellis resumed his banter, babbling to himself. "Now, we've got a freezer we gots to move, and it's running, yes sirree that's what we gots here. Plugged in and humming away." He shuffled and scratched his oily scalp and the scruffy hairs on his chin. "We gots all the goodies from that freezer in this here freezer, then why's the one outside still on?"

Mitchell's face crinkled into a puzzle. He couldn't answer. Then the creases in his skin melted. He didn't appear concerned about these two newcomers now in our kitchen. Not that I have a lot of company these days. He's a polite, trusting child, and he rarely challenges my actions or grills me with too many unnecessary questions. Doesn't pester me about why the trees cast away their leaves every fall or how come the spiders hide behind his NASCAR posters to die. Mitchell busies himself with his own notions mostly. He's a quiet boy. I like that.

I chewed on a fingernail. What did he reckon of all this, of these two odd men who had hopped out of the back of our pickup and invaded our kitchen? Mitchell never had a man in his life who showed him some respect. One who wouldn't trash him about stupid shit. Mitchell's father never came around much and yelled a lot when he did. Yet he'd been the only man in Mitchell's childhood. I had no idea what he thought about me toting those two home. He never asked me anything about them.

"Excuse me, sir," Mitchell said as he slipped past Johnny into what I refer to as the family room, although it barely has space for the television, the couch, a heavyset coffee table, a square end table, and Momma's claw-foot loveseat, let alone a family.

I never heard Mitchell and Ellis chatting together. Still, I doubt Mitchell ever addressed Ellis as "sir." If Ellis were a cartoon character, he'd be drawn up like a weasel. Maybe a smartass monkey even. Mitchell had already figured Johnny was different. He's an intelligent one, my Mitchell, and he'll go far in this world.

Just quit this shit now. Stop chasing your tail, fretting over everything and anything.

I fanned away the fog swirling about my wits, charged past Ellis, and slammed the refrigerator door.

Ellis straightened with a jerk of his neck, his hands slapping his thighs as he rolled his eyes and let out a dramatic gasp. Then his features dissolved into a pout over the loss of the appliance's cooling gusts. He opened the freezer section, allowing the frosty current to cascade over him as a bag of frozen French fries tumbled out and plummeted to the floor. He squinted his eyes and jutted his head toward the ice-crusted fringes as he inhaled the frigid air through his gaping mouth.

"Don't hold the door open! You're letting out all the cold. Idiot!" I muttered the last word as I grabbed the fries and crammed them back into the freezer.

Ellis darted from the refrigerator and started to pace and scratch his scalp again. Any other day I would have silently prayed he didn't have lice. That day I couldn't give a damn if he had cooties.

"Well sorry. But if everything in the freezer out there's in here, then why's the freezer out there, the freezer we're moving, why's it running? You squirreling some ..." he licked his lips as he scowled, "fudgesicles from us?" For a moron of a man, he suddenly demonstrated a keen curiosity.

Ellis' clamor had no effect on Johnny, who had planted himself by my kitchen sink. Johnny didn't acknowledge the broken cabinet door hanging sloppily on its hinges or the curling wall calendar celebrating April daffodils. He stood motionless, offering nothing.

I could stop Ellis' nonstop yakking and exaggerated gestures by sloshing something down his throat.

He's just a loser. Ignore him, girl. Calm down. Just breathe.

Ellis swerved toward me, slanting his head as if peering at me through bifocals for a better view. The top of his head cleared mine by an inch or two. He raised his hand to his chin, toying with his whiskered cheek as he cradled his elbow in one palm.

"What do you have in the freezer out there in that there

garage?"

I sucked in my breath. How had Ellis zeroed in on me so precisely?

I couldn't just stare stupidly at him, my lips quivering and my knees starting to buckle. I had to quench his interest somehow. "I'll unplug it when we move it."

His question dangled unanswered, but Ellis spared me further heckling. Maybe Johnny shot a glimpse that shushed him.

I could no longer stand still anticipating Ellis' next offensive or another anxiety attack to snare me. I kicked into gear and busied myself with a can of apple juice from the refrigerator and a plastic pitcher. Completely thawed, the juice blended instantly with the lukewarm tap water. I searched the cabinet for cups and plunked four mismatched ones on the counter. I accidentally toppled one into the sink. I clung to the counter and the jug's handle as the plastic mug bounced and clattered to a halt against the pitted porcelain. My hands trembled like an old lady's.

"You should sit."

My jaw flopped open. He talks! Johnny had a mellow, soothing voice projecting prairie hills at dusk. Not a deep, booming voice to fit his towering height, his broad chest, his outstretched hands the size of dinner plates. He spoke clearly, no slurring or mingling of one letter to the next. After his silence, his first words startled me. I'd almost pegged him for a mute.

Johnny gingerly freed the pitcher from my grasp and finished pouring juice into the four cups. Ellis snatched one and slurped. My brain reeled and went blank. I slumped into a chair at the kitchen table and picked at a dried-on mottled glob with my fingernail. Johnny strode to the table and set a drink in front of me.

"This will help." Again, words in a tone foreign but reassuring and from a man so refreshingly unfamiliar in my life. They rang true. Johnny did not possess a tongue that would lie or speak in anger. Nor speak unnecessarily.

The words and the world started whirling in a frantic dance. Tears welled as my throat tightened. How many glasses of apple juice would I have to drink to swallow this lump without choking?

As a child, I raced home after school and flew into Momma's embrace before sitting at the kitchen table to eat cookies and apple juice. I hated milk, so she served me cookies and juice instead. Sometimes graham crackers smeared with peanut butter, sometimes homemade chocolate chip cookies, sometimes the stale discounted ones she scored at Velva's, but always apple juice. If I straggled home sobbing because the school bully poked fun at my buck teeth, or sad because I couldn't have a shiny new bike like Amelia Patterson's, sugary treats and apple juice fixed everything. Made me happy. Made things better.

My momma would hum into my hair as she hugged me. Then Father would wander in shouting about nonsense, emphasizing his point by knocking over a stack of magazines Momma stockpiled to thumb through while waiting for water to boil or for the casserole to cool. He'd ignore me unless he identified something to holler about at me. Momma and I would stare into our laps or at the floor to skirt eye contact, praying Father wouldn't rope Grandmother into the fray as this would only spray gasoline on the fire. After his tirade ended, he would storm out of the room, letting us whisper about our day while I sipped on my juice and munched on my snack.

"Did you see Mr. Taylor's garden? The geraniums are

blooming so pretty with the rain from yesterday. And what do you want for dinner tonight, honey child, spaghetti all right? How's that book we checked out from the library last week?"

Sapped of all interest in me, Ellis slunk into the family room to join Mitchell in front of the television. Ellis' sneakers crunched stray Cocoa Puffs as he stepped. He screeched to a halt and lifted his foot to scrutinize the rubber sole. He shuffled his shoe over the linoleum to scrape off the cereal crumbs, wriggling his arms as he grimaced, and then stomped through the doorway.

What the hell's wrong with me? How could any sane woman allow two total strangers into her home? What was I thinking?

I wasn't thinking at all. And maybe, anyway, maybe I'm not all that sane.

Yet they hardly appeared dangerous. You couldn't take Ellis seriously if you tried. He pranced about like a fool or a court jester. A lame animated joke with no punch line.

Johnny, now he reminded me more of, well I would have to call him a gentleman. I bet you're saying, huh? A gentleman doesn't hitch rides in the back of a truck. A gentleman doesn't associate with a goof like Ellis. A gentleman would have his own car, a tailored business suit. A career that would cover his club membership and five- or seven-course dinners. You would certainly not find a gentleman bound for Milesdale, a nowhere sort of town with only one gas station that doubles as a pawnshop with bicycles and scratched guitars in the barred windows, a shuttered factory, some warehouses, and a railroad depot that welcomed only an occasional freight train. I don't believe they even have a church. Still, yes, yes I would definitely describe Johnny as a gentleman. Not the kind with a silk hankie in his pocket and a Rolex on his wrist.

Despite every icy stab of doubt, a peaceful breeze shooed away the disturbing jitters swarming me. Johnny would not hurt me. He would not allow anyone to hurt me. Johnny and Ellis would not, could not harm me, not in the way you might imagine. They would not beat me or rape me or touch my Mitchell. I seized my hunch about Johnny as I would a shield.

Then those hysterical voices bubbled up. "Oh yes they can hurt you." They could have ruined Mitchell and me. They could have destroyed us, taken everything, and I'm not talking about that sagging puke green couch across from the television. I seesawed between feeling safe and secure to feeling unsure as if rocking from one foot to the other.

Can I trust them? Can we get the job done? We have to. We just have to.

I had no faith in Ellis, not one bit. Johnny, however ... Right then I had no choice. They were all I had. I needed them.

Johnny was perfect. He didn't budge or say anything unless absolutely necessary. He passed no judgment. He angled his head as he drained his cup of juice with tranquil, even swallows. I followed the line of his neck. The curve of his caramel-tinted Adam's apple. He could have been twenty-four or thirty-four. Smooth and full, his features even-toned without a worry line or a blemish. His jaw shaven without the blisters and bumps from the ravages of a dull razor. His skin didn't have the grooves, the roughness, the toughened look of scuffed leather. He didn't have the life milked out of him, leaving his shoulders rounded and soft like Ellis. Not Johnny.

He set the empty cup on the counter. No excess movement. No useless words. He stationed himself where required, only performing whatever circumstances deemed essential. His calm swept over me, reassuring me that everything was OK. Practically normal. Just another listless, hot summer day with apple juice, flies buzzing overhead or crawling across the grimy windowpane. House chores, errands, and meaningless matters craving attention. Just like everybody else and his brother. I shunned the twinges in my gut Ellis had triggered with his badgering, and they wandered away.

Then someone rapped twice on the kitchen door, and my eyes bugged open.

Who the hell can that be?

I don't get many visitors, except for Sadie or maybe every once in a while a pair of short-haired missionary boys in their dark slacks, buttoned shirts, and wide ties.

Please Lord, not now. Not today of all days!

3

“Who is it?” I almost knocked over my nearly full cup of apple juice. A splash of pale orange splattered onto my stiffened fingers as I grasped the cup to keep it upright.

“Deputy … it’s … u-um … Harold. Harold F-foster. K, you alright?”

I shot out of the chair and vaulted to the door as he finished, my chest heaving. “What are you doing here?”

We had left the side door to the garage gaping open.

“Well, I was,” he gulped, “driving by and, actually it’s p- police business. Needed to … er … stop and ask you about Mike.”

Deputy Sheriff Harold Foster stood on the middle step to my porch, his shoulders slouching as he twisted the brim of his brown felt deputy’s hat with his hands. Sweating buckets in his khaki uniform, he glanced at me before his eyes plunged to his hat.

My name’s Cathy with a “C.” Harold calls me “K” instead because he stutters so badly he mangles my name. He grew up here in Willisburg like me.

We went to prom together because I needed someone, anyone, to escort me that night. Harold jockeyed to rein me in for the slow dances. I kept bolting to the bathroom and avoided dancing with him at all. He told me during prom that he loved me. What could be worse: having your boyfriend jilt you right before prom because he feared you’d wound up pregnant, or going with some guy you couldn't stomach holding hands with, let alone dance with.

"Well what's that loser done now? Who's he owe money besides me? Did he beat someone up? I never knew you all fooled with that bar nonsense. Let those overgrown five-year-olds settle their problems and sleep it off. Ain't worth the hassle." I mustered every ounce of contempt from my insides to shake the deer-in-the-headlights look on my face.

Harold had worked as a county sheriff's deputy ever since we graduated from Willisburg High School more than eighteen years ago. On that Friday night, thirty-three of us surviving seniors paraded through the gym single file and in some sort of alphabetical order to collect our diplomas, those who hadn't gotten kicked out or dropped out or quit to have a baby. That same night we graduated, I told Harold I couldn't marry him after he stammered his way through a half-assed proposal. He signed up with the sheriff's department the following month. He tried to join the army, or maybe it was the state highway patrol, but he had asthma, so they rejected him for that reason or some other. At least that's what he tells people. He married Brittany Renner six months after graduation, and now they have two obnoxious teenagers who smoke their stolen cigarettes in the parking lot by the Quikmart gas station.

"Aaaa ... actually, he's missing. But first, I, uh, I w-wanted to make sure you're OK."

"I'm," I sucked in air, "fine."

You wouldn't recognize Harold now from his senior yearbook picture. His belly spills over the front of his belted trousers. Balding for the past five years, he now sprouts a wispy mustache to recoup the loss. His colorless skin dissolves into what's left of his thinning blond hair. A regular at Larry's Tavern for beer and fried chicken wings after his shifts, Harold also serves as a deacon or whatever at First Christian Church. The locals all call him Harold, never deputy or sir or Mr. Foster even. He tries to check in on me now and again, chitchatting with me in the aisles at Velva's and waving at me while patrolling Main Street. For almost two decades, I have gritted my teeth and pasted on an unfriendly smile whenever his downcast eyes slant in my direction.

"Has he been here?"

Harold tilted his head to peek past me into the house through the half-closed screen door wedged ajar by my body. I didn't bother to block his view, yet I couldn't have him prowling around, so I frowned at him. Posing as my usual irate self masked how I really felt. I hated treating him poorly and carrying on in such a rude manner. Hated it all those years ago and hated it every time he drove by the house or flagged me while cruising the main drag to gab and see how I was "doing." He always wore that lost puppy face, and I didn't care to encourage him. I'd never wanted to hurt him.

"He bopped by last night and left." My tongue stuck to the roof of my mouth like peanut butter. That's correct, Officer Harold. Right about where you're standing, on the concrete landing, maybe four feet square with three steps down to the walkway that leads directly to the garage. Not much of a porch, as the screen door swings into anyone perched on the edge. Someone busted off the rod iron railing long before I moved in. Cracks cut a crazy pattern through the concrete surface and allow the crabgrass and tough shoots of grass to poke through.

Harold had difficulty making eye contact whenever he bumped into me. That afternoon his gaze did its typical wandering, as it never met mine for long before his eyes would dive for cover to the weeds, a fingernail, a passing insect.

He picked at a speck of lint on his slacks. A flashing alarm blared inside my skull. I'd forgotten about the laundry from the previous night. I'd never transferred it to the dryer. Had no idea whether or not it all rinsed clean or if those dark blotches clung to my clothes. I imagined the smell: a moldy odor wafting from the wad of damp cotton T-shirt, denim cutoffs, and towels sealed inside the washer all day.

"Did he ... you ... you are OK?"

Just because Mike was a loudmouth drunk who picked fights with everyone, even if they were bigger than him, as most men were, or even if their friends ganged up on him or were just as mean and pissed off at everything as Mike, well anyway, just because Mike was a nasty, foul, angry shadow of a man, everyone assumed he beat me.

He'd swagger home, jostling into bushes then kicking the crap out of them, yelling at some yelping dogs on the next street to "shut the fuck up or I'll shut you up," knocking over chairs and piles of folded clothes, stumbling over Mitchell's toys and hollering at the poor child to pick them up or he'd "teach him a lesson," slamming doors and bashing holes in the drywall. After thrashing anything in his path and punching every limp sofa pillow, Mike would collide with the couch or the mattress in a sorry heap. He wouldn't wake until the next morning, cross though quieter. Never apologetic but demanding to know when I intended to clean up "this fucking mess."

But he never struck me. He would threaten to pound me "within an inch" of my life and cursed the ground I walked, swearing he would give me what I had coming and spouting other drunken gibberish. I would shout at him awhile. As potted plants or plates and pans began crashing, I would try to calm him or hinder him from trashing the house. Eventually, I would give up and race to Mitchell's room to comfort and protect him if Mike barged in there throwing and booting anything in his sight.

Mitchell had learned not to approach Mike and wisely hid in his room when Mike hung around, loudly liquored or sullenly hungover. Mike never dared touch Mitchell either. Mike only harassed him or griped that Mitchell ate everything worth eating in the refrigerator or that he was an "expensive little bastard." That always ticked me off since Mike never covered the grocery bill or fetched anything special for Mitchell, not even a plastic trinket or such, and I would growl at Mike to get the hell out of my house if he aimed to mouth off some more.

And then Mike would bail, hurling doors open and shut, vowing never again to enter "this shithole," roaring away in whatever vehicle he conned from some moron in a lowlife bar. Most times, he arrived and departed on foot, especially after they revoked his driver's license. The last I'd hear from him, he was cussing out the shrubbery he toppled into as he staggered toward the street.

Mike would meander home with a black eye, no shoes, and once a strange, wasted woman twice his age, yet he never came home and hit me. I should have smacked myself upside the head for putting up with him. I don't remember when I gave up hoping he would change, or when I quit crying into my pillow because I knew he wouldn't. Years ago, I used to fantasize about a different man arriving on our doorstep one night.

Many nights Mike wouldn't return home at all. I would doze in spurts, awakening to every bang or tire screech, half expecting him to begin his racket. At least that was how we lived until the last year or so, as his sporadic layovers had petered out, and he scarcely bothered us with his ugliness.

No wonder everyone in town looks at me as if I'm a stray cat everyone pities but no one wants to feed.

"I'm fine, Harold. And as you can see, I've got company." I practically thumped myself on the forehead.

Damn, do I have to introduce them now? No! None of Harold's business.

We're not buddies, Harold and me, so I didn't need to play hostess.

The door had crept open behind me. Harold squinted through the mesh of the screen door and studied Johnny. The afternoon sun streaming through the windows highlighted his brawny frame. Harold casually saluted and muttered pleasantries. Johnny bowed his head in response and stared straight ahead at nothing in particular. Harold stood stiffly, probably hoping for me to invite him in. I couldn't. Sandwiched in the doorway, I pretended I didn't have a care in the world.

A swallow took a nosedive from a tree limb, landed on the front grill of my truck to pick at dead bugs stuck to the metal, then flew away with a full beak.

"Well I have to go. Thanks for checking on me, and all. But you don't have to," I said in my laziest I-don't-give-a-shit voice while backing up so I could shut the door and send Harold on his way.

"Y-you see K, um, Mrs. Nicholson, Mike's mother, she, well, she called us, me, the department, t-this morning and said Mike, he was at her house last night, took a walk and n-never returned."

I tried to appear unconcerned. Instead, my eyes scampered wildly before they latched onto the revolver nestled in a black holster secured to Harold's leather belt and resting on his hip.

"Maybe he found a rock to crawl under," I hissed. I silently begged myself not to start crying and disguised my anguish with anger.

Harold swiped at the back of his neck with his palm, inspected it, and then wiped the sweat onto his khaki-covered thigh.

"He didn't show up at w-work neither," Harold said, blinking rapidly as his mouth wrestled to form the words.

"You mean Mike has a job? He's cashing a paycheck? That cracks me up! Maybe he can pay child support. Well, if he blew off work this morning, that wouldn't be the first. He's certainly been sacked from enough jobs for that. Either that or his temper. Late, wrecking the equipment, bossing the boss." I shook my head and folded my arms over my chest, clamping my hands onto the bare skin above my elbows while ignoring the goosebumps forming under my clammy palms.

"His momma ain't bankrolling his worthless self anymore? What a hoot! Well I don't know what she's all torn up about. He's probably snoring somewhere. Somewhere in some ..." I struggled to bypass that final image of Mike cemented into my brain, the one I steered toward again and again and again. But I smashed right into it. "... some ditch or some ... somewhere he belongs. Don't worry. He doesn't shack up here no more. I'm tired of fixing busted windows and picking up after his temper tantrums. I told him that last night when he swung by, so he split." I clenched my teeth until it hurt.

"Had Mike been drinking?"

Harold didn't tumble over a single letter. His eyes locked on mine, suddenly not seeking to escape. He'd cornered me.

Mike had told me he no longer drank, that he'd traded the bottle for Jesus, and he certainly hadn't behaved tipsy. To tell the truth, who knew?

"I suppose so."

I judged that a safe answer. Harold scrunched his face and worked his teeth with his tongue like a six-year-old with a loose one. He wiped beads of sweat from his temples. I let mine run, run, run, and concentrated on that ticklish sensation the trails left behind.

"Funny thing though, Mike's mother, she says Mike d- doesn't drink anymore. He quit. Joined a church group in Cliff City where they helped him. She says he's been sober for about t- t-t, going on two months."

"Two months is a million years for an alchi. Maybe strolling the 'burg changed his tune."

"I've already been to the tavern, and they didn't see him. Velva's was closed by the time Mrs. Nicholson said he left her house, so he couldn't buy n-none there."

I ransacked other possibilities and alibis.

"The gas stations all sell beer and such. You know that, Harold. Rory's sells pints, quarts. Shit, they carry Evan Williams in jugs."

Harold nodded as if agreeing with me before countering each one of my points. "I've checked. B-but no one saw him. What time did he stop by here?"

His eyes latched onto mine again and refused to flee. It threw me off guard, and my mind emptied. I fumbled for a reply.

Well, what time was it anyway? I didn't know what to say.

Pick a time, girl, pick a time!

I could recollect everything except that. I didn't want to look flustered. It was my turn to stammer.

"Hmm, well, I was awake, getting ready for bed. Mitchell hit the sack early. I was washing dishes, or uh ... watching TV ..."

The time! Damn! It had to be right! This was how they trip you. How they catch you. You lie. You lie about the wrong things. Stupid things. Those little details you presume don't account for much, but they add up.

As a child, I saw a TV drama about this detective who deduced that the wife intentionally killed her husband. She claimed she shot him accidentally because she mistook him for a burglar. The detective accused her of replacing the good light bulb in the porch fixture by the entry door with a dud so the drunken husband couldn't see where to put his key, forcing him to break into his own house. The detective pointed out to her that dust did not cover the bulb. Someone screwed it in fresh for this stint, while an old bulb that burned out naturally definitely would feature a layer of dust. Someone had installed a spent bulb in the fixture that day the husband tottered home late at night, too drunk to open his own front door in the dark. The detective persuaded the wife to concede on this. Before the last commercial, she'd confessed.

I tried to calm myself.

I don't have to lie about this! There's nothing wrong with the time he arrived. I don't have to be exact. Cool it!

I hoped Harold wouldn't notice my trembling and how I gulped in each breath. Why couldn't I dredge up one scrap of information as simple as the time he showed up?

Why? Because for once, he didn't burst in hollering and yelling. He had quietly walked up the driveway. I barely heard the crunch of gravel every few feet and the soft thud of his heels striking the cement. He even knocked politely on my screen door. Mike never, never, ever used to knock. Just that one night. He didn't slur his words or cuss. He hadn't been drinking; he wasn't high. And it was way past five o'clock. It was dark.

I couldn't recall ever seeing him sober so late in the evening. If he hadn't drunk any booze, such as first thing in the morning, he brandished a nasty sneer. A couple beers by lunch mellowed him and made him happy for a moment or two. By that time of night, generally he was quite drunk.

The sight of Mike the night before Harold's visit shocked me as if I'd bumped into a ghost from my past. The Mike I once knew, the one I met at the factory or chilling out afterward for a beer or two. He was so friendly to me back then. And flattering. Attentive. He didn't drink as much in those days. He could rope a job in those days. I had pictured him and me together for a long time in those days. I could of just socked myself in disgust for wallowing in another one of my silly fantasies.

"I don't remember," I said as convincingly as I could. "It was dark. Mitchell had conked out. Mike popped by for a minute then left."

"Did he say where he was going?"

"No. Didn't ask, didn't care."

"Did he have a car?"

"Nope."

"What you talk about?"

Like bullets, Harold fired one right after another.

"I already told you! I hadn't seen him for ages, he turns up out of the blue and I told him I didn't want him here anymore, especially if he wasn't pitching in with Mitchell!"

I'd started shouting, then lowered my voice when I mentioned Mitchell. I prayed my boy wouldn't hear any of our words over the clamor of the television. Johnny had anchored himself to a worn strip of linoleum by my kitchen table without a hint of listening or absorbing what Harold and I discussed.

Harold didn't speak as he chewed awhile on this, staring into tufts of hairy crabgrass and patches of dirt next to the walkway. The same turf that received such a soaking the night before, no longer damp yet still brownish-green and lifeless.

Then his head sagged as his eyes focused on the ground. He had spotted something. Pursuing his attention, I sweetened my tone, except it tasted like pickle relish.

"By the way, how are your girls? I see them around town. Quite the social butterflies."

His gaze riveted on the parched grass by the porch. Besides, his teenage daughters probably didn't serve as a good distraction. I'd bet he preferred to forget they hovered over new boyfriends every other week, from what I could see.

He plodded down the steps and stooped as he inspected a jumble of dandelions busting through one of the cracks that crawled through the concrete. He tugged on his trouser legs and squatted. He picked up a small, shiny object, rolling it between his thumb and his index finger. He clutched it inches from his eyes, then far away, his face crinkling, his eyes scrunched from concentration. Then he dropped it, an object too tiny for his clumsy fingers to manage. It skated across the concrete. I swooped down the steps, scurrying after it as the screen door banged shut behind me. We bonked heads as I dove to grab it. Harold rubbed his forehead with the palm of his hand while I cupped the little red plastic thing in mine.

"It's off one of Mitchell's toys," I said. I ignored Harold's puzzled half-smile as I jogged from one foot to the other, barely able to contain my relief.

Harold's drooping eyes caught mine. We both laughed, although I'm sure we laughed about something different. I hadn't a clue what Harold found to laugh about. His queer glances careened off me. How do I rid myself of this one, ship him off without triggering more questions and suspicions? I strode up the steps, acting bored and untroubled.

"So, anyway, if you find him, tell him to send money or I'll have his ass hauled into court. I'm tired of dodging bill collectors."

Harold stuck one hand in his pocket and scrutinized his shoes. Blood flushed my cheeks. I'd been out of work since April, and I didn't want people labeling me as some welfare mother. I draw unemployment. Mitchell ate free hot lunches at school before summer vacation. I'd bagged frozen peas and carrots, loaves of day-old bread, and potpies from the food pantry the week before. Sadie always carted over ice cream and goodies food stamps won't cover. Last month I'd stumbled onto a social worker in Cliff City committed to saving the world, one form in triplicate at a time. We were getting by. Some cash from Mike would have helped us with our move to Colorado, except I'd never counted on that, and now ...

"Money. Money, money money. It is the root of all evil!"

That would be Father, hollering when the ring from a salesman's telephone call would interrupt our dinner of tuna noodle casserole and canned corn.

With Mitchell and I surviving on my minimum wage gigs, I waited until those rare occasions with Mike home and somewhat sober before hashing out expenses. I need to pay for this, or Mitchell needs that, or "Why didn't you stick with the school's maintenance department, it had benefits and ..." We would argue until Mike hurtled out the door and didn't circle back until he was ripped. Sometimes he would straggle home hours or even several days later. Other times weeks passed before we would see him again. Then months.

I didn't waste my time figuring out where he earned the dough for booze. His momma. Kind, frail Mrs. Nicholson living out her final hours a few blocks away on the corner of Oakland and Briar, down the street from a deserted shack formerly home to a meth lab. She would grope for her wallet whenever Mike sauntered over. It was his payday. Every week or so, he would tramp to her house. Eat dinner. Compliment her on the plastic flower arrangement she scored at WAL-MART to plant on his daddy's grave. Maybe grapple with a box on the highest shelf out of her reach or advise her to quit fretting over those aging biddies at the Mt. Olive Christian Church who gossiped while stitching lap robes for the seniors at Lakewood Manor in Cliff City.

Ages ago I used to go with him. Old Mrs. Nicholson, so pleased to revel in a Sunday afternoon with us. Slightly hungover, Mike and I would blow a few hours on her overstuffed sofa swimming in crochet pillows, yakking, eating Doritos or potato chips, and watching TV while she piddled and fussed as she breathlessly entertained her son and his "lady friend." Her tiny face beamed as it rose out of a pastel-flowered housedress while she chattered about her friends' great-grandchildren or presented her latest knitting project or a religious memento she received in the mail.

"Don't throw your social security away on those TV preachers! Give it to me! I'll get you to heaven quicker than those con artists." Mike teased her with his mouth full of chips, crumbs flicking from his lips as he lounged on her sofa, his feet propped on my thighs.

His mother lightly swatted him with a dish towel, declaring he would surely be the death of her someday, with all his running around and not settling down to provide grandchildren to keep her young. She tilted her head at me and winked. I smiled weakly while massaging my throbbing forehead and sipping on a soda. She'd try to persuade us to stay for dinner, which sometimes we did. Since she didn't stock liquor in the house, we usually left early. Before we'd split, she'd tuck a wad of bills into Mike's palm.

"Oh, Mom, you don't need to do that. Save it for more yarn," Mike said. He didn't mean it and readily pocketed her money with the mildest scolding. Her gaze, full of wrinkles and a hopeless sort of love, followed us out the doorway as we trod through the gobs of weeds invading her lawn.

"Call me for anything, Michael. And Cathy, you take care of him. That's my baby!"

I'm sure she stared out her front window long after we blasted away in Blue, my Camaro.

◆ ◆ ◆

Harold watched me, shifting his weight now and then to give his bad knee a break. I surveyed my sandaled feet to hide from his curious glances. His questions had rattled me and practically pushed me over the rim. But I knew better. Harold is the kindest, dumbest man in the world. He's only worried about me. My eyes darted about for somewhere safe to dock, a beam solid enough to steady me. I choked down my panic as if forced a teaspoon of bitter medicine. Would the same poisoned expression have blanketed my face if I had married him after high school?

We stood without speaking for a spell as I fretted over all that had washed downstream. The television blared with Mitchell and Ellis hooting about what I could only imagine. Johnny hadn't stirred. The sight of any other black man in my house might have alarmed Harold, but Johnny's serene demeanor apparently disarmed him.

Scrunching his face, Harold concentrated on what, I didn't know. Possibly he was thinking about me, of what could have been. Maybe he was thinking of Mike, his motive for his visit. Thinking about police stuff or paperwork piled on his desk. Thinking about what he had to go home to that night.

"How's Mrs. ... Mike's mother?" I asked.

Change the subject. Safe ground. I'd always thought well of her, although I'm sure she questioned the Lord about me. She dreamed big for us once, I'm sure. We both did, hoping I could handle Mike and shape him into the man we both desired. Mike made other plans, or at least when it came to me, he had no intentions of being a husband and father and keeper of regularly mowed lawns. Whenever Mike's mom saw me and I her, we did each other no favors on that account.

Before Mitchell hit the scene, she pulled me aside once so Mike wouldn't overhear, confiding how she had him "late in life."

"I thought I'd passed that ... well, that time for a woman," she whispered as she cradled my arm. "I'd almost given up praying for a child before Michael came to us. Little did I know I'd spend the rest of my days praying for him." Her hazy eyes narrowed. "Praying for him to be safe, praying for him to grow up right and have a good job." Her voice dwindled. "I never realized when I started praying for a child, I'd never stop." I should have treated her muffled words as a warning.

After Mitchell was born, she phoned, begging me to ferry him over. I did once or twice, and I tried a bunch of other times. That was after Mike totaled Blue, and with no car, a new baby and no job, I was hoofing it. On Judge Weaver, similar to most of the streets here in Willisburg, we don't have sidewalks. Main and a couple others sport sidewalks, even though tree roots, wild grasses, and gaping cracks have broken the concrete sections, constructing a rolling, uneven route that would easily snag a stroller wheel. So if you're on foot, you have to walk on the side of the road and pick your way through the clumps of partially mowed weeds or gravel-filled potholes.

When I managed to lug over Mitchell and all his diapers, bottles of formula, and extra burp cloths in our squeaking yard sale stroller, Mike's mom didn't know what to do about him. About me. She was at a loss. While I hoped our company would bring joy, we only brought more confusion and sadness. Her own grandchild her own son rejected. Me, the abandoned girlfriend, not even wife. She'd wrung her hands over Mike for so many years she didn't have any more energy for dealing with the squalling bundle I placed in her sunken lap. I certainly couldn't park Mitchell with her. She was ancient by then. Always clinging for support from a wall, a doorframe, or a chair as if she were about to fall. Her weepy eyes constantly sought more for her quivering hands to hang onto.

She'd paw at me to slip cash into my purse or my pockets, but I would shoo her hands away. I shouldn't have been so proud. I muddled through on government money. When I did find work, Sadie babysat Mitchell for nothing. I grew up on canned vegetables and coats from Goodwill, so I've mastered how to get along without much. I probably should have accepted what Mike's mom offered because when she doled it out to Mike, he poured it straight down his throat.

The state hired me a lawyer when I signed up for welfare so Mitchell could see a doctor for his eyes. He's got good eyes, those gorgeous green-gray eyes. Sometimes they puff up, water and itch. After several appointments consisting of hours of sitting in this doctor's office and that clinic, tests and needles and a swarm of other nonsense, they decided he suffered from allergies.

Now he takes medicine, mainly in spring and fall, when his eyes bother him. Pollen from the trees and grasses. Great, now Mother Nature's out to get us.

That lawyer created a fine mess of everything. Made Mike madder than if a bartender had dumped a whole pitcher of beer on him, which really did happen, but that's another story I won't bore you with right now. One time after Mike trashed my house and freaked the bejeebers out of both Mitchell and me and my neighbors, the lawyer claimed I required a court order to protect us from Mike. Well, I had to laugh. To expect a piece of paper could protect us. How the hell can people think that? Believe some judge's order can fix things or set things right, remodel a splintered relationship into a peaceful and loving one. Safe. Lasting. Build one with a roof and four sturdy walls. I had a piece of paper saying Mike was Mitchell's daddy, but that hadn't meant diddly to Mike. I slammed the brakes on my tears before making a fool of myself once again.

Harold studied the house's siding, both of us commenting on how Mike's mother was doing, how she's getting up there in years, isn't she around eighty-five? Yeah that's right, scares easier and doesn't take much to disturb her. I suggested she probably ought to consider a nursing home or something soon and he nodded. He explained how he had to follow up on any reports. He echoed my opinion that Mike would turn up like usual. Tanked, no doubt. No surprises there.

Everybody knew Mike. Even Harold. Mrs. Nicholson said he no longer drank, yet anybody who'd ever bumped into Mike would have gagged on the notion of him giving up booze. He'd stray awhile, weeks and months at a stretch. Then he'd backtrack to Willisburg ready to drink and settle old scores with his fists or a well-aimed empty quart-sized bottle of cheap whiskey. Certainly everyone pictured him knocked out in a drunken coma somewhere. Surely Harold felt odd worrying about Mike, the town lush. Wasn't as if Mitchell or I had disappeared.

Harold fiddled with his hat. He'd used Mike as an excuse to drop by to check on me once again. He kept finding some silliness to jaw over. I complained about the heat and the drought. "At least I don't have to mow," I said with a sarcastic snicker since I barely bothered to mow when the grass and weeds shot up like crazy anyway. He asked about Mitchell. The roar of the cicadas and the crickets and other screeching insects muted the tapping of my flip-flop on the threshold. The pressure inside me swelled as I rocked in place and pulled at my T-shirt and scratched my scalp. Crap, did I catch cooties from Ellis after all? Then Harold thought about him too.

"Who's with Mitchell? Is th-there someone ... um ... else here?"

"A friend." I almost snorted while describing Ellis as a "friend." I picked at a scab of peeling paint on the doorpost.

Harold hadn't acted too interested in Johnny, so Ellis should matter even less.

None of your concern. Keep your nose out of my business. Zilch out of the ordinary here, Harold.

I squeezed my eyelids together to make everything vanish.

Harold started chewing his lip and focused on a knot of crabgrass or at nothing in particular. When our eyes met, he would fling them elsewhere or swivel his head. He'd always been that way: nothing new there.

He still held his hat in his hands. He hadn't written down a single word.

I'm not a suspect. Not suspicious. Wound tight as wire cable, but I'm not a suspect.

I chuckled again. Harold shot me a thin grin, except he didn't seem happy. I'd bet I didn't seem happy either.

"Well, I guess, that's that. Good luck digging up that dirtbag. Don't know why anyone would want to." My heart somersaulted as Mike's momma patted me with her withered hand, a feeble smile gracing her face. "Tell Mrs. Nicholson 'hi' for me, OK?"

Harold's glum face summed up the interview. He smoothed his balding scalp with his palm as he inspected the scarred metal of the screen door. He searched for something, but not for something you'd expect from a cop on the prowl. Harold only hunted for something more to say, some reason for him to linger at my doorstep or to bring him back again. His attentions vexed me and made me huffy with him. I didn't need a middle-aged married man going nowhere pining after me.

I let the screen door bang shut as he curled the brim of his hat with his fingers. I drummed my knuckles on the kitchen counter until his patrol car backed out of the drive.

4

A smacking, thumping racket erupted from the family room. I dashed in to find Ellis slapping his leg, pounding his fist against the upholstered arm of my sofa, and stomping his feet on the floor. He laughed harshly, irritating cackles spewing from his mouth. Mitchell's squeals of delight danced through the house.

What are they watching on TV? What could possibly be so rip-roaring funny?

I trudged back to the kitchen sink. A constant buzz clogged my ears. Incessant. Relentless. And so damn loud. Sucking me into a vacuum of thousands upon thousands of thundering insects outside, hysterical cartoon characters shrieking from the next room, a clattering window air conditioner that could barely cool the place, the rumbling of the refrigerator as the motor kicked in. If someone dropped a pin, it would have boomed like an atomic bomb. I began to shake again. I gripped the counter as the gouged laminate countertop slipped from my fingers.

Then Johnny's calming voice rose above it, clearing a path wide enough for me to follow him to safety. To silence. Peace. Nothingness. No fear, no decisions, no mistakes I would have to take to the grave. He didn't utter words, more like those humming sounds a mother purrs to her child to soothe him when he's sick, or the clucking noises a rider murmurs to a skittish horse. I floated. On cushions. On wind currents strong enough to lift me, gentle enough to leave me unruffled. In water the temperature of a mother's womb, I floated away. If only I could have drifted like that forever.

His voice carried me away, but his words brought me back.

"It is time."

So evenly, so steadily. A mighty river that never loses its course and remains snug within its banks.

I clutched the kitchen counter. Jelly, coffee, and cigarette burns blemished the orange and pea green checkered laminate. No amount of soap and elbow grease could wipe clean the messes left behind by one family after another that had called this shack their home. Only fifty years old, it looked like hell and smelled like a damp basement. Sections of the fake wood paneling in the family room were peeling away from the plaster, and only my momma's claw-foot loveseat backed against the wall restrained several sheets from cascading onto the bronze shag carpet. Mike had punched holes in the drywall by the bathroom, but I'd covered those with a hanging rug of an antlered deer in the woods. Mike had taught me to stop decorating with glass picture frames.

My bedroom sits next to the kitchen. Mitchell's is off the family room. We have a small bathroom carved out of a corner of the kitchen. The concrete stoop out the front door nearest the street had crumbled and collapsed, so I block that door with the television. We go in and out the side door to the porch facing the garage.

The house forms a perfect rectangle. No basement, no attic. A simple pine box without a fancy liner. A miniature porch with a tiny landing and three concrete steps leads to the garage where I store all that junk I should sell or dump somewhere else.

Johnny was right. It was time. Time to deal with the freezer in my garage. Time to move. Yet I didn't have the strength. I could have crumpled into a heap on my kitchen floor. I could not cope with any more decisions. All my decisions up until then filled me with regret. All except Mitchell, of course.

I hooked up with his daddy when we both worked at the hot dog plant in Cliff City. "Wienie waggers," we called ourselves.

Tammy and I staffed the shipping department, labeling packages of precooked hot dogs destined for sale at grocery stores or restaurants and such. Ensuring the right boxes went on the correct refrigerated trucks, and the correct totals billed to the right customers. We didn't have to touch the raw meat, which would have turned me vegetarian without a doubt. Every once in a while I'd stumble across the guys with the bloodstained aprons and hairnets during breaks or when I delivered paperwork to a distant office. When they shuffled past, I avoided breathing through my nose to ditch the odor of death.

One afternoon I ran an errand for my supervisor, slunk downstairs to smoke a cigarette, then to my locker for change for the vending machines to snag a candy bar I could scarf while scurrying back to shipping.

As I flung my locker shut, Mike popped up behind me. He startled me, as I hadn't heard him coming. Instead of his contagious grin, I whirled around expecting to find a red-faced manager huffing that I should have returned to my post. The corporates insisted that us wienie waggers observe strict rules on breaks and locker room visits.

"Are you brave?" he asked, raising his dark eyebrows enticingly.

Stunned, I clamped my mouth.

OK, you're not management and I've never seen your face before.

I smiled cautiously, relieved I wouldn't get written up again.

Wary of any shenanigans that could cost me my job, I shook my head.

With an exaggerated pout, he cupped his stubbled jaw in one hand. His ink-black hair swept across his forehead and accented his brown eyes. Not too tall, maybe an inch or two above me with his boots on. Stocky, not fat. He looked about my age, mid- to maybe late twenties. No earrings, thank God; I can't stomach a man with pierced anything. As he spoke, his parted lips revealed a chipped bottom tooth from an encounter with a hustled pool player, a story he would act out for me at a later date.

He slowly swung his head from side to side. "This makes me sad. I would have sworn you was the adventurous type." He crossed his arms on his chest as he explored my eyes, letting out a loud, inflated sigh. He captured my curiosity.

"OK. I'm the brave type. Try me."

His face brightened. He clapped once. "Well, come on then. Follow me."

I hesitated. I said I needed to skedaddle back to shipping, but I couldn't hide the glee darting across my face.

"Well, this is on the way. I'll get you back faster than you can say 'Cheese Doodles.' Promise!"

His mischievous mood inspired me, and I was a teenager again, sneaking off campus to cut class or smoke a joint during lunch recess. I sprinted along the corridor to match his pace. I giggled as he cocked his chin and hiked his brow suggestively. He clasped my hand as we skipped down one hall and then another, outside and through an alleyway canyoned by aluminum-sided buildings and into a massive warehouse with stacks and stacks of plastic-wrapped boxes on wooden pallets. Our voices echoed against the metallic walls. I hadn't worked there long enough to know what this warehouse stored. The place appeared deserted except for Mike and me.

He waved toward a forklift. "Madam, your chariot awaits," he said in a solemn tone with a theatrical gesture of his arm. I grinned as my head pivoted "no."

"If they catch us we'll get canned."

He chuckled as if I'd told a hilarious joke. "Well I started here last week and one thing I know is this vehicle has just set there, its innards rotting away, and someone should rev up the ol' engine to keep it running right."

Blood rushed to my face. He was cute.

"No, seriously," he said, smiling slyly. "An engine sets too long, sure enough, when you need it, darn thing won't power on." He widened his eyes as if in awe. "We'd be doing the company a disservice to allow this engine to seize, the gas to go bad, and the carburetor to gum up. We wouldn't be doing our jobs, that's sure enough! They'll thank us, why, we might even get us a bonus for our dedication and foresight!"

I tittered at his zigzagging logic and his daring. I shrugged. "Can you run one of 'em?"

He smirked and threw his arms up. "Well, I would guess you jiggle the key, gas her up and thar she blows."

I smelled trouble in more ways than one. Little did I know.

He mounted the machine and fumbled with the controls. After several false starts, he managed to fire up the engine, immediately reversing it and whacking into a small mountain of boxes without knocking them to the floor. He flashed me a thumbs-up as I hugged my belly, laughing.

The roar of the engine flooded my ears. More jarring swerves and switchbacks before Mike maneuvered the machine closer and signaled for me to hop on. He couldn't have heard me, so I swayed my head wildly as I skittered backward to safety. He frowned in jest, fiddled with the joysticks, and finally pulled what I hoped was the emergency brake before clambering out of the driver's seat to approach me. He fastened his hands to my shoulders, his nudging soft yet firm, and guided me to the forklift. I didn't protest in the slightest.

"I'll teach you," he shouted into my ear. His breath glided down my neck. We toured the warehouse aisles for about fifteen minutes or so with me perched on his knee as I helped him operate the assortment of levers and buttons on the console. We loaded boxes and restacked them elsewhere. We made a mess of things. We cruised the aisles of cardboard containers and wooden pallets rising toward the ceiling, reaching speeds I'm sure that engine never achieved before or since. Mike wrapped his free arm around my waist, tightening his hold with every curve. He squealed as if our tires burned rubber while we rounded each corner. What a blast! Who could imagine motoring through a warehouse on a forklift could provide such a thrill. For me, the main thrill centered on sitting in Mike's lap, his arms brushing mine and glancing my thighs.

With the clock spinning, I began to worry someone besides a grouchy Tammy would notice my absence in shipping. Mike stuck out his lower lip when I announced that I had to go, yelling into his ear as loose locks of his hair tickled my cheek. He squeezed my hand as I climbed out of his lap and down to the concrete floor. I beamed as I hurried back to my post.

Nursing a hangover, Tammy cursed me for abandoning her as she fished through the craziness of a mixed-up order for a chain of convenience stores. I floated into the room, unable to launch anything hateful back. I cheerfully explained I'd bumped into a charming guy who required my attention and giggled away her stewing and cussing for the rest of the day.

◆ ◆ ◆

Mike handled maintenance at the plant, which included moving stuff, scaling ladders to replace light bulbs, tightening a screw here or there, and emptying waste bins from the windowless offices upstairs. We kept running into each other amidst groups of people during our breaks smoking cigarettes or sipping sodas, or after work guzzling beers and pitchers of happy hour specials. Jousting each other with pool cues or cracking up over silly stuff with our elbows propped on the bar, swiveling in our stools.

Mike was fun to be around. Always amused and entertaining, sometimes pranking an unsuspecting drunk in the crowd. He rarely got rowdy and clashed with someone. Most of the time, he was pretty attentive, scoring me another beer and conning someone else into buying it. He'd order potato skins with extra cheese, my favorite!

I donned a summer dress or two rather than my standard jeans and T-shirt. Ignored Phil's disgusting jokes instead of laughing. I shaved my legs on a more regular basis. I teased my long hair into seductive tresses free-flowing around my shoulders, instead of rubber-banding it into a ponytail.

Mike would open my bottled beers. Once, he hammed it up and uncapped one with his teeth. I used a paper napkin to wipe off the blood where he sliced his lip on the metal.

Then one Saturday, Cyn and Kyle invited a bunch of us for a potluck barbecue at their house. I almost envied them as a married couple in their forties, grown kids from previous marriages or relationships or whatever.

I experimented with a potato salad recipe I'd discovered on the label of a mayonnaise jar. Tammy decided on bratwursts boiled in beer. She lurched out of her apartment hauling the largest stockpot I'd ever seen. A frothy blend of beer and brat juice sloshed over the rim as she marched toward my car. I instructed her to nestle it between her knees because I didn't want any accidents in Blue. Although I bought her used, my Camaro Blue won first place as my prized possession, at least until Mitchell was born. Tammy dredged up her typical crude remarks, screeching that she never had this many wieners between her legs, not even in high school.

I had squished myself into this tight-fitting denim number. Mike would be there.

Some of the regulars from the Daily Deuce and a crew Kyle hung out with at Pete's Tavern and Grill greeted us with catcalls and sloppy grins. Cyn gave us a quick tour of the house so we could find the john. We partied in the chain-link fenced backyard: an untilled vegetable garden with molding, straw-colored cornstalks in one back corner and a johnboat without a motor docked on two sawhorses submerged by tall weeds in the other. Everyone carted a bowl or a bag of chips, and the spread covered the wooden picnic table. Mike actually bucked for a six-pack.

We ate and drank, then drank and drank. Phil told his disgusting jokes. Gary leaned over the waist-high fence and threw up in the neighbor's yard. Tammy and this guy she corralled started slobbering all over each other. Cyn and Kyle got into a half-hearted argument, but I guessed it didn't have anything to do with any of us. All and all, it was a nice party.

Mike invented one reason or another to touch me. My knee, my wrist. My body fluttered with each contact. I'd known him for maybe two months by then and hungered for more.

He left for a beer run. When he rejoined the party, he snuck up behind me and put his palms over my eyes. "Guess who?"

"Um. Don't know. Santa Claus."

When he pulled his hands away, he lowered them to encircle my waist. I pivoted as he cradled my hips. It was a warm summer evening. Not hot. Not a cloud in the sky, as they say. I trembled and forgot about all the people milling around us on that grassy plot of ground.

◆ ◆ ◆

The next week when we caught up with each other again for happy hour, Tammy was still pissed at me.

"Where the hell you get off? I planned on you taking me home," she said. Sacked from the hot dog factory the Thursday before, she had spent most of that week after the barbecue boozing away her final paycheck.

"Sorry, I presumed you found your ride home," I said. Her bark couldn't put a dent in my smile.

"What? We were just goofing off. I'd no intentions of going home with him. He's Leon Wilke's brother! Leon? Supervisor for the machine shop? Tattoos snaking all over his neck? Took me a while to figure out that. The Dud Brothers! Lucky for me, he passed out in his car and I hijacked it home. Thanks a hell of a lot!"

"Sorry, sorry already," I said. "I didn't realize I was your private chauffeur."

"I guess I'm ... had a shitty job interview this morning too. Did you have any brats?"

At first I thought she was messing with me, tweaking her potluck dish into another lewd comment about my conquest. I snickered wickedly.

Tammy's broad face wrinkled into a puzzle. "What's so funny? Did you get any brats or didn't you? How'd they taste? My Uncle Joe's recipe. I didn't buy buns, reckoned someone else would bring some, it being a barbecue and all."

I laughed, clapping my palms against the bar as I rocked back on my stool. She really was referring to her beer-boiled bratwurst!

"Somebody said they saw Billy wolfing down a plateful. I never did get one, then the next thing I know, the whole pot was empty. That was a lot of bratwursts! Maybe Kyle's fucking dog helped himself." She tugged at her shirt so it would cover more of her belly.

I cast her a smug glance. I did not care a hoot about Tammy's brats. Not much of a scholar or genius, Tammy had pickled her brain cells with Jack Daniels and marijuana by the time she quit school. She eventually understood my gist. A clumsy smirk crawled across her lips.

"Hooee, damn, girl! You did get some bratwurst action. Mike, huh?"

I grinned. Couldn't stop smiling all week. Couldn't have scraped off that happy face with a belt sander.

Mike came home with me a lot after that. Every Friday and Saturday and some weeknights too. He had a pad in Cliff City, but we hated going there as his tiny apartment included a meth head for a roommate, unemptied trash cans, and totally gross neighbors who raised ferrets. Mike started hanging out at my house every night and revisited his place only for loud disagreements with his landlord or his roommate. He fell further behind with rent, and when he found the eviction notice taped to his door, he moved his dirty laundry in with me on Judge Weaver.

He didn't grow up in Willisburg. His folks relocated here after Mike got booted out of Cliff City High. Maybe his mom and dad hoped Mike would thrive in a quaint country school setting. Mike had a few years on me and rarely attended class anyway. By the time he turned seventeen, he was on his own more or less, partying with the rest of his loser buddies. We never chanced upon each other on Main. Never bumped into each other gassing up or buying beer or smokes from Velva's, though he bopped in on his mom now and then. Strange, as I didn't live far from his mother. Willisburg is small-town as small-town gets. Funny how fate plays with us like throwaway plastic toys from a fast food joint.

Mike iced my cake. For years we played house. Working, drinking, arguing about who had to spend their day off with the smelly clothes, bedsheets, and towels at the coin-operated laundromat on the outskirts of Cliff City before I plugged in that used washer/dryer combo in the corner of my kitchen.

He had a side to him I did my best to dodge. A crass, brooding creature possessed him at times.

He drank every day. We both did. He'd straggle out of bed to the kitchen, bashing into the cupboards and then slamming them shut. He'd topple a mug or two before spilling coffee all over the counter.

"Shitfire! What's all this crap doing ...?"

I'd wake, smear my palms across my eyes, then chug some water and a couple Advils. He'd dial the volume to low. Not much hollering. Mostly just a grouchiness. He'd stomp off late for work or when out of work or on his days off, to the couch with the cartoons and after his stomach settled, maybe a bowl of cereal or more coffee. By noon he'd have cracked at least two beers. He preferred bottled Michelob, although as we closed in on payday, we resorted to the cheapest kind in cans and only ordered happy hour specials if we could afford to go out at all. I never started drinking until way into the afternoon, at least three o'clock even on my days off. I could expect to find him in fairly good humor by then.

By nightfall, he'd be plastered. We both would wind up stinking drunk in Cliff City after work with the crew. Sometimes we'd mosey to the local tavern if we were too bored at home and already too hammered to navigate the forty-minute round trip to the city through all the traffic intersections and past the occasional cop car or highway patrolman.

Mike got laid off from the hot dog factory shortly after we partnered. He tried security work at another factory, then construction, even did a stint bussing tables. Fed up with the bosses and the rules and the assholes, I switched jobs routinely, but even with more money or better hours, the new gig always sucked too.

I didn't have much to shout about regarding Mike and me in bed. Not after a night of boozing, which meant every night. Yet after he finished, or finished trying, he would swaddle me with his body, gathering me in his arms and legs, before passing out with his head tucked into the crook of my neck.

I've never experienced the romantic fireworks type. Guys took what they could as quickly as possible while I considered I got at least some of what I wanted in exchange.

When Mike held me so tight I could hardly move, nothing could touch me. Nothing could pry me away from him or him away from me. As he slumbered, he would toss and twirl while hugging me or clinging to me. We wriggled and spiraled through the sheets, swimming together like two tadpoles. I would attempt to untangle myself because my elbow was twisted or aching from his weight, the pins and needles beginning to burn. He would stir and call my name, grabbing me and dragging me to meld with his chest. I learned to sleep with my head tucked under his arm.

For the first months of our relationship, I floated on a magic carpet. During a smoke break or while sailing through the grocery aisles for chips or spaghetti sauce, the sensation of his limbs clamping onto me made me melt. He was my man and I was his woman. I had never before merged into one with another.

Eventually the honeymoon ended. We'd yell back and forth and then kiss and make up. I spent more time smiling at his playfulness than frowning at his ugliness. Still, our tempers flared almost daily. We fought lame fights in public places. I hung my head to weep more often than I wish to recall.

When I became pregnant during a relatively unchaotic period between us, everything seemed so perfect. You'd think an unmarried woman, whose boyfriend spent most of his time unemployed, soused, or hungover, would not have embraced this surprise. Scared of what would happen and how to manage this sudden detour. How he would handle it. But not me.

Mike was thirty-one years old. I had just hit twenty-nine. Time to nest, my body decided for us both. I didn't try to shanghai him. I was on the Pill, except that doesn't always do the trick.

It was a Friday. I'd called in sick to confirm my suspicions with one of those free tests from a pro-life group setting up shop near the mall in Cliff City. On my way home, I breezed by the PriceRight and picked up steaks, corn on the cob, and bottled beer – a reward for Mike only, of course.

I couldn't wait to tell him. My face glowed. Everything gleamed and shined more beautiful and fantastic than ever before. The leaves on the trees shimmered emerald green. The sky sparkled a brilliant blue like a priceless sapphire. The sun ricocheted off everything, brightening the world glossy and fresh. I was so in love with Mike and with this sweet baby. I patted my slightly pouching little belly all day. I throbbed with a happiness I'd never known. I would have to study on a name for a girl. For a boy, we would christen him Michael, our little angel.

I primped with various cotton frocks I'd shoved in the back of my closet, modeling sideways in the narrow mirror. I imagined my reflection doubling, tripling, quadrupling in size.

Please God, don't let it be twins!

I chose a burgundy, gold, and scarlet paisley number that showed off my legs. I set our kitchen table for what I believed would be a merry, memorable evening. We would celebrate! I cussed out myself for not having any candles.

Mike stormed through the door mid-afternoon in a lousy mood from a blown interview for which he had stayed sober. He flipped on the television, threw himself on the couch, uncapped a cold Michelob, and asked with little interest and loads of sarcasm about how my day had treated me.

I settled next to him. I couldn't contain myself. I'd planned to broadcast my news when we unwound after dinner. I couldn't wait.

He tousled my hair, a half-smile hovering over his lips. "Honey, not now, I got me a headache," he said, sniggering. He used to joke and laugh a lot. He harbored that temper he lost after too much liquor or from hosting a hangover. But back then, he could still laugh.

I clasped his left hand and placed it precisely and firmly over my belly button.

"You're gonna wear me out. I'm an old man," he said. And then in his fake hillbilly accent, "You're gonna have to go get me my vitamins!"

By then, tears slid over my smile. Mike's tired grin wrinkled, and his forehead bunched in confusion.

"Hmmm. OK, if you're gonna cry to get your way. Let me get some sustenance in me first."

He forced a brief smirk at me and then restored his attention to the television. He dragged his hand away from my belly to stroke my knee in a circular motion while he watched the baseball players flit across the screen. He swallowed another mouthful of beer. Then he looked at me with a queer expression, one eyebrow raised. I sniffled as I wiped my tears with my palm before scooping up his free hand with both of mine.

In my excitement, I wanted to sing out about this thrilling turn of events. We were going to have a baby! A family! Mike, me, and a precious baby to love. Unexpected and unplanned, but we were expecting! I couldn't conceive of Mike not sharing my joy. Our joy!

My words tumbled over each other and probably didn't make sense, yet Mike understood me clearly. He wrenched his hand from me as if I were a copperhead rousted from a woodpile. His jaw fell open. He stared at me rigid and mute. Not a muscle twitched. His chest remained still and breathless for a handful of seconds before the air escaped with a deflated whoosh. Then he pressed his lips together as his eyes circled me before pausing on my belly. He blinked as he studied the swirling patterns fashioned by the rippling material of my dress.

His bleak gaze plummeted to his lap. He sank back into the sofa. His features shriveled into a frown. His eyes glazed, focusing on nothing. His arms rested limply on the sofa's fuzzy fabric: the beer bottle steadied upright only by leaning against Mike's thigh.

His reaction didn't throw me at first. I'd never before informed a man I was carrying his baby, and so I had no idea what to expect other than a mixture of surprise and shock. Alarm maybe. My announcement jolted him, caught him unawares and unprepared, and that didn't upset me. His response was normal; at least that's how I wanted to picture it. My sheer bliss blinded me to any other possibility. I beamed, my cheeks tingling from tears. Since he pulled his hand out of my grasp right after I said my piece, I reached for him again. He yanked away once more.

"No, man, shit no!" He shook his head and then rose from the couch, clenching his right fist around his bottle of Michelob. He kneaded an eye with his left palm, then combed his fingers through his hair again and again. He took another swig from his half-empty bottle of beer before hurling it through the plate glass of the front window.

After that, Mike made himself scarce. He careened in and out of my life for the remainder of my pregnancy, sullen, drunk, or hungover. We rarely spoke. He'd fling up his arms and stomp away whenever I tried some "baby" talk.

Tammy grudgingly promised me she would chip in after I told her I couldn't possibly "have it taken care of."

"Just tell her to call me 'Aunt Tammy,'" she said. She had a friend who had a friend with a bunch of baby stuff I could borrow. Tent-shaped maternity dresses not too worn out, a used playpen and such. When I didn't have my head hanging above a sink or a toilet bowl, I boosted my spirits by reading books on loan from the doctor's office about natural childbirth. I coaxed myself into at least trying to breastfeed.

My boobs swelled, but Mike didn't notice. He never rubbed my sore back or massaged my feet after I'd spent a day standing behind the cash register. Not once did he place his hand on my hard belly in anticipation of the unearthly tremors from his child kicking and turning. Sometimes the ache in my chest punched me harder than any hormone or baby's bony heel.

It is time. That phrase echoes in my mind to this day. I slumped against the kitchen counter drowning in sad memories. Only Johnny threw me a life preserver. It is time. Time to move on.

5

I picked up the phone to reach Sadie. She would jump at the chance to have Mitchell spend the night while Johnny, Ellis, and I tended to that freezer.

These days, I lean on Sadie, although Sadie can barely walk down her own front stoop, she's so fat. In my experience, hell for most of us, people come and go. They pretend friendship or love and then drift away at the first hint of rough water. They sniff greener grass and hop the fence. But Sadie has latched onto Mitchell and me, forging a family and providing a security blanket as she embraces us both. She is a community all in herself. A queen. A saint.

Decades ago when my obnoxious teenage friends and I trawled the streets of Willisburg, we delighted in harassing Sadie whenever we stumbled across her swaying mass.

"It's that FREAK!"

We went wild at the sight of her: graying muddy brown hair hanging across the sides of her puffy face and straggling down her back, her huge shapeless shifts cloaking those pounds of jiggling flesh. She struggled with each footstep, crossing streets, navigating curbs or entryways as she lugged herself from her house to the post office or to Velva's or to the drugstore before it went out of business. She ignored our hoots and hollers and sick jokes as we exaggerated our efforts to squeeze past her in the store aisles or along the sidewalk on the main drag. She just acted like she was somewhere else or couldn't catch a single mean jab we threw at her. She didn't turn or appear flustered or upset or hurt or anything. She would scan the sidewalk ahead of her, cautiously treading over the gaps and clumps of weeds splitting the cement. Like we didn't exist.

"Sexy Sadie, hey hey hey. How about some!" The boys yelled out their car windows at her and then gunned their engines. Or honked.

She heard them. I'm glad she never glanced up. Glad she never realized that was me in the back seat laughing with my dumb girlfriends, puffing on cigarettes, and snickering at her. I hope Sadie never recognized me as one of the stupid bitches scurrying past her, giggling at the nasty taunts tossed around while she waited for the cashier to ring her up.

I never actually encountered her face to face until after I moved into the rental house on Judge Weaver, ditching my family home after Momma's death and Father's final descent into total madness. While I sifted through a hastily loaded box of dishes Father wouldn't miss, a soft rapping on the metal edge of the screen door interrupted my unpacking. I gawked through the wire mesh and gasped at the sight of Sadie filling the doorway.

Her billowing striped housedress had swished and tumbled in a washer and dryer about a thousand times during its lifetime. Sandals with gobs of flesh spilling over the flattened sides. Long strands of grayish-brown hair pasted to her cheeks. It was early summer. Warm, not hot. Still, perspiration bubbled up and dampened her shaggy eyebrows, streaked her face, and pooled in the creases created by rolls of fat. I'm sure she sweated from the effort of hiking the two hundred yards to my house as much as from the sun. Her brown eyes peeked through drooping slits of skin and floated across my door jamb. I suppose she prepared for a certain amount of revulsion, so she avoided eye contact with me.

I didn't know what to say.

A nervous sigh slipped from her mouth before she ended the awkward silence. "Popped by to introduce myself. I'm Sadie. Welcome to the neighborhood." She panted slightly between lips highlighted by a gash of pinkish-white scar tissue pulling her upper lip toward her nose. "If you need anything, I'm in the green house with the big tree." She lifted a hefty limb as if to point in the direction of her home, out of view from where she stood on my porch. Her right arm reached toward the siding beside the door – a handhold for balance I guessed.

The lightness of her tender, friendly voice stunned me. I'd never heard her speak before. Harsh, loud, barking tones belching from that mouth, from that monstrous figure, would have made more sense. Instead, she sounded like a delicate young girl, her words wafting through the air on fluffy wings.

I froze. I had no clue what to say to this creature who had only served as a source of crude wisecracks for my friends and me since we were kids. I sucked in my breath, speechless and embarrassed, as she waited on my tiny landing. She grossed me out. I only hope I didn't look too horrified.

Bulky cardboard boxes and black plastic garbage sacks brimming with clothes, shoes, linens, and an odd assortment of things I'd salvaged from the sinking ship of my family home clogged the kitchen. Two matching chairs I'd dug out of a garage sale stored stacks of books I'd already read and a plastic planter of dried-up potting soil.

I nodded and mumbled a standard "nice to meet you," or whatever. Told her my name. I didn't invite her in. From the scope of things, she couldn't have expected me to ask her to join me for a cup of tea. I swiveled this way and that to dodge staring at her as we silently shared an uncomfortable moment that stretched for an eternity. I exhaled in relief when she finally bobbed her head as she swung one of her chunky arms at me and shambled away.

A few weeks later while lounging in a plastic lawn chair in my front yard, I savored a beer and a Virginia Slim as butterflies bickered over some milkweed poking its head up through a scrawny shrub. Down the street, a front door swept open as Sadie lunged from her house. She clamped both fists onto the single handrail bordering the five stairs and started hauling herself down her stoop. She executed each step slowly and steadily, planting each foot firmly and slightly sideways one at a time. Jumbles of graying brown hair twitched to and fro as she lurched. No way I could have hoisted her back on her feet, so if she fell I'm sure it would have required an emergency response by the county fire department.

Despite my worries, she nailed it. Once at the bottom of the stoop, she surveyed the path in front of her shoes as she hobbled along her concrete walkway to the street. The stuffed handbag slung over her left shoulder pitched and bounced off her massive hip with each stride.

Sadie reached the road and angled north to Main. Then she staggered to a halt and shifted her immense body toward me, raising her lumpy right arm in a wave before her body tilted away from me. By the time I waved back, I doubt she'd seen me return hers.

I frowned at myself. While watching Sadie labor, I hadn't bothered to hoot a hello or nothing neighborly. After all, she was the one who had trudged over to welcome me to what she referred to as "the neighborhood," which consisted of her, a decrepit retiree who relied on a constant stream of teenage girls as live-in caregivers, and a middle-aged couple who only ventured outside to tend their flower gardens and a Kentucky Bluegrass lawn that put the rest of the town's yards to shame.

Judge Weaver boasts only four houses before petering out into a graveled, weedy dead end at a rusted gate to the Smithton's pasture. All of our backyards butt against the Smithton's barbed wire fence, dense with scratchy cedars, locust trees, and thorny bushes crawling with ticks that would suck you dry given half a chance. The Kentucky Bluegrass folks built a six-foot redwood privacy fence on three sides to block anything unruly from spilling into their manicured world.

Pathetic excuse for a neighborhood, however, I hadn't moved here for some sort of community spirit. A rental in Willisburg costs way less than one in Cliff City twenty miles away. And I grew up here. Everything clicked. Cheap rent, lots of space abutting the house. I'd discovered a slice of heaven when I pulled up to my new digs. Close to Main leading to the highway, to Velva's if I ran out of beer or peanut butter. Of course in Willisburg, everything is close to everything else. Eighteen years old and all I pined for was a pocket of privacy. Not visitors or company or neighbors even, not really.

Just then the insane lady roosting beneath my skull started squawking that my home resembled a three-ring circus with a sheriff's deputy banging on the door, that creepy Mr. Coble sure to roam over any minute hanging on the elbow of his latest gum-chomping "personal assistant" as he calls them, two strange men milling about under my roof, and then there's Mike.

That thought stopped me cold. My feet itched to bolt. Run away. Hide. But I couldn't escape the painful sensation of a steel trap clenching my ankle. A million cicadas chanted feverishly outside. Surrounded. I wanted to be alone. I just needed some time. A quiet, peaceful place to rest. Maybe the only true peace and quiet you will ever find is in the grave. The blazing furnace of that summer afternoon should have heated everything too damn hot to make me shiver, yet I shuddered as if slogging through a January blizzard.

Sadie, Sadie. Back to Sadie. My mind is just a pile of fraying puzzle pieces. I can't get any of them to fit. Sadie. Got to phone her.

Two days after Mitchell emerged into the world, Sadie showed up at my back door for the second time.

I'd been living here for a spell. All the while, we never chatted except for her initial flyby. Usually I was speeding in or out on my way to work, to party with friends, or hook up with some guy, and then Mike barreled into my life. I rarely hung out in my front yard, not after old Mr. Coble from across the street started straggling over to spew some meanness about this or that or to complain about crap that didn't concern me.

As Mr. Coble's frail and worthless condition worsened, he enlisted live-in helpers. Always female, but don't reckon anything nasty about that. He was too old for any hanky-panky. He would never introduce them, other than to mention them in passing, as "my personal assistant was at Velva's and she witnessed ..." blah blah blah. He put a special emphasis on "assistant." I don't know why. Maybe he was afraid we'd all mistake them for his girlfriends. Ha! Impossible to confuse that relationship.

He had trouble walking, among other things I cringed to consider since he had to rely on these girls to attend him inside his home, not just sauntering with him to pick up his social security checks at the post office. His girls kept their mouths shut and kept to themselves. They were hired help, not floozies who spoiled for a sugar daddy they could easily fleece once he forgot how to balance his checkbook. Marita, the cashier at Velva's, considered the situation good gossip. She wallowed in the notion that this old man, retired from the state transportation department, depended on high school dropouts to fix his meals and dress him.

“Did you sthee his latesth persthonal assthisthant?” Marita leered through her lashes caked with mascara, her tongue stud clacking against her teeth and leaving her lisping. She smirked and winked as if Mr. Coble engaged them for lewd stuff we could only whisper about. I couldn’t have cared less, and I’m sure the glare I shot Marita convinced her of that without a doubt. It hardly mattered to me if they were his girlfriends, drug-addled hookers, or long-lost relatives anticipating his death and the redistribution of his fortune, which to a nineteen-year-old would not have to amount to much.

He went through ’em like toilet paper. He clung to a fresh one every other month or so. They all seemed snotty, and I never saw any reason to make friends. They could barely stomach the job; you could smell that a mile off. You couldn’t have paid me to hang out with that repulsive man. Sometimes he’d confront me at Velva’s or on my way from the post office or while hauling the garbage to the curb, his liver-spotted paw attached to the forearm of some downcast girl. He spouted about some problem with his “bowel movements,” or he griped about Mike, or groused about “the youth of today” who didn’t understand the meaning of hard work or some bull. Other times he corralled me to bitch about the weather or the politicians or his doctors. He checked off anyone and everything on his shit list. I never sassed back unless I had no other choice. If you let him say his piece, he would scowl at you like you were a disgusting bug that deserved squashing, while he shook his head as if everything remained hopeless. Then he would totter away, his current blank-faced girl offering him nothing more than her slack arm for support. The two would shuffle off while I resumed fooling with Mitchell’s car seat or lugging groceries or collecting the broken glass from beer bottles taking root in my yard like dandelions. I almost pitied his “personal assistants.” Maybe I should have buddied up and encouraged them to steer the geezer away from me during their outings.

Instead, the pair would cross the street and wander nearby. "That man of yours is a menace!" the old coot would blurt through his shriveled lips quivering amidst his furrowed face.

He was referring to Mike. Tell me what I don't already know, Grandpa, I ached to spit back. If he had ever said that about Mitchell, I would have slapped him or something. Mr. Coble never smiled. He had no reason to. You wonder why people of that nature bother to live. I never noticed whether or not anyone visited him other than those girls. If he had family, they demonstrated little interest in dealing with him.

"I've a good mind to call the Law the next time he causes a ruckus like last night." Mr. Coble would jerk his head to underline his point.

You do that, asshole.

Then Mr. Coble and his girl would waddle down the road or to his house. He belonged in a nursing home. Maybe none could tolerate him.

The neighbors next to me seemed nervous about the whole setup. They were not from here. I'd bet they settled in with plans of pushing their picture-perfect young 'uns on backyard swing sets, strolling to a quaint country diner, chasing fireflies across their trimmed lawn with the children on peaceful June evenings. A crisp, wholesome small-town existence admired by the city folk in Cliff City or some far-off urban hellhole of congestion and pollution.

The babies never showed. The only greasy spoon in Willisburg burned down, to no one's surprise as the owner could barely pay his staff but never missed an insurance premium. Plenty of fireflies, but Mike usually trashed those peaceful evenings.

The husband and wife poured all their free time and attention into their red and white impatiens and their yellow and orange marigolds and their Kentucky Bluegrass, which they seeded and watered and mowed until each stalk gleamed and made your mouth water. One early, early Saturday morning after finishing their last beers in a parking lot behind a gas station off Main, some kids decided to rumble over for several fast wheelies through the damp yard, gouging out patches and forming circular tire ruts you could fall into. After weeks of intense effort raking the soil smooth, reseeding, scattering wads of straw, and scheduled watering, the grass grew back as vibrant and lush as ever. Better even.

Learning to walk, Mitchell would tug on my hand as he wobbled toward the neighbor's lawn. We'd ramble over when I assumed the house empty, removing our shoes to roll around in it. The solid blades tickled between your toes, and the thick tufts massaged the soles of your feet. Mowed in a concise diagonal pattern, the two-foot swaths seesawed from shimmering pastel green to dark. I had to gently smack Mitchell's fingers as he attempted to pull out fistfuls.

Once while hiking to Sadie's, Mitchell aimed straight for the luscious greenery with the hungry look of a starving deer. He was about two. He shucked his sandals for me to carry as he sank his bare feet into the grass bordering our road. He wore his sweet ear-to-ear grin and laughed so contagiously I didn't worry about the neighbors. Then glancing up, I saw the husband staring out their front picture window. He didn't appear peeved or nothing. As soon as I caught him watching us, he ducked out of sight as if he were the one trespassing.

Sadie!

I dialed the number.

Sadie rescued me after Mitchell was born, soon after we arrived home from the hospital. After I'd given up on Mike, and Tammy had already given me all she could.

I had reluctantly accepted Mike's indifference toward our baby. We limped through our days in a wordless agreement. When he bothered to grace our home, he would bypass me. I'd pout rather than shout when Mike hung out at home, chucking his wet bath towels on the bedroom floor and casting away his dirty dishes to the couch or the pock-marked end table. I'd pretend to sleep when he tromped in well past midnight, drunk and knocking over the nightstand. I'd shut off the faucet without a fuss after discovering he'd left the water running. I just didn't have the energy for quarrels.

He started staying away, sometimes up to a week at a time, and would explode if I asked where he had been. He ignored my protruding belly, and I never bugged him for anything unless I required someone to ferry a bulky load from the car. I reveled in my happiness over the life squirming inside me, only silently so he wouldn't trip over it and start a row.

I groaned through the morning sickness while I excitedly counted the weeks, then days between each medical appointment. The thought of labor and delivery stripped the smile from my face, however, and the birthing classes didn't help me breathe any easier. Mike refused to attend a single prenatal class or accompany me to the clinic. He ignored the articles I asked him to read, flipping aside the few pages I'd ripped from magazines in waiting rooms. Sometimes I sat through the baby classes by myself. Other times Tammy tagged along if I spoiled for a partner, but only after she chugged a beer or two.

About a week before my due date, Mike and I squabbled, and for the ten-hundredth time he swore at me, stomped off, and zoomed away in Blue. I begged Mike not to split with her, except my swollen belly and my chubby legs hampered me from chasing after him and snatching the keys out of his mitts. Weeks later, I found out he wrecked her, my Blue, abandoning her to the weeds in a ditch off a country road north of Willisburg.

When my time came, Mike had vanished. Out of work again, he left me clueless on how to track him. After my water broke, I frantically dialed everyone we knew and every dive bar in Rallis County. I wanted him by my side for this! Having Mitchell without a husband never embarrassed me. Some people at the doctor's office or the hospital or Velva's would inspect me, alone with my enormous belly and no wedding ring, and they would smirk as they turned away. I was not ashamed. A marriage license provided just one more scrap of paper to clutter my life, and though I had my moments when I wished for something like that, a piece of paper meant nothing. Momma finally got her piece of paper, yet that didn't change a thing.

That morning my agony began, some horrible smelling stuff dripped down my legs, the cramping in my low back shooting across my gut dragged through me deeper and longer, then quicker and sharper, and all the fear and worry I'd locked up revved and sped around like a crazed motorcycle gang. My arms and legs flapped in a frenzy as my heart and soul roared for Mike. How could I survive this without him? Without him holding me? He was supposed to be with me for this! Not just for the horror of childbirth, but the whole nine yards. The three a.m. feedings, the temper tantrums, the birthday parties decorated with balloons and paper cups leaking red punch, the report cards, the dented car fenders, the suspicious phone calls, the arguments over a messy bedroom, the family photos, prom.

Mike! Damn you! I needed him to help me ride out this tornado. But not just for me. For him! Mike had to shepherd me to the hospital and tend to his newborn baby to make everything right, to still the chaos rattling around inside him, to smother the twisted demons clawing at him. The experience would forge him into a whole man, not a frightened boy flitting from one toy to the next.

It struck me like a baseball bat. Mike must watch his baby come into the world! He had to hear me scream. He had to see me bleed. Then he would realize I loved him and our baby more than anything, then, now and forever, enough to suffer through the searing pain wrenching me to shreds. And he would know this only by standing next to me, by letting me squeeze his hand through each and every contraction. He had to cradle a squalling babe, fresh from the before-world, crying and reaching for the man who would guide him through this colder, crueler one. He needed to stroke those precious toes and have his finger grabbed by his baby's hungry grip, that angry little fist that would latch onto him as if it would never let go. He would understand how much we needed him. Then he would know his place. He would come home. He would come home to us. And we would be a family.

Between shrieks and moans from the pain, that god-awful burning misery I will never forget, I focused on this dream rather than my horror as I weakly braced myself for the next spasm of torment. My fantasy of how Mitchell's birth could unite the three of us granted me brief but cherished seconds of comfort and saved me from completely losing it that chilly spring morning.

I prayed somehow he would catch wind or someone would alert him, something, anything, and he would burst in last minute but there nonetheless. I clung to my hope he would screech into the delivery room to see his new baby. His paternal instinct would blast through the surface at the last minute, end his frigid treatment of us, and bring him back to me, to our baby, to our home.

What the hell was I thinking? He had wandered off again on a drinking binge somewhere. Snoring on someone else's couch or in the back seat of Blue. I should have scratched Mike's name from the birth certificate, except I couldn't do that to Mitchell. I didn't want him to grow up believing he was some kind of bastard.

After finally giving up on Mike, I rang Tammy, who managed to comprehend my desperation through my wailing. She hustled over and drove me to the hospital, gravel spraying and tires squealing. Before moving to Colorado, she still breezed by for a beer or two in my kitchen. She would tease Mitchell about how she almost delivered him in a deserted barn off the highway. But that was not true. Many, many, many hours later, he finally tore out of me and hollered louder than his father ever did.

Except his father never heard that.

6

Ellis stuck his ugly mug through the kitchen doorway.

"What y'all up to? I never would of guessed I'd say this, but I've seen enough Rocky and Bullwinkle as I can stand. We need to hit the road. Need to be in Milesdale. Where we moving that big ol' freezer, anyway?"

He threw a sneaky glance at me. Something about that man vexed me to no end. He hammed it up as a ridiculous clown. With a goofy grease-painted grin, a large plastic nose, and floppy rubber shoes slapping the ground, he pranced and performed. It struck me as an act, as if he truly understood what was what and he itched for you to know. Just like a clown, he had simply painted that stupid expression on his face.

"You figured out where we're moving that freezer of yours?" he asked once more, his ear-to-ear smirk a pure exaggeration designed to irk me once again.

I couldn't answer him because all of a sudden, I pictured the bag of groceries I bought from WAL-MART sitting on the truck's floorboard. How long had it simmered in that roasting cab? Would the milk have soured?

"Oh damn it to hell!" I hung up the phone before the first ring and bolted out of the kitchen, banging through the screen door. I grappled with the handle on the driver's side of the Ford. We had only picked up new shoes for Mitchell, toothpaste, and milk, hopefully not spoiled yet. I usually would not have commuted that distance for little more than nothing. Milk, shoot, I could have hiked down the street for some not too dated at Velva's. But I had to get far from that house for a spell. For a long time. Time to think. Mitchell hadn't minded the outing.

I'd played with the idea of just driving and driving. Not stopping. Not turning back. They would have captured me eventually. I'm not dumb. I probably could of only scrounged enough gas money to get me halfway through Kansas, and then where would I have been?

Ellis stretched his scrawny, freckled neck through the doorway between the family room and the kitchen. The television set erupted with a salvo of activity and noise. Mitchell chuckled as he sat cross-legged two feet from the screen. No longer entertained by pestering me, Ellis directed his attention back to the television, slouching against the doorframe with his backpack still strapped to him. I rearranged everything in the refrigerator to make room for the milk.

Then I punched the numbers to call Sadie.

She left her phone by her couch and had one in the kitchen and in her bedroom as well, so she never needed to travel much, generally lifting the receiver within the first three rings. One time the phone rang and rang and rang while I waited for her to chirp her friendly hello. A mini blizzard had barricaded Mitchell and me, so Sadie couldn't have left her house. I worried she'd fallen and hurt herself. Fretted myself into a frenzy as I expected to find her lying unconscious or with a busted ankle. I began planning a half-assed rescue and how I had to throw on a coat, bundle Mitchell and trek over to check on her. She answered after the tenth ring, apologizing for alarming me as she had just toweled herself off after a shower.

This time after one ring, a sunshiny voice greeted me.

"How's it going, you keeping cool?" I asked.

"Why honey, with all this insulation, I'm feeling pretty darn tropical, but the fans run and so does the TV, and I've got plenty of shade. How's your AC, landlord got it fixed?"

"You BS'ing me? He's fooling around until the first snowstorm, then he can bellyache about he's snowed in and can't it wait until the weather warms up?"

"Make his phone rattle off the hook. Let there be no rest for the wicked," Sadie said. I'd bet her rolling laugh jiggled her chin as she lounged on her sofa with plush, frilly pillows propping her head, fuzzy purple slippers on her gigantic feet, and probably the muumuu embroidered with bunches of fraying crimson raspberries draped across her short, chubby legs.

I tried to laugh along with her, except I sputtered like a flat tire.

Since Mitchell entered my life, I'd come to know Sadie well. We budded into more than neighbors. She floated into my world as my guardian angel. She saved me from certain despair. Whenever I'm in the dumps, she cheers me with words of praise and encouragement, brownies with cream cheese frosting, hugs, and sometimes sympathetic tears. She has no reason to be such a good woman. Life has treated her like shit. She just chops those lemons into lemonade, humming while she stoops to smell the roses. I truly doubt she could speak ill of the devil. What would she think of me if she knew what I'd done?

Sadie stepped up to the plate after everyone else abandoned me as I collapsed, home on my own and distraught after those days of hell in the county hospital.

Up to that time, I'd depended on Tammy, who resented pitching in for Mike and cursed his name every time I called her crying. I could not have survived all nine months without her. After I quit praying for Mike to escort me to the hospital, I called Tammy, who borrowed her sort-of boyfriend's car since she couldn't afford to bail hers out of the mechanic's shop. I had found a used car seat to bring the baby home in, but it didn't buckle quite right. Tammy wrestled it into the back seat of the Pontiac, the straps tangling with the seat belt as she growled and swore before she secured it more or less. She was a bit hungover and pissed off for me about Mike not manning up.

Tammy and I roared into the emergency room, me clutching my throbbing belly and whimpering. I wept and begged for relief; everyone ignored me as if my pleas made no sense. Tammy nixed signing anything and almost started a fistfight with the admissions lady. I guess the hospital only wanted someone to hold responsible for the mess.

Racing the hospital corridors, Tammy yelled at every wary person she lurched past to get me "some drugs, some real good drugs," until someone finally kicked her out. Preoccupied with the pain, I didn't notice her leave. The doctor on call – my regular doctor had a golf tournament or something – barked his orders at the nurses and aides within earshot and instructed me to shut up so he could hear himself think. Think?! What did he have to think about? I did all the work! The nurses wandered in and out of my room in a huff, muttering to themselves about Lord only knows what I'd done. The drugs didn't work. I groaned and bellowed while my body twisted and turned itself inside out.

"We might have to do a cesarean if you don't calm down. Can you try harder for us?" asked a young nurse whose large gold cross kept swinging away from her breastbone as she leaned over my sweat-soaked sheets.

Sure thing, bitch.

The older nurse charged in and out. "Concentrate more on

breathing and less on hollering. We can't give you any more pain medication. You've had enough." She scolded me as if I were a child who refused to put away her toys.

Fuck you! I tried to shout at her, but I yelped something unintelligible instead.

The crotchety nurse would desert me, and after an eternity, reenter my room with the doctor, who would peer between my legs then finger me while frowning and snapping at anyone within earshot. Then they would all leave. The nurses would sporadically stop by to eyeball the printout from the contraption attached to the belt wrapped around my belly.

"You're not ready to push, focus on your breath," the old nurse said in a tone flavored with vinegar.

They didn't have to cut me open. Mitchell arrived the old-fashioned way, all slimy and pink and yowling and the most beautiful sight I have ever seen, and I am sure ever will. He weighed six pounds, three ounces and measured twenty inches long.

I could barely walk afterward. My bottom hurt so bad I can't even describe it. I shuddered every time the urge to pee afflicted me, and the bathroom became my torture chamber for weeks afterward. I'd been in labor for more than twenty hours at the county hospital, so after they carted Mitchell to the nursery, I slept like the dead. They'd roust me to nurse, but I must have snoozed through that.

Then they shuffled their paperwork in order to whisk me out the door. I explained to them I had no help at home, no family, no husband. They appeared all put out that I didn't care to shove off yet. Still no Mike. I'd left word with his mother days before. She tearfully wished me luck as she had no idea of Mike's whereabouts and nothing else to offer.

The morning after Mitchell's birthday, an orderly wheeled me out to the curb with Mitchell in my lap. The orderly scratched a scab on his elbow while Tammy loaded us into the borrowed car.

Tammy drove us home with Mitchell bawling the entire trip back to Willisburg from Cliff City. Tires squealing, we nearly careened off the road on some of those sharp bends. Tammy didn't say much. The baby's racket surely needled her. She didn't dawdle at the house. Didn't sit. She escaped before I could latch onto her.

"Everything OK, now? You got everything? Go ahead and ring me if ..." she said, her fingers on the doorknob as she rushed out before she could finish or I could respond. Then I heard the Pontiac's tires peel out of my driveway. After that, I couldn't reach Tammy by phone. I would dial her number all hours of the day and night, listening while her phone rang and rang. She hadn't even left her answering machine on.

All by myself with that baby squalling endlessly and myself about torn in two. No mother's advice or casseroles in the fridge for dinner. No husband's fumbling but eager hands. No Mike. No hint of where he'd disappeared to. Whether or not he knew he had fathered a son.

That first night home I didn't sleep at all. Soon as I'd doze off, Mitchell's whimpers swelled into howls. I needed shut-eye like a fish needs water. My breasts, triple their normal size, ached and leaked constantly, drenching the front of my nightgown. All the while, Mitchell cried and cried and cried. I would rock him in the cradle of my arms, and he would cry. I would nurse him, yet nothing dripping out of my cracked, swollen nipples satisfied him. He would suck a bit, then cry, then suck a little more, then cry a lot more. We sat there on the couch, the same sagging sofa in my family room today, Mitchell's head on my chest, and together we would cry and cry and cry.

No Mike. No money. No Momma. Tammy wasn't picking up her phone. My brain, my whole body, shrieked from lack of sleep, lack of anything my body craved to survive. My pee burned me like molten lava. Mitchell had puked or pooped on every clean hand-me-down I had set aside for him. He had already soaked or soiled almost an entire package of diapers, and we were down to our last two. My check to the telephone company had bounced. The electric company threatened to unplug us in less than a month.

The sun had begun to set, fashioning geometric shadows on the carpet. I knew better than to hope for more than a blink of sleep that night. The thought of another minute on that couch with Mitchell screeching made me want to scream. I teetered on the verge of calling Harold. I was beyond desperate. Then that soft rapping on the screen door.

Mitchell wailed louder, squeezing his eyelids shut, flailing his tight fists, and kicking his blanket off of himself with his thrashing feet. I'd stopped sobbing when I heard the knock on the door. The fear welled inside me and almost gushed out.

Who is it? Will they figure out what a horrible mother I am? Have they finally realized how incompetent I am and have arrived to take him away?

I couldn't budge. I couldn't utter a word.

"Hello. Are you ... hello? It's Sadie from across the street. Is it OK? Can I come in? Don't get up now, I can let myself in if that's all right with you," said a girlish voice.

The screen door creaked open, the wooden door whining on its hinges, followed by a thud, thud, thud of plodding footsteps. Then Sadie peeked through the doorway. The enormous woman shrank backward when she caught sight of me as I gaped at her in shock.

"Honey, is there anything I can do?" she asked. She hugged a ceramic serving bowl topped with aluminum foil. The hem of her ballooning, shapeless straw-colored shift, garnished with an ivory crochet collar, ended below her knees. Coarse, dark hairs sprouted on her unshaven legs all the way to her ankles. She had crammed her feet into the biggest tennis shoes I'd ever seen, ones you must have to special order because where could you find shoes so wide?

Bone-weary, I struggled to lift my eyelids to squint into her face. Her eyes flitted from Mitchell and me to the couch to the ceiling to the floor, dodging my tear-filled gaze. Long, limp strands of dingy gray hair strayed past her rounded shoulders and hung alongside her pink cheeks. A faint scar pulled on her upper lip, producing a strange half-smile. She breathed hoarsely, from the effort of hiking from her house to mine, I assumed. Her skin glistened with perspiration. Despite the cool spring evening, Sadie sweated from the exertion of walking to my house.

Mitchell quit for exactly two seconds after Sadie crowded into the room, then he resumed his quivering clamor. I started to bawl again too.

Sadie didn't run from us. She set her bowl on the kitchen counter before gingerly scooping Mitchell out of my lap. She sandwiched him beneath her chin and on top of her jiggling, shelf-sized bosom. She stepped side to side from one foot to the other, cooing as she cuddled his trembling body.

"There there, little one. There there. Ah, yes. You're all right. You're fine. Shhhhhhh, little one. There, there."

My moans let up as her hushed murmurings calmed me too.

I watched Sadie work her magic on Mitchell, who battled every inch of the way as he eventually drifted to sleep. As soon as Mitchell snoozed in her arms, she circled in search of a safe space to set him, her body pitching back and forth as she moved her huge feet. She saw the wicker bassinet propped against the wall and lumbered across the room. She bent forward and laid him on his back as if he were a priceless crystal sculpture.

Then Sadie turned to me.

For once, I must have appeared as disgusting as her. I hadn't changed my nightgown since I left the hospital. My breasts leaked milk and left damp stains the size of basketballs on the thin cotton. I hadn't showered since my hospital ordeal. No sleep and days of weeping and exhaustion had left my face puffy and flushed. I couldn't tell you what I'd eaten. A bowl of dry cereal? Unbuttered toast maybe and an overcooked TV dinner, probably. Dirty dishes clogged my kitchen sink and covered the counters. A basket of smelly laundry blocked the entrance to my bedroom as it spilled onto the floor. I hadn't brushed my teeth since before my water broke. I sniveled as quietly as possible so I wouldn't wake the baby.

Sadie no longer stared at the floor or the walls. Her eyes rested on mine without fleeing. She walked toward me, swaying with each footstep. She eased herself down beside me. The sofa springs squeaked. The cushions underneath her sank about two feet. Then she swaddled me with her fat arms, and I sobbed into the folds of her dress to smother my blubbering until I conked out.

Sadie adopted us both instantly that day. Babied us. Babysat Mitchell. Brought food, extra diapers, formula, and playthings for Mitchell. When I did find a job, my paychecks rarely covered daycare. I would pack up Mitchell and chauffeur him over to Sadie's before my shift. Sadie would only frown pleasantly if I offered her a five or a ten when I retrieved him.

She lived like a hermit: more or less walled off from the world. A homebody who had nobody. No family. No children of her own, I assumed, at least until she let on what they did to her. She loved Mitchell as her own and ripened into a big sister to me. I would not have survived without her, and I thank God every day for granting me such a loving, selfless friend. I have always hoped that someday I can remedy all the cruelty she has suffered. I haven't cooked up anything yet.

Sadie shared her story with me now and then, spooning out bits and pieces while munching on bowls of salty popcorn or Lean Cuisine lasagna served hot and bubbly from her microwave.

Here's the jiffy version. Sadie's fifteen-year-old mother thought keeping the baby would help her keep the daddy, but even back then in the late 1950s that scheme eventually failed. She started ditching little Sadie with a drunk neighbor to snag a new man or get high herself. By the time Sadie landed on a social worker's desk, she wasn't the cream of the yearly crop of babies available for adoption. They lust for newborns, those childless couples. Preferably healthy and cute. After they winnow out the fresh ones, the husband and wife pray long and hard, and out of the goodness of their hearts, they try one like Sadie. Already a fussy toddler in an overflowing foster home, Sadie sported a cleft palate and a stomach disorder as a result of having a teenage momma who drank, smoked, and sniffed anything passed around.

The Kansas City family that took in Sadie already had adopted a newborn boy, one of those perfect blond-hair blue-eyed ones. They settled on Sadie, as the adoption agencies and the lawyers and probably the husband and wife themselves all agreed they already had the pick of the litter with their first child. And the husband and wife, they desired someone for their perfectly adorable little son to play with: a delightful little girl.

Now I don't know about you, but my experience with boys has been there's one particular game they like to play with little girls. Sadie always packed extra pounds, even at age thirteen. So she was pretty far along before the husband and wife figured out Sadie would make them grandparents. For about a month, they dragged her from one doctor to another, scrambling to hire one who would take care of Sadie's "monthly troubles." No one said "abortion" back then because it was illegal, except for the right kind of money you could find the right kind of doctor. Unfortunately for the husband and wife, they could not find the right kind.

Sadie had no clue what hit her. When she finally realized what was happening, she couldn't help but smile. The husband and wife started treating her like some diseased wild animal. All the torments her older brother inflicted, all the horrible taunts from the creeps at school, all the disappointed silences from her adoptive parents; all that began to fade. She was going to be a momma and have a baby of her own! No more dolls, no more pretend. Someone she could love who would love her back. She was only thirteen and didn't know any better.

They never allowed Sadie the chance. After her first contractions, they doped her, c-sectioned her, and put the baby up for adoption. She came to with her hands and feet bound to a gurney as an unfamiliar man in white scrubs wheeled her into the halls of the state mental hospital. The husband and wife had decided Sadie had something wrong with her that called for professional help. They signed papers naming the government her guardian. It got worse, I'm sure. Trapped in a psycho ward! Sadie never talks about that. I don't expect she has a hankering to relive that horror. I doubt I could listen to it without dying to slice up one of those monsters from her past.

After Sadie turned eighteen, she managed to convince the one doctor who actually gave a shit that she wasn't crazy and they released her. By then, Sadie had learned the truth about her own adoption and started searching for her real momma while trying to find her own child. Problem was, her real momma could not be unearthed: either dead or so strung out that she left no forwarding address. Still, Sadie kept knocking on government doors and begging for information about her family.

She finally did track down her daughter to a two-story brick home in a city near where Sadie had lived with her adoptive family. Sadie described her daughter as a beautiful girl with delicate curls and a perfect family that provided her with everything. Sadie could see that her daughter was growing up with parents who hugged and kissed her in a grand house and a yard full of toys and a swing set. When Sadie spoke of her daughter, her face glowed and her thick lips curved into a crooked smirk on account of the botched surgery on her mouth.

After locating her daughter, Sadie stalked the sidewalks nearby for a few days, observing all she could about her baby and her baby's family until the neighbors ran her off. She never explained why she didn't try to meet with her daughter or the girl's family. If someone had adopted me, I would have wanted to know. Know my beginnings. Who my real parents were. But I believe Sadie made the right decision, tough as I know it was. And I respect the hell out of her for it.

Sadie's story has somewhat of a happy ending. She did trace her grandma to the forest green vinyl-sided house Sadie inhabits now. Her grandma welcomed her into her home with arms spread wide. Not many months after their tearful reunion, her grandma died from cancer. She left her home to Sadie in her will. Now, Sadie lives rent-free and collects a monthly check from the state bureaucrats. They consider her disabled. What do they know.

Maybe my including her in our family and indulging her as

Mitchell's surrogate momma washed away some of the hurt she has carried along with all those extra slabs of flesh. I cannot imagine having to swallow all that sadness.

◆ ◆ ◆

"Hey woman, can I send you a sweet peach for the afternoon?" I sugarcoated my tongue to sound casual and cheerful.

"That would make my day. Tell my favorite man we'll bake chocolate chip cookies and he can lick the bowl."

"Don't you dare," I said, hardly meaning it. "He'll get sick from eating raw egg. He'll skedaddle over soon as I can rip him away from the TV. And, well, errr ... it would ... can he spend the night too?" My words slid sideways before bumping into each other. I would not return home until past midnight if even that. I had no idea where the night would take me. If I would be coming back.

"Of course. Send his pj's and a change of clothes. That would be fine. We'll catch a movie on TV." Sadie's voice danced with excitement. Then her tone dropped a notch. "Everything OK, honey? You sound a bit wound up."

"Yeah, well what else is new."

"I see you've got visitors."

Whenever I pop in on her, she's sitting watching TV. She's parked her couch and her television so she can scope out the world through her picture window, what little of it strays down this potholed, dead-end road. She might have even watched for Mike to leave the night before.

"Yeah, got some heavy lifting so I need some strong backs.

I'm selling my freezer. Something extra until I get a job or something going again." I puckered my lips while trying to speak slower.

Breathe. Relax, girl. You're just chatting with a friend.

I ran my finger along the razor's edge of the voice I inherited from Father, the one we whipped out when fielding questions we didn't fancy answering.

"A freezer? You referring to that chest freezer in the garage? How much are you wanting?"

My alarm pealed again, yet Sadie didn't grill me suspiciously. Just friendly. Just yakking. Mitchell and I are the only ones in town who give her the time of day. Most folks either snarl at her or look the other way when she ambles by. Children point their fingers and gawk. Everyone in these parts keeps her at arm's length. They have no clue what a beautiful person she is. Their loss.

"Not much. But it's taking up space and I don't need it. Anyway, I'll send Mitchell over, maybe five minutes."

"No really. I'd buy it. How much you asking? I always appreciate extra room here for my favorite treats. Ice cream, pizza. What do you want for it?" Her voice dwindled, and I could almost hear her rummaging for her magenta vinyl purse the size of a grocery sack, pawing through old receipts and gum wrappers, a tube of lotion and sunglasses Mitchell giggles at because they are so big they make Sadie's face seem tiny.

She knew I was broke, and she would buy a cardboard box full of dirty rags from me. That's her way of helping us without causing me to feel like a charity case. She routinely hauls food to our home: casseroles, bags of chips, cartons of Mitchell's favorite cereal, soda, warm muffins from the oven. She would stuff cash in my pockets if I let her.

"No sense you lugging that freezer all over creation in this heat. I can sure use another deep freeze. I can sure use a lot of things," she said with a short laugh. "Don't want to run out of food and a freezer sure would be handy especially if this old thing I got now breaks down. Besides I've got to defrost mine anyhow and it'd give me more storage for all my frozen goodies. I'd have a heck of a ..."

"No. I already got the dough. Couldn't be an Indian giver. Sorry. I got a lawnmower that spits black smoke if you want that."

"Oh, well hmm." Sadie's breath rattled and wheezed into my ear as I stewed.

I swatted my forehead for spewing my venom at her, for muzzling her with the crack about the lawnmower when she was only trying to help Mitchell and me. She could peg how strung out I was right through the phone lines. A regular clairvoyant. I prayed she couldn't read minds. My unflinching anger and frustration seeped through my pores at everyone and everything. Dear Sadie, of all people, you don't deserve this. Sorry. I'll stitch things up later. Somehow.

She could tell I was losing my grip, gradually slipping from the ledge. She's the dearest, kindest thing on the planet. She just wanted to catch me. Stop me from falling. Except I'd already tumbled beyond her reach.

You can't rescue me now, Sadie. You're entitled to a better friend. I'm sorry I'm a liar and a user and a terrible person and a ...

She was all smiles and sugarplums when we hung up. She doesn't hold anything against anybody. Ever.

7

Johnny, Ellis, and I followed Mitchell out of the house. Before Mitchell skipped off to Sadie's, visions of licking dough-glazed spoons swirling through his darling head, I hugged him, pressing my lips into his hair as I caressed his shoulders. He pulled away, and his grin softened as he peered at me. I handed him his school backpack, which I'd crammed with clothing for his overnighter with Sadie. He slung it across his shoulder.

"Bye, Mom."

He waved in Ellis' direction, barely acknowledging him, and then marched over to Johnny.

"Thank you, sir," he said, his back straight, his forehead high, his eyes meeting Johnny's. Mitchell didn't act like a shy boy addressing a stranger.

Johnny dropped to one knee in front of Mitchell until their eyes were level. He touched his hand to Mitchell's shoulder. They stared at each other with their eyes locked. Neither blinked. Even Ellis paused his eternal fidgeting for an instant. Johnny didn't say anything. Mitchell smiled the smile of a man, not a child. My heart erupted. A wave struck me again, toppling me and snaring my bearings as it rolled away.

God, please don't let me faint again.

Mitchell beamed at me, and I stockpiled strength from his unwavering gaze.

"I'll see you tomorrow, Mom."

So confident and assured. A grown man inside a young boy's body. Sometimes he's so serious, and he's only seven years old.

Mitchell's eyes dove deep into mine for another few seconds. Then he took off. His spindly legs flew above the grass and leaped across the foot-deep ditch between the graveled road and the weeds, his feet smacking the crumbling pavement and shattered rock. He bounced up Sadie's walkway and through her front door. He doesn't even have to knock.

I'll see you tomorrow.

I gingerly cupped his promise in my palms, swaddling it in a velvet cloth, and squirreled it away somewhere safe where it wouldn't get misplaced or damaged or stolen.

I'll see you tomorrow.

His faith inspired me and steeled me to all the fears that tore at my determination to survive this disaster. His last words guided me to the only thing that mattered. I would see my baby again. Tomorrow. Nothing else meant squat. We would reunite, our precious family. We have a family. Mitchell and I. And no one can ever destroy that.

Mitchell had presented me with hundreds of pocket-sized treasures throughout his short life. Crinkled scraps of paper with crayon drawings, shiny pebbles, or limp dandelions he plucked without completely squishing. I would open my fist to receive his gift, and carry on as if he'd rewarded me with something more valuable than gold. I taped his artwork to the refrigerator or found a small jar for the flowers, displayed the stones and odd-shaped sticks on the kitchen windowsill. Once forgotten, I tossed the rocks outside, flung the dead weeds into the grass, and eventually, I wadded up the sketches, hiding them underneath crud in the trash can so he wouldn't notice. Not this time, sweet Mitchell. I will carry this one in my left shirt pocket forever.

Clanking from the garage signaled Ellis poking around again, and that brought me back like a slap.

"We need a strong rope," Johnny said. One thing you could say about Johnny, he didn't clutter the place with unnecessary words to trip over. I gestured toward coils of tangled rope dangling from a hook on the far wall of the garage. Johnny navigated a path through the cardboard boxes and black garbage bags bulging with junk.

I shooed Ellis from the freezer and removed the old containers I'd set on the lid the night before. I'd stacked almost empty gallon cans with petrified paint drippings flowing down the rusted metal sides, a bottle of varnish, and a worthless bucket of dried plaster hardened into a concrete-like substance. I preoccupied myself with returning the jugs and cans and bottles to the lopsided bookshelf listing against the wall of the garage. Each container had left a darker spot on the shelf where the dust hadn't gathered, so I busied myself with matching them. I lifted one and angled myself between some crap I'd rearranged to construct a narrow passage between the freezer and the wooden shelves. I performed the task methodically as if my efforts would leave some lasting mark, represent some significant deed. That rectangular space was from the can of thinner. That circle, that was ... no, that was from the quart of sky blue I used on Mitchell's room when he turned two. I saved it assuming someday I would paint over his crayoned scribbles on his bedroom walls. We tacked up posters to cover his doodles instead, so what was the point? What was the point in saving it? What was the point in keeping any of this?

Mice had sprinkled their poop on the wilting boxes containing Momma's ceiling-to-floor thick-threaded drapes.

During my last visit with her in the hospital, I promised this, promised that. Promised to hang those curtains she socked away money for, swore I would not let them go to waste. I don't remember all she said during that final talk in her hospital bed. She knew she was dying. By then, so did I. Whatever she asked, I promised I would do it. Wish I'd kept a better accounting, as I've been neglecting her memory in that way. But not in others, Momma, not always.

Another tidal wave of panic surged as my heart pummeled the inside of my chest. Then a crushing fatigue hit me. I hadn't slept well the night before. Didn't sleep at all in fact.

Ellis picked up a toaster with a frayed electrical cord. His puzzled scowl soon slid into a blank expression of boredom. Johnny's frame filled the doorway, blocking the glare of the afternoon sun.

I wanted to let go. Stop thinking. Doze off. Melt into the soothing dimness of my bedroom. Slumberland. Forget. Wake up and write it all off as a terrifying nightmare.

But I could not. I ferried back and forth, back and forth. Coordinating this shape with that quart of paint, that circle with this gallon jug. After I finished clearing the top of the freezer, Johnny examined the waist-high appliance, calculating measurements or forming a plan, I supposed. Ellis knocked over an ironing board as he roamed about.

"Watch it!" I hissed, roused out of my trance.

"Well dang. Sorry, ma'am. Wouldn't want to break none of your priceless possessions out here. Sorry missy," he said, hardly disguising his contempt.

And what the hell do you have to show for yourself besides a secondhand backpack full of dingy clothes, I huffed to myself while pivoting back toward the freezer.

Under Johnny's command, the two men dragged the freezer out of the garage through the side door. Skittering to and fro, I planted my palms on the freezer lid. I feared they would raise the lid accidentally or on purpose, didn't matter which. Johnny motioned for me to stay back.

I hugged myself until I practically squeezed the breath from my lungs. My skull pounded. Had I popped any Tylenol earlier? I kept meaning to. I store it in the bathroom cabinet, next to the packages of Alka Seltzer and expired over-the-counter cold tablets. A pink bottle of Caladryl for the poison ivy and mosquito bites Mitchell scratches ferociously. Had I eaten that morning? I poured Mitchell a bowl of Cocoa Puffs, spilling half of them. They scattered, rolling across the kitchen floor. I'd snatched some potato chips from the open sack Mitchell cradled while we aimlessly paced the aisles at WAL-MART. Maybe that explained why my head throbbed and my stomach churned.

Once out the door, Johnny tilted one end of the freezer several inches up while directing Ellis to pass the rope over and under so the lid could be tied shut. Ellis bound the freezer, scrambling to his knees to shove the rope ends underneath, then pushing himself upright, skidding around to cinch the rope before slinging it across the top sideways and lengthwise again and again until Johnny grunted for Ellis to stop. Then Johnny gradually lowered the freezer until it settled level on the concrete. He tightened the rope and tied a knot with the ends, the muscles in his forearms flexing as he pulled. I released a wisp of air, and my shoulders relaxed for an instant. He'd secured the lid better than that antique clasp.

Johnny and Ellis slowly hoisted the freezer less than a foot above the ground. Johnny's side rode higher, yet he did his best to maintain the freezer level so Ellis wouldn't have to bear most of the weight. The strain barely showed on Johnny.

"Heavy, heavy. You said you didn't have nothing in here. Man, this is heavy," Ellis said.

Johnny backed up with his end and only halted when Ellis whined loud enough and threatened to drop his end. While resting, Ellis would scrunch his brow and pucker his face in disgust. "Don't you have a dolly or something, hell I never! And how the heck are we going to get it up on the tailgate? This is the heaviest darn empty freezer I've ever hauled. Bar none."

Then the two men would pry up the bottom with their fingers, heave the freezer heavenward and inch toward the tailgate.

I fluttered around with feeble attempts to help. I couldn't keep from dancing about, creating as much of a nuisance of myself as that nitwit Ellis. I shuddered, guessing how others might compare me with him. We were pretty close in age. My own face staring back at me from the bathroom mirror every morning had developed a coarser surface. Creases lingered long after I quit squinting, wrinkles slithered across my cheeks, pits from my youthful run-in with pimples crisscrossed my chin, and pouches of skin bulged beneath my eyes. Don't even get me started on my hair. What would any man see in me now? Once upon a time, I had milky smooth skin, flowing blondish hair, sparkling bluish-gray eyes, a slim but sexy ass, a shy but pleasant smile.

Sweat dripped off Ellis' sunburned nose. A loser. A drifter. Saggy jeans clung to his skinny backside. Some straw and a crow perched on his shoulder, you'd believe you'd finally met the Scarecrow from The Wizard of Oz. What woman would pick a man such as him?

Then again, what had attracted my momma to Father? Maybe he was handsome when he was younger. Interesting.

Engaging. I only remember him as a middle-aged failure. A run-down man of almost fifty when he died. My fuzzy childhood memories of him fuse with those of my teen years when the world had already passed him by. Broken and bitter. Old and out of it.

Father never discussed his past. Momma filled me in out of his earshot. A thirty-year-old grad student at the university in Cliff City, Father sipped coffee and read *The New York Times* at a diner where my momma waited tables. She was nineteen. Beautiful all the way up until she got sick. College not even an option for her, Momma built a career of pouring coffee, plying hamburgers and fries or biscuits and gravy, and clearing tables. She subsisted on the quarters and nickels left behind by the political science undergrads and pre-med majors who bustled in and out of the off-campus diner after all-nighters studying or partying and between lectures and exams.

I'd served those same morons myself during a stint at a coffee shop near the school's aging brick buildings. Full of themselves, they buried the fake wood tabletops with their books and papers, incessantly debating their foolish ideas amidst a fog of tobacco smoke. To emphasize a particular point, they would smash their fists against the vinyl cushions of their booth. The girls in their glasses and sweaters giggled along idiotically. They drank one mug after another of coffee, gobbled plates of Boston Cream Pie or Banana Meringue, and wrangled over the bill if someone didn't have enough to cough up his or her share. They didn't tip for shit. I quit after snapping at a fussy customer suited up like a bum who probably majored in math or economics. He had griped about everything from the temperature of the water for his tea to the cleanliness, or lack thereof, he exclaimed at the top of his lungs, of his fork.

For some reason, Momma had admired the budding scholars who frequented her greasy spoon. She dreamed for me to go to college, made me swear on her day of dying I would apply the next day.

I had no intention of going. I'd seen what happened to people with college ambitions. They graduated with degrees worth nothing, expensive school loans, and outdated books. Like Father.

Father racked up straight A's in high school. He enrolled in a college somewhere in New York or Connecticut where he grew up. He moved to Cliff City to attend the university for his master's. A teaching assistant gig, loans, and a scholarship paid for his textbooks, tuition, and rent. After he and Momma moved in together, he continued his classes, researched late into the night at the library, and fretted about his exams. For a long stretch he spent hours sweating over his thesis while she waitressed and tended to me, relying on the free daycare at the university when possible. But he eventually quit cracking the books. I don't have any memories of Father as a student.

Momma touted Father's academic career; why I had no clue. He rarely worked, only occasionally scrounging up day jobs as a handyman or laborer. Couldn't manage a steady job. Considered himself too good for most of the employers that would hire him. He had a college degree. An educated man. Except he never nailed that master's.

He complained that we distracted him and he couldn't concentrate. He would holler his disappointment at Momma and me while she covered my ears. She struggled to protect me from Father's anger, from his failures and his regrets. As if that would have done any good. As if that would have stopped me from discovering all the unhappiness and frustration life dishes up.

My grandmother, Father's mother, relocated from back East to live with us after I turned three, about the time my memories of childhood began to gel. Not Father's plan, I supposed, as they rarely got along. Certainly Momma hadn't suggested taking her in. These types of situations just crop up with family.

Grandmother never needed the kind of assistance required by that fossil Mr. Coble. She could dress herself, brushed her hair daily, and she smelled like soap. But she frequently forgot to stuff in her dentures and often trotted through our home with her withered lips sucked into the vacuum of her mouth. She could feed herself, although someone else had to fix her supper, as you couldn't trust her around a flame.

My momma waited tables to bankroll us all. In addition to a check the government mailed to Grandmother every month, we managed. Not long after I was born, Momma had upgraded to a black-tie restaurant with bigger tips. The manager scheduled her for evenings and most Friday and Saturday nights: even better tips and we could spend summer vacation days together, or she could greet me as I dashed home from school. Otherwise, she had to leave me with Father and Grandmother when she worked. She always prepared a Crock-Pot full of stew for dinner or set a casserole warming in the oven before rushing off for a shift.

We moved to Willisburg for cheaper rent. We also had to move because of Grandmother. She caused one ruckus or another with the tenants in the apartment downstairs. I adjusted without a hitch to swapping our small apartment in Cliff City for the two-bedroom one-story ranch-style house in Willisburg. Grandmother slept in the hall on a cot Momma stretched out every evening and folded up every morning. A neighborhood with grass and trees and a short stroll to a public park with a pond for Father to fish and while away the hours between the odd jobs he landed before he gave up entirely.

When Grandmother first arrived, she had only physically aged sixty-one years, except she had mentally deteriorated way beyond that. Her crab-like hands clutched at anything wandering too close. I learned to dodge her, or she would pinch me without a word or a warning shot. Oftentimes she hummed to herself. She bickered over jigsaw puzzles with Father, criticized my momma's cooking, bad-mouthed me, and moaned about anything and everything.

She hovered ever alert and on the hunt for one of the few things that brought her joy. Her eyes lit up like firecrackers every Halloween and Easter or any other special occasion calling for candy in the house. Momma joined me for trick-or-treating, entrusting a bowl of lollipops with Father while both he and Grandmother terrorized any children parading up to our front door. We stopped doling out Halloween candy after parents complained about Grandmother poking through the youngsters' bags as they stood on our porch anticipating their treat.

After trick-or-treating, I would sprint through the front door, my cheeks flushed from the cold and my lips smudged with chocolate. I'd prance across the room in a fairy costume or princess gown Momma bought from a discount shop, twirling a milky white pillowcase that toted a pound or two of goodies. Grandmother would try to snatch my loot while Father cursed at her and demanded she go to her "room," which consisted of the cot in the hallway outside our bedrooms.

Momma and I stashed our sweets like squirrels with their nuts. If I didn't protect my candy, Grandmother would nab and eat every morsel in one sitting. When we shopped for chocolate chips for cookies or cream cheese frosting for cupcakes, Momma smuggled them into the house, storing them in the basement behind the Christmas decorations. Once Grandmother snitched a heart-shaped carton of candies my momma gave me for Valentine's. She holed up in the bathroom and ate each cream-filled chocolate-covered bite, burying the emptied container and ridged paper wrappers underneath the folded bath towels. I bawled up a storm. Momma promised to bring me more. Father yelled himself blue. Grandmother denied his accusations just as loudly, growling and swatting at the air surrounding her.

As I invented new hiding spots for my sugary treasures, Grandmother developed a habit of constantly opening drawers and snooping into closets. If I blundered near her, she would slam shut whatever she had ajar and start a racket.

“What? Stealing up on me like that, you ... you ... Go to your room!” she cried.

Sometimes she would scamper through the house seeking something, I never understood what, then snarl at me for swiping it, whatever it was.

Grandmother couldn’t leave the house by herself. She insisted on tagging along with my momma on every shopping expedition or errand unless Momma could hit the store on her way home from work. Grandmother wreaked havoc with the clerks and jeered at them when they confiscated merchandise from her as she ripped the packaging or spilled the contents.

We didn’t worry about her home alone until she began amusing herself by tripping the smoke alarms. She didn’t set them off by just pressing the tester button. She would strike a match to a rolled newspaper, an old TV Guide, or wads of Kleenex and raise the flames to the device. After it started beeping, she’d scurry around the house flapping her arms and cackling. She burned her fingers, except that didn’t teach her nothing. Momma bandaged my grandmother’s scorched hands, threw out all the matchbooks she stored in the kitchen cabinet, and stowed the neon-yellow lighter in the shed out back. Grandmother found the lighter, and after she torched a curtain, we never left her home alone again. I was six years old then and even I knew better.

Father skirted anything to do with his mother other than reluctantly allowing her to assemble puzzles with him. Grandmother and Father spent hours analyzing and arguing over three-thousand-piece jigsaw puzzles they erected on a folding card table that I'd get spanked or at least scolded for accidentally bumping. European castles, stampeding horses, and quaint countrysides with windmills and meandering streams materialized in the middle of the living room. As Momma hustled me to school, we would zip by a shell of a puzzle, the borders forming a multihued rectangle of blurred images. When I revisited the scene after school, portions of a bridge spanned a river, a tree branched out, lilacs blossomed. Morning, noon, and night, Father and his mother huddled over the table, circling and cussing at fragments that should have fit but refused, until a flock of birds would appear.

Father and Grandmother derived a manic delight in placing the last piece of each puzzle. They would hastily collect the remaining pieces of cut cardboard during the final moments, racing toward the finish line, while the picturesque spectacle fanned across the table before them. A gaping hole usually dominated the middle of a strip of sky or a grassy meadow, the similarity of their colors and lack of detail proving the most challenging. Whoever clung to the final piece gloated over his or her victory while the other sulked.

Their obsession with the last piece grew stronger and more frantic. They both started slipping pieces into their pockets, hoping to savor that final triumph until puzzle pieces whirled through the washer and dryer then ran off with the missing socks. Father would howl and swear as he ransacked the sofa pillows and combed his fingers through the shag carpet for a stray piece before flinging one last hostile grimace at the puzzle pocked with several blank spaces. Eventually, with both hands he would scoop up huge chunks of the incomplete puzzle and toss them into the kitchen trash can, scattering a trail for Momma to pick up.

Once as I sat at the kitchen table reading a book while Momma scrubbed dishes, an explosion of angry cries in the living room rocked the house.

"Give it to me! Give it to me now! I had that piece and just set it down," Father said.

"No, you didn't."

"Yes, I did, damn it! Give it to me now!"

"No, you didn't! No, you didn't!" Grandmother screamed, her voice mimicking claws on a chalkboard. "Now move so I can finish the puzzle. Get out of my way. Stop that! Stop!"

Rooted to my chair, I prayed the madness in the next room would not swamp the rest of the house. Momma's gaze riveted on the sudsy water dousing her arms up to her elbows. She carefully swished through the pots and plates so they wouldn't clink and draw attention.

"Hand it over right now! You have been hiding it all along. That is not fair!" Father tattled like a grade school child. He punctuated his rant by slugging a chair with a pillow again and again. "You hand that over right now!"

"It's my piece. I found it. It's my turn to set the last piece. Fair's fair. You had your chance. Now it's mine."

"I was looking for that piece yesterday." Father contradicted his previous claim to have just held it. "I kept trying for one that fit. Wasted half the afternoon searching. Why ... you kept it all this time! You've been hiding it." He sounded amazed, as if anything that batty woman would do could possibly shock you. "You hid that piece. There, right there in your pocket, you lousy cheat, so you could ..."

"So what of it." Grandmother shrieked a harsh, frenzied laugh that must have punched him on the chin.

"Fair's fair. It's my turn. You've had your turn. It's my turn! My turn now, mister!"

"Why you ... you ..." Father grew too furious to speak.

Father never threw a puzzle away if it retained all the pieces and sometimes would take out his favorites to redo.

"Damnation! Why do they never get any easier?" He glared at a collection of greenish-colored pieces designed to produce a dense field of grass flanking a lake full of ducks. Most days, he dressed in the same T-shirt and sweatpants as the day before, his gray bangs shoved behind his ears, his fists clenched as he paced, his eyeballs sunken into a sea of crow's-feet, wiry eyebrows, and darkened semi-circles.

One puzzle totally unhinged him. A Christmas present from Momma, it consisted of five thousand pieces. The puzzle depicted a Monet watercolor recreated using teensy-weensy snapshots of other famous paintings. A Van Gogh here, a Renoir there. Difficult to match the colors. The lines. While in the kitchen coating peanut butter on a cracker, I was startled by a roar followed by the crash of the table and five thousand jigsaw pieces flying across the living room before bashing into the four-chair dinette set. We'd already buried Grandmother by then, so she hadn't screwed up anything to cause that eruption.

Through it all, Momma sanded the rough edges for me. She always made time for me somehow. We arranged elaborate fashion shows with my Barbie dolls as she helped me pull those elegant outfits over their pointy tits and excavated the shag rug for the tiny plastic stilettos I kept losing. We played Chutes and Ladders and Candyland, Momma acting excited or at least pleased with every game. We experimented with Monopoly. I would cry when I had to fork over those white ones coupled with pink five-dollar bills or pastel green twenties for landing on a piece of real estate she owned. So Momma rewrote the rules, and we started playing what Father scornfully labeled the "socialist version" where no one owed anyone anything and we all lived scot-free, borrowing from the bank anytime we needed more cash to purchase property or a miniature plastic house.

When young enough to still expect an answer for everything, I asked Momma why Father yelled and frowned. She directed me to hold the dustpan and gently hushed me so we wouldn't disturb him.

Now I understand why. Father had lots of time to think. Too much time to think about things that infuriated him. After he had quit his hunt for a regular job, he rarely bothered to change into outerwear, stomping around the house wearing a dishwater gray terry cloth robe over his T-shirt and boxer shorts or cotton pajama bottoms or stained sweats. Except when weather allowing, he left the house to go fishing at the public pond down the road.

Father loved to fish. Didn't matter that the locals depleted the pond years ago. Never mind that he never ushered home a stringer of fish, not a single crappie to fry up for dinner. He would spend hours preparing his tackle box and fingering his lures, calling the convenience stores to check their supply of wriggling worms for bait, fiddling with his pole to confirm the reel operated smooth and the line reeled in right. He warmed up by practicing his casting behind the house in the backyard, having already removed the hook so it wouldn't snag on a tuft of weeds, a tree limb, or a fence.

Once when I was about five, I spied him out back fooling with his gear. Father's slight smirk and the occasional whistling from his lips signaled a safe spell to approach him.

"Whatcha doing, Daddy?"

"Writing my obituary," he sang out without a glance in my direction.

He seemed so graceful and at peace. The almost invisible nylon thread with a small leaden ball tethered to the end flicking back and forth, back and forth. His statement corkscrewed through my childish thoughts, confusing me. Daddy wasn't writing anything from what I could tell. I was old enough to know about writing. My momma had begun teaching me how to scrawl my ABCs. I'd just started kindergarten.

I toyed with the word on my tongue before seeking an answer from Momma.

"What's Daddy doing?"

"Daddy's going fishing, dear." Momma maneuvered a rag around the kitchen faucet.

"But we don't have no fish in our yard." I weighed the odd explanations my parents provided to satisfy my curiosity.

"No, of course not dear. Why don't you grab the broom for me, sweetie. Momma needs to finish before I leave for work." She glanced at the clock above the sink. "Oh, I'll save the bathroom for tomorrow."

"Momma?"

"Yes, baby."

"What's an obitchery?"

"What? I'm sorry, dear. Bring the broom to Momma and get the ... oh, don't bother. I'll finish this later. Is that the phone ringing?"

I scooted away to find Grandmother stroking the quilted fabric of Momma's loveseat as she perched on the cushioned edge staring into space. Her dentures absent, she grinned toothlessly at something I could not see. She still entertained moments of pleasantness back then. I would talk to her once in a while until I learned my lesson. Grandmother's good humor could last for a day or two or only for several seconds. I had yet to comprehend how rapidly her mood could splinter.

"Grandmamma, what's a bitchery?"

As if waking from a trance, Grandmother reared back, her half-smile vanishing.

"What?" she blustered.

"B-bitcher ..." I stuttered as my voice tumbled to a whisper. Grandmother sucked in a mouthful of air and aimed her chin upward, then raised her hand above me before slapping it across my cheek.

Stunned, I suffered in silence for an instant before exploding into cries for my momma. Grandmother, all five-foot-two, one hundred and thirty pounds of her, stormed off to the kitchen, swearing in a loud wail.

"That brat, she called me a bitch!"

Momma sprinted to me from the kitchen.

"Why you ... what do you expect from such a ... such a bastard!" Grandmother cried while Momma tried to hush my bawling so I wouldn't alert Father and draft him into combat mode.

That grumpy old woman lived with us until she died.

Tough to stomach, my grandmother, but at least she wasn't smearing-shit-on-the-walls crazy like some. Losing her mind gradually, one piece at a time, then her bladder control all at once. Placing pennies throughout the house so she could collect them and squeal, "A lucky penny, a lucky penny! Today's my lucky day!" After she croaked in her sleep, lucky dog, Momma and I had only Father to bark at us. If Grandmother had lingered much longer, she would have wound up in a nursing home like one where that pathetic Mr. Coble belongs.

Father flew with her body to Boston for the funeral. Momma and I turned the ordeal into an adventurous road trip. We made it for the church service, where I met Father's brother and sister, my uncle and aunt. I had no idea why they wept nonstop for that hateful woman. Even Father looked sort of green around the gills. I was about ten when we buried her.

The day after the funeral, Momma took me to a beach nearby. She watched from the towel she'd spread on the sand while I played near the shore in the surf. I laughed and giggled as the waves tickled my toes, splashed my face, then washed over me and knocked me down as cold, salty water surged through my nose, leaving me gasping.

8

Ellis whimpered about the weight of the freezer.

"Break, break. Man, I need a rest." He wiped his brow with the bottom of his T-shirt, exposing a beer belly that sported curly brownish-red hairs and a couple reddish-black moles. I shuddered as I quickly averted my glance. The three of us formed a semicircle as we examined the ancient freezer while soaking up the sun, listening to the whirring of insects' wings and the chirping of birds. A fly droned by lazily, docking on the freezer's chrome latch briefly before buzzing away.

"Let me do it, let me help," I said, tired of twisting and kneading my damp hands.

Ellis swiftly reeled away from his end of the freezer and made a sweeping movement with his arms, like a TV game show host gesturing toward a brand new frost-free appliance I'd won for guessing the correct number of how many angels could dance on the head of a pin.

Johnny would have none of it. He raised his hand, his palm facing me to nix my offer. "Back the truck in," he said in a style thwarting any debate. I scurried away to do his bidding as he unhitched the tailgate and swung it downward.

It took at least three tries before the engine kicked in. After reversing out of the driveway, I spun the steering wheel and did a one-eighty before backing in as far as I could without crashing into the garage. Ellis delighted in his recess from physical work and threw himself into his new task as our conductor, directing with his arms and then thrusting his palms out as he yelped "Stop!" when the pickup's tailgate lurched within less than a foot of the corner of the garage.

I bought the old thing for about five hundred bucks. The pickup that is. I keep expecting it to die on me for good one of these days, but it keeps on trucking. The Ford only stranded me once, and with just one night's rest, it revved into gear, and she hasn't given me any grief since.

Today would be a bad day to die. Please don't fail me now!

I peered at the cloudless sky. Not a hint of anyone up there to answer my pleas.

Ellis grumbled to himself as Johnny motioned for him to boost his end of the freezer once again. Ellis clamped onto the bottom edge, and they moved it a few inches before another mandatory halt and a round of protests about the temperature, the weight of the freezer, and how the hell would this ever get them to Milesdale. Nearly an eternity later, they lugged the freezer next to the truck's tailgate. Ellis abandoned his end and occupied himself with swiping his forehead, stuffing his sweat-stained T-shirt into his jeans, then tugging it out again.

"Oh, boy! And it's hot! Hot, hot, hot! Perfect weather for melted ice cream, wouldn't you say there, J?"

Johnny ignored him and studied the freezer and the back of my pickup. I had hopped out of the driver's seat and stood to the side, studying the scene but staying out of the way. I knew I was no use.

"No way! No how! That thing's too darn heavy to lift into that pickup. Let's go ... you know anybody 'round here with a dolly? You got to have a dolly. Then you set two two-by-fours, maybe, no two-by-sixes or … well, err … like you got some planks of wood lying around? Then we can, wouldn't be much to it then. How about those neighbors of yours? Tell 'em today instead of a cup of sugar, we need some …" Ellis trailed off, his jaw hanging open like an overheated Labrador plopping on the porch after a hard run.

Johnny had grasped one side of the freezer and hoisted it at a slant so he could set one of the four bottom corners of the freezer on the lowered tailgate. Using the tailgate as a lever, he then tilted and pushed. The strain visible on his face only as a wince or two, his taut arm muscles bulging as if to burst. With one last grand thrust, he heaved the appliance up and over the tailgate and then shoved it in, bracing it against the cab. I didn't know if Johnny heard the thud, or if I'd only imagined it. Afterward, Johnny straightened and scanned the freezer settled in the pickup bed. He said nothing.

"Hallelujah! That's quite an awesome stunt there, J. Heeeeere's Johnny!" Ellis jammed his hands in his pockets and jerked them out again to corkscrew the edge of his T-shirt around his right trigger finger. Then he began whooping and squawking loud enough to wake the dead, so I shushed him.

"Well, excuse me! But I can't control myself, witnessing such an amazing feat of strength and power. My hat's off to you, bro. Don't mind if you do. You're a better man. And the best man always wins!" He jabbered on in his meaningless fashion, flashing his idiotic smirk at everyone and no one.

He struck me as useless. A nuisance. And a noisy one at that. Able only to attract attention I preferred to dodge. They seemed to come as a pair, so I thanked whoever responsible for bringing me Johnny even though it meant tolerating Ellis as well, and let it go at that.

Well, that son of a bitch Ellis hadn't set up enough of a ruckus to wake the dead. Just the living dead. I sighed as Mr. Coble hobbled across the street with a strung-out creature that looked way older than the nineteen or twenty-year-old cosmetology school reject I took her for. Coble had finally resorted to using a walker, although he had needed one for quite a spell. His fingers trembled as he ferried the aluminum walker, skidding the rubber-bottomed silver legs a couple inches forward every few moments while his feet shuffled to keep up. Each footstep an effort in concentration.

The listless eyes of this month's personal assistant drooped toward the ground through eyelids blackened with makeup. The rhinestone stud in her nose winked in the sunshine. The spaghetti strap of her maroon top had slipped to flaunt a copper-fringed tattoo peeping out from her left breast. She obviously didn't care if someone as creepy as Ellis leered at her.

Mr. Coble hacked and wheezed as if choking on some disgusting thing clogging his throat. Something that could have, should have choked him to death. His skin flaked and oozed with sores that would never heal. He grossed me out. I could almost sympathize with the girl if I wasn't so preoccupied. She had to collar his arm to steady him, her right hand cupping the sagging flap of skin above his elbow, grimacing as if she would puke any minute. Her ebony-dyed hair magnified the paleness of her face. Her teeth grinded a wad of gum, then she blew a small bubble from her mouth. As it popped, her tongue flicked out to recover the goo before it stuck to her lips.

Opaque green shades covering Mr. Coble's glasses protected his sunken eyes from the sun. His beige slacks could have fit a man twice his size. The belt suspending his pants puckered the extra material around his pelvis, while the excess belt strap slapped obscenely against his trousered thigh with every step. No one had bothered to iron his once-white buttoned dress shirt, now smeared with prunes or whatever splatters from his spoon or dribbles from his mouth. An extra-large baseball cap advertising the state association for soybean growers shrouded his hairless scalp. Every movement appeared to hurt him.

"You are," Mr. Coble paused to cough, "are despicable." He and his assistant huddled at the edge of my short driveway on the dead-end road skirting my yard. His hunched shoulders quivered, and his hands shook with every word. He sucked in each breath with a raspy wheeze. I prayed he had finished, but no such luck. I gritted my teeth until my jaw ached.

"I pity that," retching sounds interrupted him, "boy of yours." He gagged into his handkerchief for about five minutes.

I wanted to fling a snippy remark at him. But if I would zip my mouth, he'd wander off eventually, as any comment from me would only rile him and detain him longer. My stomach flip-flopped, and I felt like throwing up.

"You bring ... any man ... into your home. Someone ... should call ... the Law!"

The old fart always spoke menacingly to me, really to anyone within range of his poisonous tongue. This was a different version of the same shit I tried to tune out since dropping anchor here, except his venom seeped in this time. Something in his manner disturbed me more than usual. I wilted beneath the withering scowl on his gnarled features. As if he possessed some special insight into my very nature, a bird's-eye view of my soul. Despite the unseasonable, unbearable blaze of a hotter than hot Midwestern summer afternoon, I shivered and hugged myself tighter.

Mr. Coble weaved as if to retreat. The sullen girl with the rounded spine slouched to the left and slightly behind him as she cracked her gum. Then Mr. Coble veered back toward the three of us, glowering yet saying nothing. What the hell was he waiting for? Did he expect me to respond?

I'd learned to ignore him. I would shoo Mitchell into the house if Coble swayed across the street so my son wouldn't have to listen to his crap. I tossed away anything he said as quickly as I would a moldy slice of bread. What a repulsive, wretched man. He carped about life in general or Mike in particular or the teenage "ruffians" he encountered. Sometimes about me, and I would frown and stomp into the house after Mitchell. Flip the finger to his crooked back, out of Mitchell's sight, of course.

I'd never let him or the terrible things he said get to me before. Yet that day, something changed. His toxic speech left me shuddering and sweating and dry-mouthed. I couldn't see the slivered, hateful eyes through his plastic shades. I felt them. His glare bored into me. His eyes ripped through my flesh. If only I could hide. Vanish.

Ellis curled into a crouched stance as he switched his weight side to side, his eyes darting back and forth from me to Mr. Coble, from Mr. Coble to me. Maybe wondering if I would spit back? Scratch his eyes out? Ellis glowed with excitement, his mouth gaping, his eyes shouting Fight! Fight! Rooting for blood.

It was Johnny who sent Mr. Coble on his way. Stiffening as he straightened taller, Johnny gazed at the old man. Not threatening. No emotion on that face of polished stone. If Mr. Coble considered engineering another ugly observation, he thought again. He gawked at Johnny, then at me. His chin slumped to his chest as he concentrated on the fractured asphalt ahead of him. He aimed himself and his walker at Main, and he and his personal assistant staggered up the street.

I wobbled like a bowl of warm Jell-O. If I had tried to speak, I would have stuttered worse than Harold.

Let's scram the hell out of here before the Law does show up.

Again.

With another hunk of thick twine he scrounged from the garage, Johnny tied the freezer in place to hinder it from budging once we motored off. He'd already planned for a bumpy ride. Then Johnny seized the tailgate, and the metal latches screeched as he closed it. Ellis opened the passenger door and climbed in. I would have hollered at him to jump in the back with the freezer, but I couldn't muster the energy. As it was, the three of us would have to cram ourselves in the cab and rub elbows the entire trip.

Somehow I crawled out of the hole I'd collapsed into and commanded my leaden feet toward the vehicle. I hauled myself up and behind the wheel. Johnny tugged the ropes one last tug and then slid in next to Ellis, who grunted as he squirmed to the center seat next to me. Ellis sat so near me, the heat radiating from his arm warmed mine. His days-old stench repelled me. I scrunched as far to the left as I could to make more room for the three of us and stay as far as possible from Ellis. I resigned myself to fate and turned the key.

Once the engine started rumbling, I shifted into Drive. I braked. I had forgotten my purse. Can't go anywhere without that token of security, although there's rarely any cash in it. My driver's license, a hairbrush, a checkbook I dared not use, some fast food coupons, an old tube of hand lotion, a dried-up ballpoint pen stashed inside.

Maybe I'll need that where I'm going. A plastic-handled hairbrush. Should I pack my toothbrush and some spare underwear too? Do they let you bring that stuff to jail?

I slammed the lever back into Park and killed the engine.

"Back in a sec," I said.

I careened through the house, hunting for my purse. Why

can't I ever track it down when I'm in a hurry? Do these damn things sprout legs and stroll away on their own? As I paced through the kitchen, my foot landed on a bit of cereal that exploded like a firecracker. I halted, momentarily stunned, then continued into my closet-sized bedroom swallowed whole by my queen-sized bed and a shoulder-high chest of drawers bloated with unfolded clothing. The bedding formed a pile, and for the ten-hundredth time, that mound of linen stirred to gradually reveal a dozing Mike entangled in the sheets, sleeping off another one. Then the image shattered into a million pieces before my eyes.

I wheeled about, then padded over the linoleum and into the family room before trekking across the carpet and sticking my head into Mitchell's crowded bedroom, plastic critters and miniature cars scattered on every speck of floor.

Where's my purse? Where am I going? How the hell can we get rid of that goddamn freezer? It's huge!

I had toyed with the idea of the river, but things wind up bobbing downstream. They're always discovering bodies drifting along or snagged in an eddy, and then there'd be more visits from the cops. A ravine? Off a cliff? Maybe bury it at the old Stolte farm: six hundred acres of locust trees and thorn bushes. No one goes there.

"Then we'll need shovels," I said to the vacant house.

After pacing through each room, I jolted to a stop. There's only four rooms if you don't count the bathroom. Every doorway I passed through, I smacked into one memory or another, a faded remnant of my past, good or bad. I've always complained about this dump. What if I don't come back?

Memories blasted me: the cold winter nights broken up by heat leaking from the gas furnace, lying in my bed shivering with only a soused Mike to warm me, snuggling beside him as he tossed, kicked off the bedspread, and then clasped my arm. A toothless Mitchell army crawling toward me across the pockmarked linoleum that's curling up in the far corner of the kitchen. Sadie tickling Mitchell into giggles while I lounged on my back porch, sipping on a beer, pulling on a cigarette, and watching the June bugs try to right themselves. Tammy and I drunker than shit and laughing so hysterically we almost peed in our pants as we slipped on the kitchen floor wet from spilled margaritas. Mitchell conking out in my lap while we caught the ballgame on TV.

Then less than twenty-four hours earlier, those three firm raps on my back door. He stood at the farthest edge of the concrete landing. I refused to open the door and railed at him through the screen's torn wire mesh.

"Well, guess what the cat drug in," I hissed, ready to splash more fuel to rekindle the firefight still smoldering from years of battle. From habit.

I hadn't seen Mike for two months, one week and three days, after our last and most horrible clash. Every night since that dreadful night, I listened for his racket – the clattering and cussing that trumpeted his return. When would he storm back into our lives? After dinner? After Mitchell's gone to bed? Drunk, mumbling something I couldn't confuse for a half-assed apology, more likely a demand for something to eat or drink.

In the past when he breezed by unannounced after a binge, he never knocked. Just shambled in. He'd poke through the fridge, prepared for a skirmish if I volunteered one, but somewhat subdued as he longed to crash on a mattress with sheets for a change, not the back seat of someone's car or the chaise lounge in the garden shed behind his mother's house. My puky couch would do when no one else would welcome him, not even his own mother.

Except that last night, that awful night before Johnny arrived to rescue me, Mike had knocked. I'd almost given up expecting him. He had strayed for an especially long while this stretch, and I assumed he was in jail or had found some dumb broad to shack up with. I was surprised yet pissed enough to be a bitch.

"What the hell do you want! I'm out of beer and Mitchell's asleep. I don't miss your trouble here no more. Just got used to you not bulldozing over and busting everything," I said through the screen.

He shifted his weight and stared at his feet. He looked different. His bangs didn't hang in his eyes. Someone had taken a pair of clippers to his customary rats' nest, grooming the once-tangled locks into straight swatches of freshly washed hair. I scoured his face, his clothes, the way he stood, and I could see it clear as a cloudless, sunny day. He hadn't drunk a drop. I recoiled.

"Mike?" Maybe I'd made a mistake and it was someone else on my doorstep.

"I'm ... I ... sorry. I should have called. Sorry to intrude like this."

He was nervous but not in an awkward way. Calm. Solid. He was almost in control. Still, he wrestled with something; I could see it in his eyes. Sharp brown eyes surrounded by a sea of pearl white, not the yellowed, droopy ones underlined with plump, charcoal half-moons I'd grown to know. He was thirty-nine. His face lined and shaven. He wasn't wearing a tie, too hot for that, though he struck me as the type of man who would feel at home in one. I could hardly connect him to the Mike I knew. Maybe a sleeker version of the one I first met, before the hard partying floored him. Only older, wiser. In charge.

"We need to talk. I'm ..."

He slid his hands from the pockets of his pants and spread them to his sides in a gesture of helplessness.

"I'm sorry about everything that's happened. I wish I could ..."

His words died as he examined the door jamb before pivoting his gaze to me. Handsome. Yes. He was handsome. Not the pinup pretty boy kind of cute. His once ink-black hair now streaked with silver strands whispering through his evenly parted hair and trimmed sideburns. A scar crossed through his eyebrow from some stupid brawl years back. And those eyes I could get lost in. Still had that gut, but don't we all now.

I yearned to sniff him. Would he have that same odor? The liquor-weeping-through-the-pores stink of an alcoholic: that sickly sweet stench of spoiled fruit? Or would I smell aftershave? Old Spice? Menthol-scented shaving cream? Would a minty chocolate after-dinner treat flavor his breath?

His skin gleamed as if recently shaved, and here it was late in the evening. Someone had ironed the button-down short-sleeve bleached shirt tucked into his pleated tan slacks. Suede dress shoes. When had he ever worn anything but cutoffs and T-shirts with holes? Jeans and dirty boots or tennis shoes? He reminded me of those Wonder Bread boys, the ones who letter in sports and staff the upstairs offices poring over balance sheets or selling insurance. Not my Mike, no he did not resemble my Michael.

Yet I studied his eyes, and deep down I saw him peeking back. I saw my Michael. I also saw fear. Was he afraid of what I would dredge up? Maybe afraid of what I would want. What I would need. Was he afraid of me? I expected those eyes to narrow, swapping clear and alert for bloodshot and dazed, his lips to twitch and his hand to paw his hair, then the slamming and the shouting and the stumbling would resume as if it had never ended.

"I'm sorry how things have turned out, Cathy. I'm sorry I haven't always been ... I'm sorry I haven't been there for you and ... Mitchell. I wasn't a good person. I am sorry for all ..." His features contorted into a frown aimed inward. Not at me.

"You deserve better. I should have been there for you both. I know it's been difficult," he said with a sigh, pain searing his eyes as they focused on mine again before dropping to the threshold once more.

You could have flattened me with a wet noodle. Sorry? Mike apologizing? When had anything ever been his fault? He blamed everything and everyone, the moon and the stars, the dented metal trash can, the sprawling weeds, his father, someone he worked with, the good Lord himself before he would ever accept any responsibility for one damn thing. Everything was someone else's fault: every failed interview, every pink slip, every opportunity stolen by some asshole, every smudge or accident caused by someone or something beyond his command. He would not fess up for a mangled fender if discovered passed out on the steering wheel. Everyone else had fucked up, blown it, and messed with everything. That's why he always put up his fists when someone pointed at him. He had to defend himself from everything. From everyone.

Not that night. Not this time. He had changed as if a wizard waved a wand at him while sprinkling magic fairy dust. A new man!

I must have looked pretty awful, with my mouth hanging open, my tattered cutoffs hugging my thighs a tad tight. Beer breath. Braless with a T-shirt spritzed by dishwater and barefoot in the moonlight of a hot summer evening.

I had no idea what to say. What would you say? What could you say? What do you say when the son of a bitch who trampled your dreams and screwed up the life of your lovable, fatherless boy ... what the fuck could I do when that asshole shows up at my door and ... says he's sorry? Seeks forgiveness, I suppose? Wants back into our lives maybe?

A different man, or maybe the same man, with those beautiful high cheekbones, the hard jaw, the strong shoulders, the roughened palms that could hold on tight, so desperately tight, squeezing the air out of me, as if I were the most precious treasure that he would never, ever surrender.

I had never experienced that with anyone else. That I was essential. Desired and totally possessed. Despite the boozing, the arguing, his inability to buy groceries or cover doctors' bills, Mike made me believe I had a place, a special place in this world only I could fill. A place in Mike's heart.

Most days when I rose, he'd cop z's as long as possible. Hungover, burying his head in a pillow to block the blinding light of day from seeping into his throbbing skull, he would flail his arm in search of me, thrashing at the vacant spot on our bed.

"Don't leave me." The pillow would partially smother his moan.

I'd drape my chuckle in sarcasm as I smiled. "Someone's got to scrape together the rent."

"Come back. Come back soon as you can."

Then the full force of morning struck him like a sledgehammer, and his body screamed for a drink. Or maybe while still somewhat stoned from the night before.

"Come back. Bring beer."

I had grown to hate him. I would curse him when he smashed through our lives and damn him when he stayed away. Rearing a child all alone, even with Sadie's aid, left me with a hefty load.

Whenever Mike barged in, Sadie withdrew. She knew our tiny house afforded no room for four when it included one of her size. Mike would badger Sadie and laugh idiotically at his own crass remarks if he ever lumbered through the doorway during her frequent visits. She would say nothing, lower her head, survey the floor and shuffle for the door as soon as physically possible. She'd navigate the porch steps cautiously. Teetering with her arms outstretched for balance or with one hand tagging the vinyl siding to catch herself if she fell, she slowly maneuvered downward, stepping off the side of the bottom step within reach of the stability permitted by the house's exterior wall. Mike would hoot and howl after her as she lugged herself across the driveway. I would bop him with a rolled magazine or snap at him to shush.

Mitchell would sandwich his ears with a pillow, training his eyes on Simba, Kermit, or Goofy prancing across the television screen. As things started to fly, Mitchell would duck into his room. The broken windows, the bottles of Jack Daniels and beer whacked against the side of the house left in piles of jagged pieces for Mitchell to slash his feet open. I'd sweep or rake up the shards of glass after Mike left or while he snored in the bedroom.

When he'd come to, I'd yell some more. He'd grumble then rummage through my handbag for money before I could snatch it from his fist. He'd shoot me that don't-try-it-bitch-or-I'll-have-to-slap-you stare. It was a front. He'd never hit me. Something he threw might sail past me, but for some strange reason, he drew the line. I have to thank him for that. Even I couldn't stop from crossing that one.

There I go again, dragging out all those memories best left locked away. Once I open that closet, it's hard to shut because all the crap keeps falling off the shelves.

My purse, my purse, a shovel, my purse ... what ... what the hell?

Images fluttered about me like so many dead leaves on a windy mid-November day. With my feet glued to the floor of my kitchen, I faced the dirt-streaked window above the sink. A cedar tree growing next to the house attempted to break in by thrusting its bristly branches against the glass pane. My tears let loose. I was bawling by the time Johnny pulled the screen door open. I collapsed in a heap on the linoleum. He knelt beside me and laid his hand on my shoulder. I kept sobbing, but an incredible wave of relief washed over me from his touch. I squinted through my tears into his eyes. Two deep wells of cool, refreshing water gleamed back.

Damn. I can't stand acting so pathetic. I hadn't felt that worthless since Mitchell was born. I had a good excuse then. I guess I had a good excuse that day Johnny appeared on my horizon.

He helped me onto my feet.

"Shovel. I got one in the garage. Somewhere. I can find it."

"We won't need a shovel," Johnny said.

"What?" I asked.

He bewildered me. Johnny seemed to know everything. So assured and confident. My watery eyes struggled to pierce through his expressionless ones, bore through his forehead, and understand, really understand what transpired in there. What did he know? He knew more than he let on. And he understood. He accepted everything. He had taken control. He had taken charge. He found me. I had not found him. He came to me. And he would snip this loose thread before it completely unraveled everything.

He led me to the vehicle as one would a child. He cupped my elbow and guided me into the driver's seat. He had tried to steer me toward the passenger's side, except I resisted.

I'm driving! You're running this dog and pony show. You're in charge. You tell me where the hell to go.

I aimed my brainwaves straight at Johnny.

But I'm driving my own damn truck!

As I clambered in, Ellis cradled my purse in his lap. I grabbed it and shoved the vinyl bag behind the seat as we glared at each other.

9

The Ford fired up without a complaint. I turned onto Judge Weaver. I targeted my eyes straight ahead, skirting the ones I knew pursued me from the forest green house with the towering cedar tree.

We crunched gravel and chunks of pavement as the road snaked toward Main. Right at the corner. Hardly anyone out on that scalding afternoon except that jackass old man Coble. Hearts & Kisses displayed its handwritten "CLOSED" sign taped to the door. Velva's looked dead. A couple scarred pickups rumbled along Main bound for somewhere else. We maneuvered by Leroy's rusted Chevy jutting into the street in front of the tavern, a grime-encrusted push lawnmower and a half-empty sack of concrete mix in the truck bed.

A phantom gust of hot wind blasted from out of nowhere, chasing several plastic cups and empty sodas across the blacktop. A stray beer can followed, clanking a zigzagged course along Main. Then as abruptly as it began, the wind quit.

Ellis danced in his seat, gaping past Johnny's chest out the window and twisting to gawk out my window at the blackened plate glass of the abandoned storefronts, the scattered few without BB gun pellet holes or boarded over with plywood.

After entering the bank, Mr. Coble's assistant pulled the door shut behind them. She watched us through the glass door as we passed, and my eyes met hers.

We tooled along at the legal limit, twenty miles per hour. Instead, the pickup seemed to crawl at two miles per hour. Moving that slow only wisps of air wafted through the open windows, providing no relief from the heat. Harold's patrol car was parked next to city hall. I ached to speed up. I repeatedly verified the needle hovered near the twenty-mark.

The rearview mirror revealed a car tailgating my Ford: a pack of teenagers in an aging Oldsmobile with a missing driver-side headlight. One asshole hung through the window frame whooping at us. I couldn't catch a word, but I'm sure they just wanted to drive faster. Their obnoxious jeers certainly had nothing to do with the cargo we carried.

Then the driver veered into the oncoming lane and sped up next to me. I lifted my foot off the gas and angled a tad to the right, taking us as far as I could without sideswiping a parked car. We drove neck and neck for several seconds. As the car accelerated, a skinny, pimpled brat in the passenger's seat stuck out his head and bellowed.

"Mooooove, cow! Mooooove!"

I jumped as he hollered at me through my window. The car zoomed by as the driver gassed his engine and then swerved in front of us. My bumper almost dinged its tail. I punched the brakes. Johnny braced himself with one hand on the window frame before pivoting his head to check on the freezer. I clung to the steering wheel. Ellis banged his hand against the dashboard.

"Those bastards! What the hell are they trying to pull?" I gasped.

The car pitched forward, then the brake lights flared briefly as the sedan suddenly cut a sharp left into the Gas & Go, tires squealing.

I used to burn rubber with them some twenty years ago. I would have been there in the back seat clapping the tops of my thighs as I laughed, spewing tobacco smoke.

I eased onto the gas pedal. We approached the outskirts, ushered by a whiff of the town's sewage lagoon. Only a few more run-down rentals and another deserted building before we could weave our way through the countryside. Fleeing Willisburg with that heavy freezer did not pose the challenge I had dreaded.

I glanced at the gas gauge, yet I didn't need to.

Damnit!

When I hit Route A after collecting Johnny and Ellis, the needle perched just above E. We didn't have enough gas to make it to the next station at Englewood. Maybe we could have except with this truck, you never knew. If you taxied downhill, sometimes you could run on fumes. I thumped the dashboard with my palm.

"What the hell's the problem now?" Ellis asked.

I despised that man.

"Out of gas," I said, sick to my stomach again because that meant backtracking to Willisburg. A foul taste surged to my throat.

I aimed for a graveled driveway. Rocks flew as the tires spun. I whipped into reverse, and the spray of gravel pinged against the wheel wells and the undercarriage. My foot pounded the brake pedal, and the vehicle staggered to a halt in the middle of the road.

Ellis moaned as he tried to start in on me again.

"I don't want to hear it!" I barked in his face. I stifled an irresistible urge to clobber him. My fingers clutched the steering wheel. The heat stirred in my gut. Johnny calmly reached past Ellis and put his left palm on my hand. His cool touch soothed me. He didn't need to say anything. It was as if he had drained me of all the hatefulness. I shifted the lever into Drive.

I chose Rory's. You had to pay ahead for gas, as all the drive-offs had pissed off the owner beyond belief, but you saved a nickel a gallon with cash.

I plowed through the swinging glass door into an arctic draft of airconditioned air. I flung enough dough on the counter to top off my tank and tapped my toe while the clerk jabbered into the store's telephone. I didn't know her. Still in her late teens, she'd splurged on too much makeup for a day gig. Her Hard Rock Cafe London T-shirt barely concealed her bulging belly.

Yeah, you been there, girl. Is that where you got knocked up?

She wore flip-flops and baggy jeans shredding at the hems from being walked on and plucked at. With a cigarette between her fingers smoldering to ash and the phone nestled between her jaw and her shoulder, she picked at the polish chipping from the nails of her other hand. She hadn't bothered to acknowledge me. I rubbed my arms for warmth as the shop AC blasted at way below sixty-eight degrees. At home I can't afford to crank up the AC, but I have worked where I could flip the thermostat as high in winter or as low in summer as I fancied. When someone else foots the bill, who gives a rat's ass about global warming.

"He's always telling me he's going to call and he doesn't. He just got himself a cell phone. I called to find out where he'd been all weekend. Finally called his mom's. She answers and he takes his sweet time picking up the phone. I'm like, well, what the fuck are you up to? And he's like, hey what business is it of yours, you're not my mother, and I'm like, fuck you! Don't talk shit to me! You said you'd call. I could have gone to Becka's, she was having a party, well some people over, did you go? ... No fucking way! Who else was there? ... No shit! Jackson Thompson? That turkey. Wait someone's calling ... I might have to get it, nope. Well, anyway ... No, I didn't sit around but I didn't tell him that, went out for smokes and sodas, ran into Jesse and Marla and that girl, what's her name, I keep forgetting her name, Bailey, Hailey, Hillary. Something like that. Isn't she a number? Showing off her tits with those see-through shirts. What a slut."

I curbed the desire to bash in her face with a six-pack of motor oil from a nearby display.

"There, there," the winged angel floating by my ear hummed. "Relax."

"Excuse me," I said as politely as I could. You should have guessed by now I'm not what you would describe as "polite." I don't tolerate this kind of nonsense well, and with the circumstances facing me that day, that bitch should thank her lucky stars I didn't sock her, pregnant or not.

The girl kept yakking. She didn't even look at me.

Don't create a scene. Breathe. In. Breathe. Out. That's the ticket out of here.

I scooped up my cash and fluttered it through the air above the counter. "Can you please switch on number two," I said through gnashing teeth. Stupid broad deserved to get fired. In all my years behind counters, I'd never treated a customer so rudely, even when they begged for it.

The girl took a drag and rolled her eyes. "Just a second." I'd no idea if she meant it for me or the idiot on the other end with nothing better to do but listen to her drivel.

She swiped loose strands of her bleached hair from her face. She leaned from her chair, almost losing her balance and falling onto the floor, punched some keys on the register, punctuating her efforts with some choice cuss words, and then clasped my stack of bills before continuing with her rant.

Long, yellow hair spilled down her cheeks past the cracking foundation on her nose. Smoke swirled about her purple eyeshadowed lids. She paid me no more notice than she would a passing breeze.

I retraced my steps to the truck and found Ellis pummeling the dashboard with his palms to a wild tempo that lacked a rhythm.

Johnny worked the gas pump. What a gentleman. When had Mike ever filled my tank? I'd end up with the gasoline stench and a thinner wallet while he'd prop his dirty bare feet on my dashboard or dangle them out the window on summer days, growling at me to hurry so we could vamoose. Never offered to mess with the hose, check the oil, wash the windshield. And forget about paying for gas.

I banged the driver-side door shut. I started gnawing on a fingernail again.

We would hit the road soon with a full tank. Stationed by the rear tire next to the gas cap, Johnny watched the numbers click, click, click. I counted the mounds of broken concrete and tires piled in the neighboring vacant lot. Ellis yelped and bounced in his seat, bumping into my elbow. I snarled at him, wishing I could slap him silly instead.

"Gimme a minute," he said as he fiddled with the passenger door handle before finally heaving it open, hopping out and marching stiff-legged toward the store, his skinny arms flicking to and fro.

Johnny anchored his focus to the fuel pump while the machine chugged gas into the tank. The truck gulp, gulp, gulped.

Damn, maybe we'll never escape.

I sank into my seat as if a cinder block tied to my leg dragged me down, down, down into murky water.

Let's go! What if Harold swings by? Maybe this isn't going to fly. Maybe we're going to get caught. They'll arrest me and send me to jail! But I can't. I can't go to jail! What would happen to my baby? What would happen to my Mitchell? What would they do to him? They can do anything they want to me, I don't care. But I can't let anything happen to my boy!

Johnny finished gassing up and walked past the rear of the pickup toward the passenger side. Ellis had left the door yawning open. I didn't mind until a Toyota station wagon covered in tiny dents from hailstorms puttered by us within spitting distance. Johnny squeezed himself against the wheel well so he wouldn't get grazed. My truck's passenger door fanned out far enough for the car to clip it. Just in time, Johnny's arm shot out and shoved the door out of harm's way. Quicker than snot, he averted an accident that would have demolished the door of my sorry old truck and more, a hell of a lot more.

Just-in-time Johnny.

I began laughing so hard I almost lost it. I quit for a moment so I could say it out loud.

"Just-in-time Johnny." More hysterical laughter. "Can I call you that?"

He didn't say anything. The corners of his mouth barely curled as he boosted himself into the cab and slid over the bench seat to the spot next to me, a hint of a smile tugging at those full lips.

A million years later, Ellis clambered in. "Had to take a whiz," he said.

I glared at him.

Ellis' eyeballs swiveled in their sockets. "Well, I had to visit the little boy's room! That apple juice ran right through me. Shoot, you'd expect it would have soaked in, being such a hot day and us not having much to drink all day. Nor eat," he said with a leer.

How revolting for Ellis to broadcast his private business.

Shut up already.

An odd shape bulged from Ellis' shirt. He smirked in that gross manner of his as he removed a package of powdered sugar donuts from underneath his T-shirt. He grunted while hoisting up his pelvis so his hand could dig into his jeans' front pockets. He fished out a 3 Musketeers bar and a bag of roasted peanuts.

"Ellis, you idiot!"

Johnny stared straight ahead.

"You want some? Here, I got Twinkies. Oops, must have dropped those," he said as he snickered. He wiggled his nose like a rabbit and raised his eyebrows at me.

Johnny turned to Ellis. He probably shot him a look that should have silenced the weasel, but Ellis shrilly justified his actions. "I was hungry! Starving! Haven't eaten since that stale Egg McMuffin this morning. I'm a growing boy! Can't expect me to live on air and water alone." Ellis scowled at me as he cradled his booty in his lap, his gangly limbs protecting the junk food as if he cuddled a newborn babe.

"Shut up, would you." I kicked the floorboard. "I'm ready to leave you here! Toss you into the nettles! You are not worth the space you pollute on God's green earth! Asshole!"

"Now, no way. Johnny and me, we are a team, aren't we, Johnny. We're a team, Johnny, and you're my man. Joh-NEE! Joh-NEE!" Ellis chanted, thrusting his fist upward with each syllable of Johnny's name. "We stick together like bread and butter, me and Johnny ..." Ellis' whiny voice tapered off. I could have spit I was so mad.

Then his mood steeled harshly, stabbing me with its pointed edge. He jerked his head toward the load Johnny had strapped in so securely. "You need to move your ... your *freezer*," he said slyly. "Me and Johnny work together. You need me and Johnny. Johnny and ME!"

His menacing tone threw me off-kilter. His cunning eyes bored into mine, probing through me and reading my thoughts as if he lifted my shirt, strummed his dirty-nailed fingers through my dresser drawer, peeped behind the door at me. And I was helpless to stop him. I wanted to cry. I did need him. Needed him out of town, miles and miles from here. If anyone were going to blab, it would be that sour-smelling piece of shit. If he hung around with Johnny he wouldn't. Johnny would keep him quiet.

"Start the engine," Johnny said. Not rudely nor as if to boss me. He only provided guidance and sensible advice. And I needed that. If I'd kicked Ellis out, then there would have been a commotion, and with his shoplifting, then there would have been Harold or the other deputy assigned to Willisburg. And then ...

How many disasters have I skated through today? I've been lucky so far. After last night, I need a lot of luck. A whole potful, thank you very much.

The fresh fuel revived the Ford, and the engine turned over with a roar. I steered for the lane aiming away from Willisburg.

Will we make it out this time? We have to. We just have to.

Whoever designed this road to the main highway possessed an incredible sense of humor or toked too much bad weed. It weaved and wavered. No shoulders, just a shallow ditch full of fescue and scrub grass. No room for error. I almost wound up in the ditch once, scuttling back from some bar with Mike grabbing for the wheel while proclaiming I sucked as a driver. Sometimes he conked out in the back seat, and I managed to skid home without losing traction. If Mitchell napped during the trip, his head flopped back and forth as the tires hugged each corner. I loved cruising this two-lane in my Camaro with the windows rolled down, my hair whipping my cheeks, and the empties crashing into each other on the floorboards. I always drove fast with Blue – the closest I'd ever come to flying.

The truck gradually gained speed. We coasted at fifty to fifty-five. The signs said I could go that fast. However, you probably should travel Route A slower, much slower.

Shoulder to shoulder, Ellis, Johnny, and I leaned as the vehicle took each curve. First this way, then that way. A short straightaway where we righted ourselves, then back to that gentle rocking motion. Like a porch swing on a lazy summer afternoon. Decelerating for a few sharp bends, then up and down. The crest of each hill allowed us a quick glimpse of the horizon before we descended into the rollercoasting pavement. I checked my mirrors every other second to screen what, if anything or anyone, trailed us. Nothing except baked asphalt behind us. Pockets of trees and thinning pastures of milling cattle lined the roadway. I knew Route A by heart and could have navigated it in my sleep. Only ice storms could scare me off it. Left, then right. Up, then down. Left, then …

Holy shit!

Ellis wasn't paying attention, but Johnny saw it. He flung his arms out straight to brace himself against the dash. My tires screeched as I pounded the brake pedal with both feet and veered off the pavement into the fescue bordering the road. The engine died with a shout. Ellis' forehead thumped against the windshield.

The ropes strained, the knots clinched, but the freezer held.

"Goddamn, woman, what the hell did you stop for? We might as well walk. This is some goddamn shit!" Powdered sugar smeared Ellis' face, and bits of donut spewed from his lips as he shrieked.

Through gritted teeth, my hands gripping the wheel, I moaned.

Oh my God! How can this happen now?

Johnny radiated calm as Ellis squirmed in his seat, kneaded his temples, and swore I was a crazy, stupid bitch, his words exactly.

"I think I hit him. Go look, please. I hope he isn't dead. I can't look. Maybe I missed him. He could have jumped out of the way. Please! Go, just go look." My shoulders sagged as I slumped forward, my forehead pounding the steering wheel. Once, twice, three times I banged my head on the Ford logo.

Ellis erupted into a twitching, sputtering wreck. Johnny released his grasp on the dashboard, reached across the wriggling Ellis, and tugged on the door handle. He eased Ellis out of the cab with both hands before stepping out himself. He paced the front of the pickup, examining the bumper, then ducked to scope underneath the chassis. He straightened and strode to the back of the truck. I pinned my eyes on Johnny in the rearview mirror, bypassing the pavement so I wouldn't see the gory, mangled hump.

What if someone motors by, pulls over, offers to help? Someone could identify us, someone like Harold or a local yokel. Or maybe someone smarter.

The state trooper who trawls through town would have radioed in my plates before strutting over to innocently ask, "What's that there you're hauling? Care if I take a peek?"

A car hurtled past us heading in the opposite direction. As Ellis stood by the pickup, he chattered while whacking his palm against his thigh. He babbled hysterically as he debated with himself, his speech rising and falling like a yo-yo. I tried to tune him out. From then on, I would pretend he didn't exist. And if I couldn't block him out, then I'd dismiss him like a fly buzzing by that I didn't have the energy to swat.

Johnny returned to the cab. Ellis climbed in after him, fussing and cussing and slamming the door. Johnny sat unruffled as Ellis goddamned this and goddamned that while rubbing his forehead in between clenching his fists open and shut.

"Did I kill him?"

Johnny nodded. Then he turned to me. His eyes sank into mine.

"He ran into the road. You could not have avoided him." He didn't burst out and say it. Johnny didn't say, "It wasn't your fault. You didn't mean to do it. It was an accident. You didn't do anything wrong." He didn't say it out loud, but his eyes told me everything. Everything I craved to hear. A swell of relief bathed me from head to toe. A slow-moving wave that didn't knock me off my feet but rinsed me clean and left me refreshed. I started to float again, drifting out to sea.

I shut my eyes, but I could still picture it. A baby fawn lying crumpled on the pavement, blood pooling around its corpse, the pink tongue hanging out, the glassy dark eyes, the wisp of a cream-colored puffy tail, the spotted fur coat drenched red.

The air spiraled about me like syrup, too thick to breathe. The muggy heat wrapped wet wool blankets over my arms and legs. Not tight, just lots of bulky layers. Billowing, hazy clouds waltzed before me.

Am I dreaming? Am I somewhere between awake and asleep, somewhere, back in my bed, lying in that shallow dip in the middle where the springs poke my ribs?

I couldn't focus on Johnny's features anymore. The jet-black brows, the almond-shaped eyes, the skin the hue and texture of melted chocolate with a dash of cinnamon.

My lips trembled, yet I could not separate them or move my tongue.

Did he suffer? I didn't say it aloud.

He died instantly, a voice in my head echoed. Didn't know what was coming, what hit him. The baby deer loped across the pavement, planted his four spindly legs on the asphalt, and stared straight at my truck as we bore down on him, not even trying to escape.

"A dog! You almost killed us over a goddamn dog that don't have enough brains to stay off the goddamn road," Ellis said.

"A deer," I mumbled, correcting him. A baby deer. A little

fawn.

"A deer, hell, we would of felt a deer! I did not feel no bump. A deer would have bashed in the front end. That was no deer, no siree George, that was a dog! I'll go check this out myself."

My mind, full of fog and dusty cobwebs, suddenly cleared and rocketed into action. "Stay in the car and shut the fuck up! I don't want any more of your crap!"

That stunned Ellis, and he froze for all of two seconds. "Well excuse me, ma'am. What the hell is your problem? I swear. Goddamn! All we needed was a lift. Just a goddamned ride. And now we're all caught up in some bullshit over a freezer and a deer or dog or whatever the hell it was you killed."

"A baby deer," I said, gazing through the windshield smudged with a film of crud and dead bug juice.

The racket from the cicadas fused with the clatter of a zillion other bugs beating their wings as they flitted from stalks of grass to tree branches to leaves and then back again.

Where's his momma? Is she watching us from behind those trees? Why did she skip out on her baby? He was just standing in the middle of the road! Sure wasn't my fault!

I stared straight ahead, seeing nothing, while I grieved for the baby deer.

Johnny didn't stir. Ellis rambled to himself as he dragged his scrawny fingers through his mop of hair.

"Why did he run in front of us like that and stop? That makes no sense," I said. But nothing ever makes any sense, so why do I keep asking? Why the hell should life make sense anyhow?

"I'll tell you what makes no sense. Us driving nowhere with

a dumb bitch who can't ... shit, Johnny, all we needed, Johnny, all I'm saying, all we needed was a ride, a simple ride to Milesdale." He teased out the name with a nasal pitch. "We need to be there tomorrow afternoon. We had plenty of time. We coulda walked there faster. Truman told me they got a job lined up that'll keep us in smokes and biscuits for two weeks. Room and board, Johnny! A sweet deal! But we gots to ... he warned me not to show up late. He told me we gotta be there at the warehouse in Milesdale no later than one o'clock. Now we're moving a piece of shit, murdering animals, hotter than shit and we're going nowhere! Nowhere, I tell you."

He ranted some more. Then he started flapping his limbs in an attempt to unlatch the door and exit the pickup as if he planned to split and stomp off in the middle of nowhere. Johnny turned toward him, and that was that. Ellis cussed again, folded his arms across his chest, let out an exasperated huff, and leaned forward to sneer at me.

My hands locked onto the wheel with the ferocity of a snapping turtle while the crushed fawn bled out on the asphalt behind us. Bolted to my seat, I couldn't budge.

I'd grown numb to the roadkill I raced by on my way to work or home from errands in Cliff City. The stray dogs, the tomcats, the possums squashed into the asphalt while a vulture or two feasted on their rotting flesh, some lugged to the side by larger scavengers to fester amidst Queen Anne's Lace and Bachelor's Buttons.

You couldn't dodge the squirrels that darted out rather than waiting for you to pass. The box turtles, now they made it easy. Tooling along the broken yellow line marking the center of the blacktop, you'd spot their itty-bitty lumps up ahead. The turtles drew in their heads and legs and holed up. Tack slightly to the left or right and you sail over the humped form. After catching a breath, the turtle would edge out of its shell and creep another inch or two before another hunk of metal would zoom overhead. Usually, they reached the other side without a scratch. Sometimes you'd find their cracked, bloody shells strewn across the road. Damn teenagers. They'd aim for the poor things. Where the hell did those turtles have to go so badly they would cross this dangerous stretch of pavement?

A baby deer. They have those quarter-sized milky white dots in their copper fur for camouflage. Supposed to protect the fawns, prevent predators from detecting them while they hide in the tall grass or the forest undergrowth, helping them blend into a carpet of fallen leaves or some bushes. Those little camo dots didn't do squat to protect that baby from my truck's dented chrome bumper.

Last October, an entire family died because a deer sprinted in front of their car one night as they traveled to Huxton. Mom, Dad, and the two girls. The buck crashed through the windshield of their minivan, which rolled down the embankment off Route Z, then landed belly up in a shallow stream. The deer's antlers gored the mother's neck. Both kids and their momma died instantly. The father hung in there a couple days before he gave up the ghost. The deer died too, of course. KILLER DEER, the headline screamed. Justice, the Bambi-lovers and tree-huggers would say.

I called it plain sad.

Mitchell always buckled up, but I was kind of lazy about myself. Not that a seat belt would mean shit if one of those crazy deer rammed through your windshield, casting you and your vehicle careening into a ravine.

In all my years, all those thousands and thousands of miles, drunk, sober, tired, middle of the night, you name it, I never had an accident. Guess I've been fortunate that way. Not in much else. Hell, I'd been having the worst luck since Mike ... Why does everything in my life keep fucking up? If it weren't for Mitchell, I'd swear I'd been cursed. One thing for goddamn sure, I am unlucky in love. From the very beginning. From that very first fuck. Travis Williams. Asshole.

10

Travis, Travis, Travis. Oh my, I got bit bad. He would press himself against me until the bulging fly on his jeans jabbed through my skirt, his hands grasping my ass, pulling my hips into his. His lips caressing my neck. I thought I'd died and gone to heaven.

Then he shoved my heart through a meat grinder.

I'd just begun my senior year. Twenty-one-year-old Travis had already graduated from Willisburg High and farmed with his father on the family spread raising beef cattle on about five hundred acres south of town. I first laid eyes on him at a honky-tonk bar, his back against the wooden counter as he soaked in the scene. He was only a few inches taller than me with his boots on. After he'd kick them off, we fit like two pieces of a puzzle. Thick brown lashes surrounded his steel-gray eyes. He had a bent nose from a boyhood brawl and teeth not too straight, not too crooked. He often stashed a wad of tobacco between his cheek and gums. Travis didn't gab. He listened and nodded, chuckled at my girlish banter, and stroked his roughened palms up and down my back as I curled and stretched like a pussycat. He would brush his chin against mine to trigger the tingling and twirling that only one thing could stop. He didn't smile much. He'd squint at everything as if he found even the shadows too bright. He came across sort of tough and out of reach. But not to me.

I met him soon after I turned seventeen, a virgin still if you can believe it. In my high school, you had to dig deep to discover any virgins who survived eleventh grade. Even the ugly girls would put out. We did have plenty of pimply-faced boys fumbling about desperately inexperienced. Like Harold. I made it to my senior year intact. Sure, I'd fooled around up to a point. I'd almost gone all the way with a boyfriend behind the desk in Coach Bauer's office one Friday after school. Yet I managed to fight off or dissuade the ones scheming on me. They'd beg and plead, made complete morons of themselves. One jerk I dated actually got mad, called me a prick tease, and accused me of leading him on. He claimed he deserved a treat for all his trouble.

Before Travis, I'd entertained close encounters with fewer than five boys. I am not a forward type of girl. I never flirted recklessly or obviously. I'd let them make their move, and I'd either approve or deny them to continue. By the time I collided with Travis, I had stayed pure, more or less.

Travis didn't ask. He didn't beg. He didn't have to.

A sweaty August Saturday night. School had already started back up, except they had to let us out early the day before on account of the suffocating heat in our unairconditioned classrooms. We reveled in the fleeting freedom of summer, running about half-naked and almost barefoot in our tank tops and our tight, short skirts, searching for something to quench our thirst.

We planned a girls' night out at a country dance hall. Shelly borrowed her mother's ancient Ford Torino station wagon with its flaking fake wood side panels and two of its four hubcaps missing. Rachel, Christy, Jill, and I scrambled across the split vinyl for a seat. Jill won the battle for shotgun and celebrated by guzzling a pint of Everclear she had mooched off her older brother. The rest of us sipped from a liter-sized plastic bottle of Seven-Up watered down with cheap whiskey that Christy stole from her parents. When we arrived at the parking area, Jill was too wasted to walk and spent the remainder of the evening puking out the passenger window or sprawled on the back seat in a comatose state.

Shelly parked next to a van in a jammed gravel lot. We jostled to examine ourselves in the rearview mirror for smeared lipstick and stray hairs. I tugged at my bra, wishing the lacy contraption had more to work with. I had dressed for a standard night out, not slutty though definitely sexy. Slinky skin-hugging velour camisole. My silver hoop earrings played hide-and-seek with my hair. A denim skirt drawn taut over my slim hips and thighs. Glossy black sandals with a three-inch heel.

We had worked to pass for eighteen even though the guy at the door would let us in anyhow. They only hassled you if you showed up with runny-nosed teenage boys or your baby sister. They served beer to anyone with ID. Most schlepped in with their own pocket flasks of grain alcohol or some other poison of choice and bought setups from the hefty, grizzled man behind the counter. The bar changed its name every so often to sidestep debt collectors or regain its liquor license. Those days they called it the Hitchin' Post. I'm pretty positive it's shuttered now. Set off the two-lane that somersaults to Osage Springs, the metal-sided roadhouse attracted all kinds: the college kids from Cliff City slumming with the country yokels, married couples out for a good time, dancers who swirled you until you saw stars, and of course, creeps scheming to sweet talk young girls into a stroll through the parking lot.

After paying our cover, we left the moonless sky behind and entered a wicked den of booze and loud music you could dance to but only with a good buzz.

"It's Naked George. I hear they got a new drummer," Shelly screeched in my ear.

"What?" I shouted, pivoting my hips as I strutted to the beat of something loud and indistinguishable from the chatter, whoops, and laughter. Men in cowboy hats and plaid shirts checked us out as we bobbed our heads hunting for a familiar face or a perch to roost. A tipsy woman with a curly hairdo dyed the color of an overripe pumpkin knocked into Shelly and Christy.

"Hey! Look where you're going," Christy yelped.

The woman's eyes scurried wildly as she grabbed the backrest of a good ol' boy's stool. She started toppling. A man lurched forward to seize her arm and steady her.

"Now there, be careful hun. Watch your step," he yelled.

A pack of his friends huddled nearby guffawing and pointing while gulping from plastic cups, their faces flushed and merry. One with a scruffy beard cupped his hands around his words so they would soar above the racket. "Go get her, Charlie. That one's a keeper." The others hooted and howled, clapping each other on the back before taking another swig and surveying the festivities for more cheap entertainment.

Folks of all shapes and sizes crammed the bar. The overhead fluorescents blazed onto a tossing sea of denim, polyester snap shirts, belt buckles as big as pie plates, leather cowboy boots with fancy stitching, baseball caps embroidered with tractor company logos, and murky clouds of cigarette smoke. The stench of stale beer and tobacco mixed poorly with Rachel's stifling perfume.

I dove into my purse for my pack, and instantly everyone bummed off me.

"Go buy your own! These things cost money," I said. I fiddled with my lighter, scraping my thumb raw as the four of us bunched up, cigarettes to our lips.

"It's dead," Shelly said, her ruby red lips barely anchoring her unlit cigarette as she spoke. A squat man in a brown vinyl vest that hardly hid his bulging gut slid up to us and whipped out a shiny metal lighter, flipping the cover with his thumb and sheltering the flame with his other palm. He grinned at us all, his lips peeling back to reveal a gold-capped front tooth.

We took turns sticking the ends of our cigarettes, my cigarettes actually, into the fire and sucked and huffed until you could mistake us for dragons. We only offered grim smiles in gratitude before quickly swinging our attention elsewhere, ignoring his feeble bid to connect.

"Where you ladies all from?"

Shelly gestured toward her ears and held her palms up. Too loud to converse, she signaled to him. She swiveled her back to us as she inspected the horde for hotties. At least twice as old as my girlfriends and I, the man lingered for several minutes, smiling awkwardly as he wrangled to engage at least one of us before wrinkling his nose in disgust and stomping away to the bar. Christy caught my gaze, and we both erupted into giggles.

Rachel frowned while puffing, not even inhaling. She patted my shoulder. I crinkled my face as if to ask "what?" before resuming my scan of the crowd for anything appealing. Conversation required shouting in someone's ear, so you learned to communicate through gesture. Body language. I shook my hips and shuffled my feet to the music, although I had difficulty feeling the rhythm. The music roared. I couldn't identify the competing bursts of the different instruments, let alone comprehend the lyrics the singer screamed into the microphone. I didn't recognize the song or the style of music. Rockabilly country something or other.

Rachel pressed her mouth next to my ear.

"What?" I groaned, somewhat annoyed and not interested in what she said anyway.

She uncrossed her scrawny limbs and smoothed a satiny sheer blouse tucked into her skirt. She clamped onto my wrist to tug me, pulling my hair away from my ear, squealing so loud it hurt. “Should we see how Jill’s doing?”

I wrenched my arm from her and swabbed my ear as I scowled. I spotted a group of guys clumped against a wall high fiving each other while hooting and snorting.

I edged away from Rachel. Christy, then Shelly jockeyed toward the band. I followed, veering this way and that, bumping, scuttling, and squishing sideways through bodies. I sensed my high heels sticking to the floor. I landed wrong, almost losing my balance. I grabbed Shelly’s arm for support. She swerved toward me, rolling her eyes.

“Watch out!” she mouthed.

“It’s the floor. It’s gross,” I said in a wail no one heeded.

A cutie with a goatee chatted up Christy. She smirked and jutted her ear toward him, pretending to listen to his banter. He wasn’t close enough and didn’t know her well enough to burrow his mouth into her hair so she could actually listen. She led him on all the same.

Rachel tagged along at my heels.

“I need a drink,” Shelly said.

The three of us stared at each other. No chance they’d serve us alcohol. A girl our age would have to finagle someone to buy her a beer or get herself a soda and find someone to top it off with booze. A slug or two pooled in the bottle left behind in the car, except that meant checking on sick Jill, which did not sound appetizing. And that would have corralled us away from the action.

We glanced around, clasping our handbags and contemplating our options. Men and women swarmed every table surrounding the dance floor. Plastic cups littered the fake wood laminate tabletops, some half-empty, others lying on their sides with their contents either spilled or already guzzled. Every table featured an ashtray heaped with spent butts, and in several, a smoldering forgotten cigarette.

A skinny middle-aged woman with blond hair cascading down her shoulders and blue-tinted sunglasses nestled on the tip of her nose flopped onto the lap of a mustachioed man wearing a Lynyrd Skynyrd T-shirt. She threw her head back laughing, catapulting both of them backward to land spread-eagle on the floor.

At another table, an argument brewed as an enormous man with a withered limb clutched to his chest hollered and wagged the index finger of his good hand at a seated man in overalls shaking his head like an angry bull as he tilted back and forth in his chair with a bitter expression. I couldn't hear what the man barked. However, you could measure the feverish temperature of his words as his face reddened, while rowdy onlookers cautiously preserved their distance.

I attempted to poke Shelly with my finger to point out a lip-locked couple on the dance floor who required a motel room. I found nothing but a vacant space next to Rachel, who tapped my arm once again.

"What is it?" I hissed. A man braced against the wall leered at us before returning his bored gaze to a game of pool.

Rachel lowered her eyebrows and pouted as she toyed with a lock of chestnut hair gathered behind her ear.

I mouthed, "I'm going to the bathroom."

"What?" she asked. The music clogged my ears, but I could read her lips. I gestured toward the back of the building and paved my way through the crowd. She trotted behind. For the ten-hundredth time I asked myself why we always had to cart Rachel around.

I shouldered through a herd of women surging toward the sink, the doorway, or lining up for the single toilet stall. As soon as I finished brushing my hair and checking myself in the mirror, I ditched Rachel in the bathroom, slamming through the saloon-style door.

On my own, I plowed through clusters of bodies. Three middle-aged men sidled up to a group of girls so fortified with lipstick, mascara, and eyeshadow you could have mistaken them for old hookers. A pasty-faced boy stumbled by, leaning against the wall as he weaved toward the patio where the drunks went to hang their heads over the rail and barf.

"Jerk!" I said as he grazed me. He plunged toward me and uttered something that hardly suggested an apology. Then he pitched toward the back door. I swatted at my shoulder to wipe off his touch and straightened my denim skirt.

A brood of cackling women rushed by me as I strutted quickly to distance myself from Rachel. A crash of beer bottles followed by raucous laughter riveted the mob. Then Naked George's singer started howling again and drowned out everything.

I didn't notice him right off. He had propped himself against the bar with his elbows resting on the edge, thumbs in his belt loops. I spied the opening next to him and skated over, plopping my purse on the counter and fishing for my Virginia Slims.

His head drifted toward me as he said something. The corners of his thin lips curled upward. I couldn't hear diddly, so I tossed a smirk and shrugged as if to say "maybe," though to what I had no idea. He did not have the sort of face I would immediately say "no" to, not like the graying losers lining the walls or trawling for easy women. I took him for a couple years older than me. His eyelids formed slits that peered out from under the brim of his cowboy hat. Unlike most of the men there who sported cheap cowboy hats purchased from the local feed store, Travis carried his like a crown.

He had tucked his plaid shirt with silver ribbing and metal snaps into his belted button-fly Levis. His boots looked worn but clean. My eyes darted over his roughened knuckles free of jewelry. A working man. Not married or at least trying to pass as single. He sipped from a plastic cup, but he didn't strike me as intoxicated. He certainly wasn't a college boy trying to blend.

Travis angled toward me without disturbing his post at the bar. I smiled shyly. He was gorgeous. He tried again, leaning closer and speaking louder though not obnoxiously. His breath warmed my ear.

"You want to dance?"

He didn't smell as if he had spilled a bottle of aftershave on his shirt or if he had showered with scented soap. A hint of fresh sweat and a whiff of chewing tobacco. I flipped the strap of my purse over my shoulder and trailed him into the gyrating mass of bodies. And a nice ass!

And he could dance. I didn't know the steps, but he spun me to the left and then right, the right foot and then left. I had never danced that way before. He led me where he aimed us both to go. After a while, I got the knack, and he didn't have to sidestep to prevent me from kicking the toe of his boots. We cut loose to the next song. Then the next. I don't think I heard the music even. I just moved to a throbbing pulse, following the pressure from his knees and thighs, his palms and arms as he nudged me in one direction, then pulled me to the right, then whirled me again. He beamed at me. His relaxed grin hid his teeth. We danced nonstop. The perspiration bubbling up from my pores made my hands slippery.

Once I lost his grasp and sailed into a sloshed couple bolstering each other in the middle of the dance floor.

"Sorry," I burst out with a laugh. I covered my mouth. "Ooops!" my eyes said to Travis. The pair ignored me, swaying with their chins on each other's shoulders, completely out of sync with the fast-tempo music. The woman's eyelids drooped, and her jaw gaped as if she dozed.

The music stopped as the lead singer barked into the microphone. You couldn't follow any of his gibberish, except the dancers understood and released a collective sigh as mismatched partners left the dance floor. Those lingering merged, mingling limbs as the music softened into a leisurely beat. The lights dimmed. I swept away any distractions as I focused on Travis.

He squinted at me with his half-smile, his gaze latched onto mine. He slid his arms around my waist and drew me toward him, our bodies melding as one. I laid my head on his chest as he tilted his head, so his hat brim shaded my forehead. My hands found each other behind his neck and interlaced. Then he sliced between my legs with his knee, boosting me onto his thigh and rocking me, reeling us in circles now and again. He would nuzzle my cheek and brush his lips against my ear, murmuring something and sparking sharp tingles to shoot through me. My senses shut out anyone or anything but him. I was terrified and exhilarated all in the same instant. I don't know how long we cuddled each other, but I can still taste the sweetness of his arms enveloping me. In less than twenty minutes, I'd fallen in love.

After another slow dance, the band took a break before the final set. Travis led me off the dance floor and outside into a humid summer evening. A flurry of bugs attacked the one working light bulb that flickered by the entry. The stars took advantage of the moonless heavens and glittered, glazing the sky with a fairy-tale glow. A thunderstorm earlier in the day left the ground mushy in places, and our steps kept time to a soundtrack of squishy noises as I walked hand in hand with Travis. He tenderly squeezed my fingers in his leathery palm as we picked a path through puddles and gobs of weeds amidst the graveled lot, small batches of stoners passing joints, or twosomes grinding against each other while backed up to parked cars. We strolled by a man and woman squabbling while sitting in their front seat, the doors yawning open as their harsh shouts ricocheted through the night.

Travis steered me toward the back of the parking lot to his truck. He lifted me onto the lowered tailgate. He stood in front of me with his palms on my knees, massaging the soft parts and tracing my kneecaps with his fingertips. I scooted closer, my hem snagging on the roughened steel of the tailgate, and cinched my knees on each side of his pelvis, right against the bone. I'd never done anything like that before. It seemed natural.

His hands gradually traveled up my legs to my thighs then to my hips. A low moan slipped from him as he nestled his jaw against my chin. His first kiss on my cheek felt like a butterfly wing had grazed my skin. We linked lips and tongues, arms intertwining and hands exploring each other.

Then Travis retreated half a step as his eyes locked onto mine. He undid his buttons and peeled his jeans back to the tops of his hips. He guided me onto my back while he remained standing, his pelvis pressed against the tailgate. My eyes flitted across his face as he unraveled my underwear from my hips, my ass, and away from my legs and feet. Then he grabbed my thighs, pulling me onto him as he pushed himself against me. I let out all the air in my lungs I'd bottled up for ages. One almost loud WHOOSH! I wrapped my legs around his waist as his fingers prodded and raked my thighs while he thrust himself inside me. He pumped away before gradually speeding up, reaching a fury that left us both panting.

I'd expected it to hurt a little. That's what everyone said should happen. I was too wound up to notice. And Travis wasn't some kind of giant: just a normal size for a man, I suppose. The only sore spot five minutes later was the back of my scalp, chafed from being bounced against the metal bed.

After his silent explosion, his thin lips clamped together to form a straight line, smothering his strained gasps as he struggled to catch his breath. Then a stillness settled as our eyes wandered over each other.

"Ow," I said with a giggle as he tugged up his boxers and redid the buttons of his jeans.

"Ouch?" He sniggered seductively. "I wasn't trying to hurt you."

I sat up on the tailgate, letting my legs dangle off the edge, and tamed my helter-skelter hair with my palms. I looked around for where he'd flung my underwear. I crossed my legs.

"Ouch my head," I tittered. In the darkness, I could barely make out his lips.

"We can fix that," he growled low as he fiddled with my bra strap. His fingers tiptoed across my neck. He hoisted himself onto the tailgate next to me. Then snatching one of my wrists while his other slinked around my waist, he hauled me on top of him as he leaned backward. Keeping our laughter quiet and private, we inched higher into the pickup bed. I clung to him, scrabbling to balance on him as he slid his backside along the bed's raised grooves, squirming toward the cab like worms until our feet cleared the tailgate's edge. Then I kissed him. His fingers fondled my ass and kneaded my flesh while my hands scooped his face as if I readied to sip water from a mountain spring. Our arms and legs, fingers and tongues tangled as we kissed and pawed each other. He wriggled out from under me as he rolled me onto my back before climbing on top of me. With his knees between my legs, he raised his hips as I unfastened his jeans, one sparkling stud at a time. I shucked his jeans and boxers down his thighs. Then his pelvis dove down and we did it again, the old-fashioned way.

◆ ◆ ◆

Travis and I stole away whenever we could and spent our precious afternoons and evenings swirling and spinning in each other's embrace. I never arranged for him to meet my family, fearing Father's deranged reaction. By then, Momma spent most days in bed when she didn't run errands or work. Travis lived on his family's cattle farm a half-dozen miles from Willisburg. He never bothered to introduce me to his folks either.

On Friday and Saturday nights, we'd hook up at the roadhouse if I started the evening out with the girls, or he'd pluck me up after school in his Chevy or earlier after he'd cajole me into cutting class. We'd order burgers and fries to go from the Hamburger Hut before it permanently shuttered its drive-thru and walk-up windows. Then we'd roam through the countryside until we unearthed a private niche in the woods off a gravel road or tucked between the cottonwoods next to the river. In the pickup bed, he would spread his mother's fraying quilts with their machine-sewn calico and checkered squares faded from years of washings and flapping in the sun to dry. Then he would lay me on the quilts and mash me into a potato pancake. Afterward, I would lie on my back, my legs unable to coax themselves together for a spell and my spine bruised from smacking against the metal truck bed. His momma's old quilts couldn't protect me from that.

The winter cold hindered us from romping outside, so we snuggled in a cheap motel outside Cliff City where the desk clerk didn't give a hoot who you were or what you did or why you were there as long as you could pay cash. Sometimes we settled for the cab of his pickup, and after we finished, we fogged the glass until I could write in the wetness. Using the tip of my index finger, I looped our names with a heart and pierced it with an arrow as he watched with his close-mouthed grin.

We saw each other regularly. Like clockwork. Except for one week out of every month when Travis attended to "business" with his buddies at the tavern or for poker in someone's den. Go ahead and guess which week of every month that was.

Travis never introduced me to his friends, a bunch of guys who worked farms or construction. We'd drive by them in town or rambling a country lane as they hailed each other by hollering through their truck windows. The lanky blond one always glanced at me while he jawed with Travis about a tractor part or vaccinating and deworming a herd of cows and calves.

Once while cruising Main Street, Travis elbowed me as he snapped, "Get down!" I concentrated on his muscular, roughened hands as he waved nervously at a car or a person I couldn't see as my head rested on his cab's vinyl seat. His parents or maybe his preacher, I supposed. Too much in love with him to even jealously imagine another girl. Too stupid to fuss and ask why he treated me like something he had to hide.

Then one early April afternoon, with the jonquils unfurling their white and yellow hoods and the trees budding wispy pale green sprouts, I followed a whim and borrowed Momma's car after school to track him. I had to report my good news. My period hadn't started, so we didn't need to start our routine breather yet!

I found him with his friends at the local pool hall in the aluminum-sided building that now houses the flea market. Travis blushed slightly when heckled by a boy bending over the table as he prepared his shot. Travis strode toward me with a flustered expression stealing across his face. He leaned closer as I purred into his ear that I needed to speak with him. Alone. His friends jeered at us.

"Which game you playing, Travis," one said.

Not one of them acknowledged me directly, although the tall blond gawked at me.

Sandwiching his wrist with my fingers, I drew Travis farther away from the table with its colored balls clacking against each other.

I whispered in his ear. I knew no other way to put it. "My friend didn't stop by for her monthly visit."

I'd never been this forward before. Never had to before, yet my thirst for Travis swamped any sense of modesty. And it wasn't that I desired him for sex. I yearned to see him, chat with him and hear his voice. Inhale his scent. I'd grown accustomed to his monthly buddy time coinciding with my monthly time. Of course he needed to hang out with his friends. I never questioned why he didn't need to see me for the entire week.

Travis appeared confused at first. Then a shadow submerged his features. He grabbed my arm and hustled me toward the door. His pack of friends licked their lips and blew kisses, taunting him to "shake a leg." The blond leered at me as if he owned me. Travis and I tromped outside to the sloping sidewalk.

"Why'd you come here?"

His sharp manner threw me for a minute. Silly me, I'd believed my situation would please him. I'd styled my hair with a curling iron and dressed seductively in a diamond-patterned miniskirt with a practically see-through lacy blouse.

"I ... I thought you'd want to maybe go for a drive. Maybe check out the dogwoods by the river?" Then I pouted at him flirtatiously, angling my head so my eyes slanted upward to gaze into his.

He'd never spoken testily to me before. Sometimes he'd remain quiet when I babbled about this or that. He'd never said a mean or hateful thing in the more than seven months we dated.

I waited patiently for the day I knew, just knew steered my way. The day he would hum in my ear how he loved me. I'd teased him about it on and off. He'd pull back, smiling and raising his eyebrows in mock surprise. I'd never even hinted about getting married. About him bending the knee to me and promising to stand at the end of the aisle as I sashayed toward him. A church wedding. I'd never mentioned it. I only dreamed about it every fucking day.

"You know I'm busy. We've some sick cows and it's calving season. I'm waking early and working past dark. This is my only day off this week."

I guessed I'd thrown him off guard. He hadn't figured on me popping by. I softly strummed his cheek with my pointer finger, but he didn't respond. He kept his fists in the pockets of his jeans, his eyes scanning mine. He chewed on his lower lip, his eyes boring into me. I let my hand drop and then crossed my limbs over my waist.

"Well fine, then. Sorry to disturb you." My half-smile dissolved into a frown as I glared at my sandaled foot. I had no inkling why he would react so unfriendly to my unexpected arrival. I had not prepared myself for the sting of such a stunning rejection.

"You're only a ... a few days late?" His voice cracked as he swallowed.

Then it dawned on me. I wasn't pregnant, or at least in my youthful foolishness, assumed correctly. That's why he acted so huffy with me. Travis wasn't mad. He was scared. His fear tinted his skin a limestone gray as his eyes darted about me.

I forced a girlish laugh as I gently slapped at the air between us. "Don't worry, I'm taking care of things."

"You sure?"

He never quizzed me before about "taking care of things." He had never concerned himself with any of my girl business until that moment.

I giggled awkwardly.

Travis shifted his weight, pulled his hands out of his pockets, and folded his arms firmly across his chest.

"Now Travis, do we really need to discuss this right here, right now?" I spooned sugar onto my tongue as I lifted my palms to the sky, my eyes coyly searching his. I held back nothing from him in the privacy of his truck or a cheap motel room, but I preferred not to discuss the details of my embarrassing experience at the county health department shortly after we hooked up. I took my pill every morning and never skipped nor forgot, not once. Two of his friends hurled gestures at us through the window.

I simmered. My arms collapsed to my sides, lifeless.

"Well I don't know. Maybe we can get together ... later." His lips barely moved as he talked.

"Fine. That's just fine," I grimaced as scalding steam escaped from me. Still hadn't mastered the artistry of letting 'em have it. My face burned as I stomped back to my momma's car. I would show him. Go ahead, cool your heels, sweetie pie, I glowered. Next time he readied himself for fun, I aimed to blow him off. I sped away, furiously puffing a cigarette. The wind gushing through the car windows knotted my hair into a ragged mess.

I never saw Travis again. I watched for his truck to coast by after school, hugging my handbag while I trampled the grassy corner where we'd always rendezvoused as the minutes ticked into hours, the days into weeks. I listened for the telephone to ring, moping around the house that first weekend assuming he'd phone me as before. I rang his house despite promising never to call him. I banged down the phone every time his mother answered.

Decked out in my discount store finery, I prowled the honky-tonk or our other haunts with Shelly and Christy, once out of desperation with a somewhat sober Jill and that pain-in-the-ass Rachel. But I never bumped into Travis again. I ran across one of his friends gassing up. He didn't remember me or just plain ignored me. Not even a slice of attention. I sobbed myself dry and rubbed my eyes raw. By the first of May, I pocketed my heartache. My love for him wilted, turning me bitter. As all the other girls preened and prattled about their prom dresses and dates, I smoldered.

Months after that miserable prom night with Harold and after we buried Momma in a peach and maroon silk nightgown, I found out Mother Nature bucked off Travis' family. That summer's drought had sucked all the moisture from the soil leaving the pastures brown and the livestock hungry, so they shipped their herd south to federal land hoping the cows and calves would find enough grass to fatten up. Travis had signed on at a dairy three hours from Willisburg. The ad for the farm auction hung on the bulletin board at Velva's. And that's the last I heard of Travis Williams. Fucking asshole.

11

"Let's get the hell going, wherever the hell that is. Just get this show on the road, puhLEASE!" Ellis whacked the tops of his thighs for emphasis.

You'd have thought killing that deer, especially a baby deer, would have tossed me into the deep end. Unnerved, I rattled worse than a coffee can full of nails. Yet something steeled inside me. I twisted the key and gunned the engine. It fired right up. Thank you, Lord.

My front tire dipped into the ditch. I gassed it, and the pickup heaved and wheezed back onto the highway. I fought against glancing through the rear window. Luckily I didn't run into the path of another car as I didn't check for one. I latched onto the steering wheel and drove. Fast. Fast as I could.

We weaved and swayed with the rhythm of the road once again. Hot. So hot the gusts surging through the cab slammed us like heat from a furnace switched on High. Ellis, silent for a change, stared at the blacktop ahead, pursing his lips and scowling. Johnny remained Johnny. Thank God for Johnny.

We met several cars aiming toward Willisburg or beyond. No one I recognized. When we hit the main four-lane at Englewood, Johnny motioned for me to head south. South toward Milesdale. Except we had one stop before traveling on to Milesdale that afternoon.

Thwack thwack thwack, the tires struck the asphalt. So hot,

the tar melted and oozed in spots. Temperatures that steep sometimes buckle the pavement. Almost four o'clock. Hottest part of the day. The thermometer must have topped one hundred. And it was only mid-June, with the feverish fury of July and August ahead.

With it this damn hot, what's July gonna do to us?

Ellis fiddled with the radio until he realized it didn't work. The AM/FM stereo in my rig only plays static interrupted by hate radio and a random country western station that flits in and out of range. Some jerk busted the antenna two summers ago. Ellis slid a pack of smokes from his pocket and lit one, cupping his hand against the wind racing through the cab. I itched to ask how he stole the cigarettes from behind the counter but ate my words instead. Maybe he paid for those.

Ellis squawked as he smacked at his fingers that had grappled with the lighter. He had torched himself.

I guffawed. Served him right. I'd bet he stole the lighter too. Now that was justice. The wind hurried the cigarette's fire, and soon Ellis threw the butt out the window, saddling us with the ashes swirling around the cab. I used to burn through a pack a day before I discovered I was pregnant with Mitchell. I sneak one now and then. I rassled with the temptation to bum one off Ellis, as I couldn't stand granting him an edge over me. Besides, I probably could not have peeled my fists from the wheel.

We bounced along for miles. Quiet except for the air pouring through and Ellis, who whistled, hummed, and occasionally sang snippets of some jingle from a TV commercial. He'd drum his fingers against the dashboard, his thighs, the slight paunch of his belly. The truck rumbled past Eastley, past the turnoff for Huxton, Carlton, then past the state conservation park. The blanched sky bore a fuzzy, hazy coating as if someone left it to hang on the clothesline too long.

Not much traffic. Cars and trucks whizzed by us, their windows sealed against the heat with the AC blasting. Every once in a while, we'd glide by some that didn't look as if they'd make it. A two-door sedan crammed full of little kids grumbled and sputtered unsteadily. We rode up behind a pickup loaded with plastic patio furniture and a mattress, the vehicle's engine grinding away at less than the speed limit. We breezed by a gooseneck trailer stuffed with shit-covered cattle on their way to the sale barn. One bellowing steer was wedged so tight against a slit between the steel slats that only his right eye could roam wild with fear. In the back of a contractor's truck, a black plastic trash bag snagged in the closed lid of an aluminum toolbox waved frantically at us while we waited for a chance to pass. I moved over for a convoy of eighteen-wheelers breaking the law as they barreled by in the left lane, rushing to fork over crap for people to buy or fret about.

The billboards lining the highway displayed huge ads with large-breasted women advertising Live! Young! Girls! Girls! GIRLS! They screamed for attention every mile or so until the massive women began competing with a succession of pro-life billboards picturing enormous babies flapping their arms and giggling at you. Someone had spray-painted "Jacks Cafe 5 miles" in gigantic purple letters on a deserted mobile home parked catawampus off the four-lane. We coasted another five miles and found nothing. Not even a turnoff.

Ellis sniggered to himself as he lit another cigarette without scorching himself. The wind roaring through the windows whipped my hair about as wads of coarse strands slapped my face.

Then my Ford uttered a sickening rattle. My ears perked. I rolled up my window and shushed Ellis. Had I imagined it? There it went again.

Damn. Not now, please not today!

The pickup hurdled past the fading broken lines like an aging racehorse. But that noise alarmed me.

The last time my truck croaked like that I wound up stranded not far from Cliff City.

Speeding home after a late shift last fall, the truck lost steam shortly after the gagging intensified. I punched the gas pedal with my foot as it slowed to a crawl. I steered the choking hunk of metal onto the shoulder, where it coughed and then shuddered into silence. I fiddled with the key and gassed the engine, yet it wouldn't stir. The fuel tank meter measured half-empty. Maybe a filter or the fuel hose? I have no clue about car mechanics other than to fill the tank and haul it in for service if I can afford it. I had no chance of repairing what ailed my truck at that hour of night on that stretch of pavement.

I'd zoomed by the well-lit convenience store not far from where my truck died, so I pulled out the key, slammed the door without bothering to lock it, and marched, cussing myself for the ten-hundredth time for not buying a cell phone along with everyone else. I've always scrimped and cut corners to survive, but I always end up paying anyway.

Nice evening for a walk, I strained to convince myself. Cool wind, cool enough to snuff the bugs and turn the tree leaves a million shades of red, orange, brown, and yellow. At least it wasn't raining. I sank one fist into the pocket of my windbreaker and squeezed my purse against my chest with the other. A couple drivers offered me a lift, but I shook a firm "No!" I almost caved in to the guy wearing a starched white shirt and tuned in to a Christian radio station who gawked at me hungrily. I figured he would either try to convert me or kill me, so I risked the hike rather than whatever he would suggest besides a ride. That quickened my pace.

After a thirty-minute trek, I arrived at the gas station in one piece. I sprinted across the driveway as the fluorescents above the pumps switched off. I reached the entrance, the two glass doors barricaded by a padlocked rod iron gate. The lights inside still burned. I stuck my face between the bars and clapped my palm on the glass twice as I scanned the aisles. Nothing. I rapped louder with my knuckles until a woman with hair dyed coal black poked her head out of an office doorway. She frowned as she withdrew. I knocked again, harder and quicker. She looked wearily at me, knitting her eyebrows with a twinge of suspicion.

Open the door pretty please? I smiled in the most sincere manner I could muster. She shrugged her slouching shoulders and walked toward the door, pausing to cough into her wrist and clear her throat. We inspected each other through the glass in between the plastered stickers and taped-on signs threatening to card all minors and prosecute all drive-offs.

"My truck broke down. Can I use your phone?" I raised my voice so she could hear me through the glass.

The woman's aging features froze into a grimace as she checked me out. Her straight blackened hair, parted dead center, merged with thinning, ashen gray roots. She exhaled a lungful of smoke with a sigh.

"Why not. Just don't knife me or rob me, that's all I ask," she screeched.

She trudged back to the office and retraced her path with a cluster of keys attached to an arm's-length section of untreated wood smudged gray and polished smooth from years of handling. She unlocked the glass door. After tugging it ajar, she braced it with her body as she unbolted the rod iron security bars. She battled with the accordion-style gate and finally folded it out of the way while shooing my attempts to assist. "It don't like strangers," she said without striking me as mean or snarky. After she forged a half-foot gap, she stuck out her head, peering around casually and then at me.

"Where's your vehicle?"

"About a mile south of here. I just need a phone. I can get someone to pick me up."

I didn't know many who would bail me out, especially at that hour. Sadie, already tending Mitchell for me, didn't even drive let alone own a car. Tammy had already lit out for Colorado. I was chummy enough with a couple gals from the plant. We never did much after shifts, instead keeping busy as single moms or making ends meet with lousy relationships. One of them would hit for me in a pinch like this. First I'd try Terry, who had worked the same shift. Then Liz. No, maybe not Liz. That David character would have given his right arm to retrieve me, but I was not going there.

"What's wrong, you out of gas?" the lady asked with only a flicker of interest, her eyelids drooping over her hazel eyes. Her lipstick had worn off, leaving magenta streaks in the fissures of her lips. She teetered between falling asleep or passing out.

If I hadn't responded, I doubt she would have noticed. As she acted so helpful and all, I yakked anyway even though it'd be a waste of breath. "I'm not out of gas. Could be a problem with the fuel hose or the filter or something. I filled it yesterday. Maybe just bad gas. It started choking then the engine quit."

The woman's tiny figure blocked the entrance while propping open the glass door behind her. She tilted her head as if expecting to hear something. She nursed her cigarette and let out a noisy gust of smoke before clawing at the security gate to widen the opening. I grinned my thanks and edged sideways through the metal bars and the glass doors.

The woman shuffled to the office with me in tow. She stopped to brush her polyester slacks with her palm and take another drag. I followed her through a swinging door and into a room smaller than a public john clogged with a desk buried in boxes and two tall filing cabinets. Shelving gobbled up every speck of wall space and overflowed with piles of catalogs and folders and assorted loose papers. She rooted through the debris on the desk, unearthing the telephone, and tried to untangle the cord so it would reach me from my perch in the doorway. She grappled with it a few seconds, her blood red manicured nails clicking against each other. Huge silver rings embedded with chunks of marbled stones and buffed turquoise glimmered on every finger. Then she grunted in disgust, scooped up the entire contraption, lugged it toward the edge of the desk, jerked her head toward the wheeled office chair, and shoved the receiver at me. She leaned back against a filing cabinet that towered over her and asked without any enthusiasm if it was local.

"Cliff City."

She puffed and stared at the ceiling as if aiming to arrange some privacy the cramped room could not afford. I counted the copper-singed water stains in the ceiling tiles as the phone rang.

Once, twice, now three rings.

Hmmm. Didn't go straight home, huh Terry?

Maybe she had accidentally or intentionally unplugged the phone. Couldn't depend on Liz. She recently had taken in her daughter, her daughter's six-month-old, and the daughter's boyfriend, who wasn't even the baby's daddy. Liz had broken out in hives, and she constantly snapped at everyone on our line, even the boss. Who else did I know well enough to roust out of bed in the middle of the night?

Damn!

After ten rings, I gingerly set the receiver in its cradle.

Mike had vanished, wallowing in the midst of one of his "away" periods. Not that he could have rescued me if I had tracked him down, as he'd lost his driver's license again the year before after running a red in someone else's car and drunkenly resisting arrest. They'd threatened him with jail if they caught him driving without a license. And he had no car, of course.

"Try again. Sometimes, you know, the phone company." The woman uttered each word with obvious effort, her voice gruff and wheezy.

I didn't have any better ideas, so I dialed Terry's number again. A mother of two teenagers, she probably was accustomed to the telephone ringing later than this. I counted five rings as I twirled strands of hair around my pointer finger before Terry huffed a garbled "What?" Must have assumed I was one of her kids, although she didn't say so. She promised she'd skedaddle, knew exactly which gas station I called her from, maybe twenty minutes or so?

"You're gonna have to bunk here. I ain't chauffeuring you all the way to your pad tonight. You can have my daughter's bed. She doesn't seem to need it," Terry said. "We'll deal with your truck tomorrow."

I told her that'd be fine. Sadie would fix pancakes or cinnamon toast for Mitchell's breakfast before whisking him out the door to school.

"What I tell you about that phone company," said the woman through a plume of smoke and a scratchy laugh.

"She'll be here soon, so I'll ... well, thanks for the help."

The woman parted her lips as if to speak and took a drag instead as her gaze floated around. I scooted out of the office to the entryway.

"Where you going to wait?" she asked.

I twitched my head toward the door. "Right outside. Thanks again."

"You can't wait out there with the kind of people out this late." She sounded a tad more awake. Skirting me as she ignored my weak protests, she plodded to the front with her collection of keys and secured the entrance.

"Wait at my place. The headlights from your friend's car will shine in when she hits the driveway. No use waiting outside in the dark."

I was numb and drained after a ten-hour day assembling microwave ovens. I had to wake up early to get Mitchell to school during the week, so by midnight, I'm usually sort of hammered anyway. I wasn't too keen on hanging out with her, but pacing in the cold with God knows what slithering by excited me even less. So I tagged behind her as she turned off the store fluorescents.

She offered me a cigarette and something to drink. I agreed to both. "Soda's fine." I craved a beer, but that could have made things weird. I preferred to remain as alert as possible.

She gestured toward the refrigerated cases, and I selected a Dr. Pepper. Then we trod toward the back, past crates of Diet Coke and Pepsi in plastic bottles, stacked boxes of bagged pretzels and Doritos.

She tossed me a cigarette. Funny, no one's tossed me a cigarette since high school. I caught it in my palm, my fingers floundering awkwardly without breaking it. She didn't provide a light until we exited the back door. She keyed the deadbolt as she flicked her spent cigarette into the night. She started to lift a fresh one when a hacking fit cornered her attention. Afterward, she lit up and extended the flame to me with one hand while pointing with the other at a single-wide trailer nestled against a handful of trees. No lights on inside or out. I'd sped by there a million times and never noticed it before.

I matched her short footsteps toward the unlit structure. The metal keys whirled and jangled against each other as our shoes crunched gravel. The woman halted twice to puff her cigarette. She exhaled as she surveyed the ground before her feet. I was taller than her, and I'm not tall. She was probably one of those women who shrank with age. Stooped, rounding back, matchsticks for arms and legs. No hips. She almost sported the figure of a young girl. Her thinning hair trickled down her shoulders. Her carrot-colored hoodless sweatshirt swamped her and made her appear tinier.

I trailed her to the mobile home sprouting amidst a crop of locust trees, heaps of milk crates, and dense stands of weeds. As we reached it, I recoiled and reconsidered entering. Before, I'd been the stranger, the potential danger. Unknown. Now, who was this woman after all? Just a tired old lady. It was dark, it was late, and who knew when Terry would hustle over.

I pictured myself sitting cross-legged on the pavement, hiding in the shadows, hugging myself to stay warm, yawning while scuffling with the sandman as I prayed for Terry's dented Ford Taurus to putter up the driveway. Exhaustion ruled that out, so I blindly followed the woman through the door.

She flipped a switch. The overhead bulb barely illuminated the place enough to see the cluttered main room, which consisted of a couch, a reclining chair, and assorted furniture on one side, a kitchen on the other, with an open counter separating the kitchen and the sitting area. The hushed buzz of a television from a room beyond the kitchen filtered through. The woman huffed as she bent her slight frame toward the vinyl couch and cleared a seat for me, tossing to one side mail-order catalogs, unopened envelopes, and a stray sweater.

She patted the cushion. "Sit," she muttered. She chomped her jaw and ground her teeth as she smoothed her hair behind one ear with a liver-spotted hand, her silver and stone rings clacking against each other. I plunked on the couch and half-smiled before hoisting my cigarette to my lips, then my soda.

Damn Terry, don't take the scenic route.

The woman plucked a wrinkled T-shirt and a wadded-up paper sack from the beige recliner, dumping both on a neighboring table as she plopped into the chair. "Well, that's better. Can't ask for better than this," she said. I guessed her at somewhere between seventy and a hundred years old. Grooves deep enough to trip over crisscrossed her cheeks. Either smoke from an endless stream of cigarettes or her drowsiness tinged her eyes bloodshot, or maybe that was how they usually looked. Her head slumped backward as she spewed a column like a steam stack. Then clenching the filter between her yellowed, not quite straight teeth, she bent forward to untie her shoelaces before sinking back into her chair as she pried each shoe off with her opposite foot. "Yes," she murmured to herself. "Much better." The woman stretched back in her recliner, flinging up the footrest.

She closed her eyes for a few seconds then wrested them open. She studied me. I should have said something, yet I had nothing to say, so I slurped my bottle of soda and puffed my cigarette. The lady smoked menthols. Gag me! But beggars can't be choosers. I'm always trying to quit by not buying a pack; besides, they're so expensive! If someone offers, I can't say no even if I discover they're those puky menthol ones. I rose to find an ashtray, cupping my palm underneath the smoldering end so

I wouldn't spark a mess.

"There, on the coffee table by the lamp, no, should be there. Over there." She swung her arm at across the room, except the dimness blurred the square table wedged between the couch and the wall. I spied one half-full of butts on the kitchen counter and ferried it to the round table between her lounger and the sofa.

She stamped out her cigarette with one hand while plunging the fingers of her other hand into a pink-and-purple checkered slick case for another. After firing up, she coughed as she shoved the lighter into the case. Not even glancing my way, she jabbed the cigarette case at me, providing me another as she hacked, attempting to cover her mouth with the back of her wrist.

"One of the benefits with this job: lung cancer." She snickered before diving into another coughing jag. I lit the cigarette, vowing it would be my last from her. I tried to appear concerned despite not spoiling to listen to her troubles.

"No, no, just wishful thinking," she said, her words smeared with sarcasm. She squinted at me again through the haze. She clucked her tongue as she focused on me. "You come here for gas?"

I sailed past practically every day. I didn't recollect ever stopping in, as I could always locate a gas station in Cliff City selling at a couple cents a gallon less.

"Oh, sure." I tapped my cigarette against the speckled blue and tan ceramic ashtray. "I commute a lot, for work and stuff." I spoke rapidly as I rocked back and forth.

Damn Terry, hurry.

She stared at me with growing curiosity, and I squirmed as if a pebble stuck in my shoe pestered my toe. How would we see Terry drive up? How would I catch her headlights from where I sat in that trailer with all the fuzzy maroon curtains in the main room pulled shut.

"You said we'll see the car headlights?"

She tilted her head toward the room nearest the highway, her eyes fastened on mine. "Headlights shine through that bedroom window. Can't miss 'em. If they're on, they'll wake us," she said. "Bright enough to wake the dead," she drawled, or was it an accent? "Sure do look familiar. Guess I've seen you here. Buying gas. Cigs maybe."

I nodded.

She chewed on her lip before another puff and a long pause. "Now, I know I seen you before. Where you live?"

"Willisburg." I wasn't in a chatty mood. I smirked and drew another hit. Yuck. Lite cigarettes I could have managed, but menthol? You might as well quit. I stubbed out the half-spent cigarette. Smoke gushed from my nostrils as I examined my dirty fingernails.

"Willisburg, Willisburg, that south of here?"

"Yeah."

"Out in the country, right?"

Hells bells, lady, we're all out in the country once we whizz by the Cliff City line, so what's your point?

"Willisburg, why, that's off ..."

"Yeah, right at Englewood, then about four maybe five miles before Main." I stifled another yawn while imagining my head hitting a pillow as I tugged a bedspread up to my neck.

"Willisburg," she said dreamily as she rubbed her chin, the

tobacco smoke wreathing her face like a cheap veil. The static from the television in the other room blared and then dwindled. This must have snared the woman's attention too. She leaned forward a tad.

"Did you sign those papers?" she crowed in the direction of the TV clamor. Startled, I sat up more alert. We had company. I had not expected that. No response from the person or persons next to the television.

"Vince? You awake in there?" No sound besides the hum of a late-night broadcast. The woman let out a sigh and then sank into her chair. She didn't offer me an explanation about the guy in the other room, and I didn't request one. She lost interest in "Vince" and his papers. Her gaze wandered. The ash from her cigarette fell to the floor.

She puckered her lips and stroked her cheek before piping up again. "Wait a minute. I knew a girl from Willisburg. Well, she was a girl then. A young thing." She shot a glimpse at me again. "You have eyes like hers. Same color. Ain't that a strange one." Her stockinged feet massaged each other. "That was years ago. Heard she died. Of course, we all do eventually." She cackled wryly. After a lengthy pull on her cigarette, she sputtered and wheezed before she became silent. Her gaze sagged to her lap.

I started thumping my toe against the matted shag rug, the thick threads a darkened shade you couldn't describe.

"She was quite the sweet thing. All pretty, had a baby and all. We used to fuss over her. She was younger than the rest of us. Rushed around that restaurant like a ... like a ... like one of those African gazelles on TV." The woman's eyes misted. The ash on her cigarette threatened to collapse again. She flicked the ashes to the carpet before bringing it to her mouth. Without taking a drag, she resumed talking.

"A little baby girl. She brought her in once to show her off. Just the cutest thing! All dressed up like a doll." The woman smiled, her eyes glistening. The ruts on her face softened. She didn't seem so old anymore or so bitter. "Some of us had kids, bigger kids. It had been a while since most of us held a new baby. Especially a sweet one like that. She didn't cry, didn't even fuss." The woman wiggled one arm about in the air. "We passed her 'round like a bowl of candy."

My ears perked.

She gabbed nonstop, prattling to the walls and the ceilings and all the spaces in between. "I forget the last time I cuddled a baby that tiny. I never had one of my own. Nope. No babies for me." She cleared her throat, choking and gasping. "One day you wake up and you're forty, forty-five, fifty. And it's like, 'hey – what happened to my life?' I always assumed I'd have kids. Never supposed I wouldn't have, you know, the normal stuff we all expect. Well my momma would tell me not every girl gets to be a princess. We can't all wear that diamond tiara!" Her shrill drawl rebounded off the low ceiling and the fake wood-paneled walls.

Then her tone sparkled again. "That Louise, she had it all! A husband, a home, a beautiful baby girl. What a cute thing! Louise shared pictures of her every year. We sort of watched her grow. At least 'til I got canned." The woman scowled. "Too old for the suits to pinch on the ass while chugging their three-martini lunches."

At the first mention of her name, I froze. Then I felt as if someone had picked me up by the waist in a tender hug. Louise?

"You were a w-waitress? At the Braxton House?" I stopped obsessing about Terry springing me from that dump.

She slung her head toward me as if discovering me wafting

in a fog. "Worked there seven fricking years. Gave them my best years 'til they fired me. Bastards! I didn't steal that money! They knew it! Those bastards. They couldn't prove nothing!" She punched the air as fiercely as an elderly lady could with her puny, gnarled fist smothered by those grand silver and turquoise rings. "I gave good service. Excellent service. Got the tips to prove it!" She snorted while studying her cigarette. It bordered the filter, so she milked another small puff and then stamped out the fiery end before abandoning it to the brimming ashtray. She hacked as she hunched forward and pounded the armrest with her jeweled hand.

My jaw slid open, and my eyes widened as if an alarm clock had shaken me awake. No longer tuckered out and aching for sleep, I scrutinized the woman and saw her again as if for the first time. She had known my momma! A soft breeze flowed over me, shooing away the stale haze.

Then the woman cocked her head at me. "How'd you know about the Braxton? They went out of business more than ten years this Christmas. Wouldn't of been your kind of joint neither." She droned on without enthusiasm as she lit up another cigarette.

"Louise was, well, my mother's name was Louise. She worked at the Braxton House when I was young and before she ... well, she got sick and died just before I turned eighteen." Tears swamped my eyes. I hadn't thought of Momma for forever. Worries over Mitchell and Mike and eking out a living crowded my memories of Momma. I'd not forgotten her. I'd only moved her out of the way on the highest shelf in a closet where you store winter coats and mittens and photo albums.

Then old snapshots fluttered before me. Momma cutting the crust from my banana-and-peanut-butter sandwiches. Singing along with me "... and on that farm they had some chickens, E-I-E-I-O ..." to muffle the ugly clatter from Grandmother and Father feuding. That day I finally realized she was dying. As she sunk into her hospital bed, her eyes only slits and her skin a sickening gray, she kept promising me she would mend. She said she just needed to rest.

The wrinkled woman before me inspected me through dull eyes that started to water as well, gleaming pink around the edges. She cupped both cheeks with her palms. "Oh my God, Louise, why you're Louise's precious little Catherine! My lordy!" The woman cooed. "Louisa! What a gem! My, your mother would be proud. What a sight!" She contemplated me in awe and sighed. "It's like you've come back from the dead! Yes, I see it now. I knew I'd seen you before. Knew I'd known that face! I couldn't figure where or how! Now I see, the hair and those eyes. Yes, that's it. Louise! What a miracle!" She clapped her thin, leathery hands, the metal rings clanking as the tobacco smoke curled heavenward.

"Stand up, let me take a good gander at you."

I swiped my cheek with the back of my hand as I rose, spread my arms, and spun in a slow circle. Before I could flop back on the couch, the lady bolted from her chair and grabbed me in a surprisingly strong bear hug. I draped my arms around her waist and hugged her in return. We both beamed at each other as she squeezed me. "Sweet baby Catherine. My, what a ... now you are, yes, looking like your momma, well, almost. Except for that nose and Louise had some freckles, didn't she?"

My head pumped up and down. Then she lowered her voice, fastened her gaze on mine, and said, "I'm so sorry, honey. I would have gone to the funeral if I'd known. Didn't hear about her 'til months later. I wasn't waitressing at the Braxton with Louise when she got ... sick." Then we both retreated from each other, and as the moment evaporated, I searched for a wall clock. At least twenty minutes had ticked by since the phone call, hadn't it? What was taking Terry so damn long?

The lady seized my hands again and began babbling about the good ol' days. The change surging through her amazed me. The dreary creature transformed into a ball of energy. She'd pause only to cough or clear her throat. She told me stories about the restaurant, always tossing in something about my momma and how she juggled everything just so. She painted a cheery picture of my momma, how she always smiled and laughed and put a positive spin on problems, chuckling instead of snarling at dropped trays, rude customers, and lousy tips. I pulled my hands from her grasp and rammed them into my pockets. The woman yapped away. While she skipped down memory lane, I pined for a glaring light to shine through the near darkness of the single-wide mobile home. More than thirty years had elapsed since she waited tables with Momma, yet you could have supposed it all occurred yesterday from the way she carried on.

"Yes, she showed pictures of you, you as a baby with a bow in your hair, you with your favorite doll, you all dressed up for Halloween and Christmas. We watched you grow up. But you're young. You got plenty of time, child," she said, ignoring how my smile withered. "You're young, you're still a pretty young thing."

I didn't bother to correct her.

"You've got plenty of time to marry and have a family of your own. But don't wait too long. Don't wait too long like me. My dear momma would say, 'If you put all your eggs in one basket some asshole's bound to knock it over,'" she said hurriedly, as another attack ambushed her last words. She pawed the table for her cigarette case. I refused her third offer. The smoke had started searing my eyes, and the hammering in my skull throbbed louder. She sprawled back in her chair. I reluctantly retrieved my seat on the couch as I wasn't going anywhere soon.

"My momma was full of good advice. She also used to say, 'Don't go clinging onto some man like he's a life raft, he'll drag you down and drown you,'" she spat out, hostility skidding across her crinkled features.

Ending the awkward silence that followed, I said I already had a son. A boy named Mitchell. No mention of Michael. Her momma was right about those assholes and that damn basket.

She brightened, inhaling as deeply as she could. "You do!" she said through a film of smoke. "You got pictures of your boy? Let me see!" I considered her request. I recalled the wallet-sized portrait of Mitchell from years before when he was a baby, one of those when they're changing so fast you can hardly keep up. It was from a Sears studio and a bit dog-eared. I shook my head. This disappointed her momentarily before she perked up.

"Then you must look at my pictures from when I was a girl!" She swatted the armrest with her palm as she spoke and then pushed herself out of the recliner. She scampered over to a bookshelf against the wall by the far bedroom, the room whose window would signal my escape from that quicksand any goddamn minute.

Clamping her lips around her cigarette, the lady sifted through layers of papers, books, assorted ceramic knickknacks, and a varnished plaque of a blond Jesus. She dug out a dust-covered vinyl-bound book with both hands. She scurried to a spot next to me on the couch, creating room by nudging a pile of papers onto the floor, and then sat beside me. She cradled the book in her lap and sucked on her cigarette before setting it in the ashtray to smolder into nothing.

"My momma told me to keep a scrapbook. The older you get, the easier you forget, she always said. I want to remember it all. Almost all of it." She displayed the first page of blurred black and white portraits of a baby in a bassinet pasted onto the felt-like black paper. She turned the page. An out-of-focus baby in a bonnet. A shy child perched in the lap of a man donning a hat.

"That wasn't my daddy."

She flipped the pages. A fuzzy print revealed a woman in a camel hair coat with a corsage on the lapel, the little girl frowning with her arms crossed. "I suspect we was heading to church." The woman hooted as if she had cracked a joke.

I pretended the album interested me, smiling blandly and oohing or ahhing at the appropriate interval. Most of the photographs were black and white with bent corners, while the colored ones had faded, the once brilliant hues dissolving into sickly pastels. Others dangled from the album's pages as the yellowed tape had exhausted its sticking power. She waded through pages and pages of photos, raking her pointed nails across the images while mumbling, tittering, or identifying this face or that. We pored over flocks of children, couples, adults sitting shoulder to shoulder on a couch, a grinning woman snuggling up to a grinning man, all to the tune of her unending commentary that blended into nothingness to me. Only her coughing interrupted her.

Newsprint from decades earlier blanketed the next sheets. The stiffened, amber paper crackled from the woman's touch. Tiny bits flaked off and spiraled downward. An advertisement heralding the circus coming to town, several others of grainy photos with captions depicting a woman in a leotard and feathered headpiece posing by an elephant or hurling hula-hoops. Then one of what resembled the same woman with a girl of about eleven also in a leotard, both posturing with their arms swept upward.

"Yes, can you believe it! My mother and I ran off and joined the circus! We had such a wild time!" Then her eyes narrowed, and the woman panted. After struggling to regain her breath, she resumed. "Momma performed with the magician and the acrobats. Don't worry, she never tried that high-wire stuff. Mostly trampolines and cartwheels. Sometimes I jumped on the trampoline and tossed the balls to the jugglers. I handed out programs, hung flyers, and got things set up and packed away. I didn't have, you know, some special talent required of circus folk." Her wheezing had grown louder and more constant. "I was afraid of heights! Sometimes I'd help Alvin with his dog tricks too. By the time I was thirteen, well Momma decided ..." She stopped as another hacking fit buried the rest of her tale. Lasting longer than the others, this one alarmed me.

"Can I get you something to drink? Some water?"

She bobbed her head up and down, which I interpreted as a "yes," while she fought the violent coughs wracking her chest, causing her entire body to heave back and forth on the couch. The scrapbook skated to the floor. I dashed to the kitchen, opening cabinets as I hunted for a clean glass. Dirty cups, plates, and bowls spilled from the sink onto the counters. I found a chipped mug in one of the cupboards and filled it from the faucet. Static mingled with the TV drivel. I strained my ears yet couldn't detect anything else. The TV patter died into the background as I pivoted and delivered the woman her drink.

She gasped as she swallowed. She squeezed her watery eyes shut. After a few huffs and another sip, she opened her eyes, and they darted about in search of her almost empty cigarette case. Her gnarled hands snatched up the case from the cluttered coffee table, and she clutched it to her chest. Her energy spent, she sank into the couch as her sluggish eyes drifted through the murky trailer.

Then it slammed me like an explosion. A blazing shaft of brilliance flooded the room. I grabbed my purse and darted for the door.

"Thanks, thanks so much for ... err, your help and everything. It was nice meeting you." I flung open the door as she lifted her head. Confusion clouded her features.

“Stop by sometime with your boy! I’ll let him pick out a treat, only if it’s OK with his momma! And take care, dear. My momma always said ‘Never drive faster than your guardian angel!’”

I threw a goodbye wave as I leaped through the doorway toward Terry’s glowing headlights. It struck me I’d forgotten to get her name, but I kept running.

12

I didn't ask where Johnny planned on taking us ... us and that freezer. I stewed over the truck and prayed that gagging noise did not signal engine trouble that could stall us out. After it broke down on the highway that night, it started the next day without a hitch. I never had it checked by a mechanic or anything expensive like that. Probably just bad gas, I skittishly reassured myself at the time.

I backpedaled from my anxiety over the truck and concentrated on driving, almost humming aloud to deaden Ellis' idiotic blather. He griped about the heat, the unlevel asphalt patches and fissures in the road that jogged the pickup, and the uncertainty of our destination as he tugged on his hands and toyed with the hem of his T-shirt. Johnny sat still, palms on his thighs, staring straight forward. He paid Ellis no heed.

I didn't need to sneak glimpses of Johnny anymore. I knew exactly what I would see. As if I'd known him forever. The dingy blue denim shirt. The cuffed jeans. The scuffed boots. The curve of his chin. The smoothness of his cheek. The calmness enveloping him.

We drove and drove and drove. The minutes melted into hours. Farther ahead, pools of water loomed on the highway's horizon, only to vaporize into nothingness as we approached. We passed pastures full of black locust trees brandishing their outstretched nail-like thorns. Store-bought FOR SALE signs stapled to barbed wire fences. Not much civilization this far south of Cliff City. Just fields, a couple gas stations, and the titty bar off Route J.

Traffic motored alongside us before zooming by. Some early model sedans actually overtook us, but I didn't want to push my truck too hard on that hot afternoon. I was running on autopilot. Not much to eat either, just some potato chips I shared with Mitchell at WAL-MART. I licked my lips, hunting for salt. Instead, I tasted those margaritas Tammy and I used to cook up in my kitchen when we were too broke or too lazy to hit the bars.

I first met Tammy at Marsey's Super Clean in Cliff City, wrestling starched shirts onto wire hangers and lugging bagfuls of pleated skirts and silk blouses for dry cleaning. I'd just turned twenty-one and chucked my fake ID. Paid my bills more or less on time. Except for that bad call with Steve, I fooled around, scoped my prospects, and scoured the horizon for the one. A keeper.

In between men, I caroused with my girlfriends from high school. Christy and I lost touch after graduation; I heard she left town for who knows where. Then Shelly got married and started having babies. Rachel hired on as a dancer for one of those skanky juice bars off the highway. I can only shrug at that one. Maybe she got a boob job.

Tammy and I joined at the hip after my last scrap with Jill when we practically scratched out each other's eyes after she barfed on my cashmere sweater.

My drinking buddy, my confessor, my judge and jury, my best friend bar none. Tammy had a few years on me as well as a lot more miles. She reveled in her role as the caped demon that grappled with my good-girl angel.

With a slew of ear piercings and jeans losing their battle at the seams, Tammy slid behind my wheel and floored it.

"Come on! Let's go to Toggy's. Wild gorgeous guys'll be there. Darts, dollar pitchers, sweaty guys, what more could you ask for on a Thursday night? And if we're lucky, maybe some good sex, some nasty and crazy shit to keep us in smiles for a day or two."

"Tam, we gotta work. I can't be late anymore. I can't keep going hungover. The fumes are getting to me as it is. Cindy ..."

"Oh, fuck Windy Cindy. She needs us and if she don't appreciate us, well hell, there's lotsa jobs, plenty of other joints that'll scoop up two hustling, nose-to-the-grindstone kind of gals like us."

A chuckle and a smirk would spread across her cauliflowered skin, scarred from raging teenage hormones years before. She preferred Marlboros, persuading me to swap brands as she had grown tired of bumming my high school habit of Virginia Slims.

"That's a wuss smoke," she said.

She parted her long, wavy reddish-brown hair more or less in the center. If we lived elsewhere, I guess you'd call it auburn, but here we say reddish-brown. Her underbite jutted her chin forward and supplied her with a shit-eating grin.

Tammy drank her coffee straight and fancied her men clean-shaven and tall with broad hands. She rarely left a bar before last call or went to bed prior to two a.m., no matter when she had to work the next morning. She dragged me into a pickle with almost every boss on my cluttered resume.

She broadcasted her views on sex whenever she felt inclined, whether or not anyone asked. Tammy believed fiercely that each and every woman had earned at least one mind-blowing good fuck as compensation for all the suffering in our lives, periods, pregnancies, rapes, etc. She argued many women merited rights to more than one, claiming she deserved a greater payback to reimburse her for her third stepfather. It was her perverted version of Mr. Right. Justice on a sexually twisted scale.

She found it totally outrageous that every person born on this planet, past, present, and forever, represented a man's ecstasy and a woman's physical agony. Add that to the billions of miscarriages and abortions women have endured since the beginning, my lordy she would explode when you accidentally bumped into the subject. The miserable business of being female made her hot-poker mad and probably explained why she spurned churches and any religious creed asserting how women should behave.

"God is a man, and he hates us women," she said more than once.

Tammy butted horns with a religious type behind us in line at the grocery one afternoon with our cart full of liquor, chips, and soda. The woman hassled us about our hedonistic beverage of choice, or that we wore our shirts too tight: something those bitches presume they have a right to harass other women about. Tammy responded with an obscene comment about the packages of meat in the woman's basket. The lady misunderstood Tammy's bawdy jest and instead harped at her that God created man, not animals, in his own image, quoting from the bible of course. Thus pigs and cows belonged within "man's" domain to rule. And eat.

Now Tammy is no vegetarian, but the scripture-quoting set her off.

"If man is made in God's image, then God is one hell of an asshole!" Tammy said.

The woman's indignant expression warped to one of shock. I sighed and warned Tammy to shut up or we'd get booted out. Then she tore into me, and I held up my palm to shush her, which generally worked when she wasn't drunk yet.

We usually partied at my house, as the string of apartments she squatted in typically included a surly roommate – Tammy rarely paid her rent by the first – and an odor of pepperoni pizza and stale beer.

One night at my house, long before Mitchell and around the time I hooked up with Mike, Tammy and I spent an evening wading through cheap tequila, a tub of coarse salt, and limes we cut with a dull knife.

It was past midnight. I started diluting the poison with water so I could face the next day without my skull cracking in two. Tammy, always between boyfriends, and me, savoring the attention of a certain cute guy, resumed our ongoing conversation about men and sex.

Tammy never lost her virginity. She got rid of it. Since that memorable afternoon on the back seat of her next-door neighbor's car – and no, she wasn't with the next-door neighbor – if she wasn't trying to get laid, she was describing getting laid, and if she tired of that, she would discuss someone else's options about getting laid.

That night Tammy swigged until the well ran dry, abandoning the pre-mixed margarita concoction for straight tequila. I nursed a cup of lukewarm water. Tammy repeatedly pried open her plump, sagging eyelids as she struggled to corral her hair back into a loose ponytail that slumped against her neck, all the while preaching her gospel in a throaty voice.

It wasn't anything I hadn't heard before. Most of what she said that night made sense, but not always.

"No, no no. He's a shithead. Messed up the sheets is all. No broken heart, not for me. I'm a happy clam now he's gone.

Fucking A! Nothing but a lowlifer. A real waste of rubber. No more than half a hard-on. Pigs before shwine and all that shit," she said. Her speech winded her and she abruptly opened her eyes wide as she sucked in a lungful of air with a screechy gasp.

She scratched her squared chin while leaning back with two chair legs off the ground. She started tipping and almost crashed to the floor, slamming her hands on the table for support at the last minute.

"Let me get this straight. You, you meet this Tom." I squinted as if searching for her in a fog.

"Pete."

"Pete? Wasn't, was it Pete? Wasn't we talking about Tom?"

"Tom?"

"Yeah. Yeah, Tom."

"Tom from warehouse Tom?"

"Yeah. Yeah."

"No. No, I never brought him, never let him follow me home, no ..."

"Well, what Pete? No, we was talking about ..." I said.

Slouching in the chair at my kitchen dinette, corkscrewing her ponytail in her chubby fingers, trying to focus on the individual strands for split ends, Tammy sharply veered off course. "Should I cut it?"

My brain reeled through a haze thick as a marshmallow. Cut what? Then interrupting my own giggles, I squealed, "Don't pull a Bobbitt!" My laughter ricocheted off the walls and echoed around the house.

She scrunched her face in confusion, then we both whacked our palms on the table and howled. Tammy sank from her chair onto the floor.

More excessive hilarity. Then, what were we laughing about?

"Pete?"

"No. Peter."

"No Peter? Was that his problem?"

More hysterical shrieks. Tammy rolling and tossing like a six-month-old fighting a diaper change, throwing her legs up then banging them on the linoleum again and again. Our wheezy peals of merriment gradually subsided. Spent, Tammy sprawled on her back, her eyelids sealed as if asleep. The room spun as my eyelids flickered.

Then Tammy wriggled onto her belly. After a brief spell, she scrambled up from my dirty kitchen floor using her hands and knees and plunked back onto the vinyl chair. We both revisited our tumblers of tequila and tap water, respectively.

Tammy's goofy grin wrinkled into a puzzled expression. "Where am I sleeping?"

"Couch." I had piles of crap on the narrow twin bed in my extra bedroom and zilch interest in making space for an overnight guest at that moment.

"Couch? That puky thing?"

I frowned. "Don't call my couch puky."

"Puky. Puky, puky, puky. Smells puky. A Goodwill reject. Puky. Besides, hurts my back when I sleep on it."

"Then sleep in your car," I snapped, a bit insulted. "But you ain't driving home."

"Bullshit! I can make it. Gimme cup of coffee, some soda. I make it," she said, coaxing her eyelids wider as she swiveled her head and hunted frantically for something steady to focus on. Then Tammy's darting eyes closed, and she sat lifeless. She could have nodded off in my kitchen, slumped in the armless chair, resting her temple against the wallpaper of bowls, measuring spoons, and sprigs of dried herbs someone slapped up years and years ago.

"Eh. I can do it. I can ... What time's it anyway?"

"You ain't leaving," I said sternly, sitting more erect and striking the tabletop for emphasis. "We'll drive together. We'll take your car. We got wienies to wag. Save me gas."

"Then how you plan on getting home? If I drive ... if you driving with me? Tomorrow?" Tammy crinkled her forehead as she wrangled with logistics complicated by hours of alcohol.

I sandwiched my palms as if in prayer, pouting in exaggerated innocence. "Oh, I'll arrange a ride home somehow," I said sweetly.

The clock ticked before Tammy figured the score. "You devil woman," she said, her eyebrows lifted, her eyelids forming only slits.

I snickered wickedly.

"Mike! Get a ride, real ride home from that real man. That Mike man." Tammy's laughter rippled through her rolls of fat. "Well, well. You two lovebirds." Her eyes widened, then drooped ajar. "You burning rubber with the Mike man?"

"Nope." My cheeks flushed a bit: a little from the booze, a little from the topic.

Tammy wasn't pretty, and she knew it. She never flirted with men, at least not with a titter or a fluttering of her lashes. If a tall and not too ugly dude intrigued her, she'd strut over and straddle him with a stare as he slid a pool cue through his fingers while he eyed the solids or the stripes. He'd cast an occasional glance in her direction, reeling off a joke or remark, something racy to see if she blushed or if she laughed along. She laughed along, loud and hard. Then she would launch into a raunchy story or a string of crass terms. Tammy never blushed. And she loved to talk about sex.

Men made me squirrelly. I tiptoed amongst them while hanging back out of reach. Elbows on the bar with the other girls, tapping my toes on the footrest of my barstool, I'd brush away the dance requests or the lame offers unless an enticing one arose. Sort of cute. Funny. Not too tipsy. Not coming on too strong. I didn't care for anyone calling me a slut. And after I learned my lesson with Travis, I avoided hopping into some man's bed at the first opportunity.

Mike and I bumped into each other during breaks at the hot dog factory, smoking in the parking lot with Jack, Trish, and a bunch of others, or after work on our way to one hangout or another.

Mike would smooth his rich black hair with his muscled hands, then rub his palms together. "Let me show you how it's done. Watch the master, watch the side pocket," he would say with a dramatic flourish of a cue stick. Then he would miss and snigger, swig his beer and flash me a grin.

Or he'd sneak off to the jukebox with somebody's change or the waiter's tip. "L-9, L-9. That's a nice slow one. You like both kinds of music, don't you? Which you prefer, country or western?"

An easy laugh, a contagious smile. A slight raising of his eyebrows. I always smiled at Mike, except shyly. I was never a tease. Didn't act coy, sling back the innuendos, the come-ons, flip my hair, giggle at all their one-liners. I would sit with my knees glued as one, my grip on my drink for support. I'd pull at my shirt to ensure it covered everything. I bantered back and forth, though I skirted the crude comments. Just pretended I hadn't heard it.

Adam, Phil, Trent, Kyle, Howard in receiving, they could dish it out, and I would slop it right back. To them, I was one of the guys, and they knew better than to hit on me. One look, that's how you mark your territory.

Keep your distance, bud. Don't even think about it. No way.

Mike was new. His gravelly voice grew soft and whispery when he spoke to me. He jockeyed plenty to get my attention. He had it.

"Mmm good Mmmike. Mike. Michael. Miko. Mike. Mikey. Mmmick." Tammy toyed with his name on her tongue. I enjoyed the taste of it too.

Then I turned red.

"I don't know. Maybe not. Too soon," I said. I slammed the door on my romantic notions and delusions that could jinx everything by wishing for more than what life had in store.

Tammy let out a sigh as she heaved herself upright, wobbled, and then deposited her backside on the dinette chair again, a palm against the wall to brace herself.

After she regained her bearings, she leered. "He ask you out?"

I hate it when your girlfriends pose those pointed questions. Puts the stink eye on everything. And anything confided to her got around quicker than crabs. If word of my crush spread to Mike and everyone, I would end up the butt of all their lewd wisecracks, especially if I'd misread that gleam in his eyes.

"Not really. It's not like we don't all go out after work and stuff. Weekends. I see him a lot, you know."

"Yeah, I know," Tammy said slyly, her head tilted sideways in her palm bolstered by her elbow on the table. Her elbow kept sliding, sending her head flopping. She combated gravity, seeking a comfortable position that would maintain her partially upright. Then she surrendered and plopped her head on the table. Normally she would have lit into the opportunity to feast on this potential source of gossip and sex rap. The tequila had taken its toll. Tammy slipped toward a comatose state.

I licked my finger and dabbed at a sprinkle of salt we'd spilled while dunking our rims hours earlier.

Dumb from drink, I continued to think out loud. "Maybe I'm ready for another shot at it. I ... it's been over five years since I, well ..."

"Five years?" Tammy's eyes flared open as she tottered backward and almost fell out of her chair again. She clamped her palms on the table to catch her balance. "Gimme cigarette," she said as her gaze wandered before riveting onto my pack. She stared at the white and red box, the lighter tucked inside the plastic wrapper, lying on the telephone book on the kitchen table.

"Don't go bumming all my cigarettes."

"Where mine?"

"They're in your purse."

"Where'd my purse go?"

"I don't know. Go ahead and give me one too."

She scuffled with the package for an eternity before I grabbed it. I popped one in my mouth and flicked the lighter while she waited for hers.

"Gimme," she mumbled, her arm flailing toward me. I planted one between her fingers and tossed the pack onto the counter behind her. She fumbled with the orange Bic and torched the cigarette black. She exhaled a billow of smoke and frowned.

"Now wait minute." Tammy had regained the scent of our earlier chat and backtracked. "Five years, whaddya mean five?"

As the liquor wore off, the lateness of the hour collided with me. I yawned. "What the hell are you babbling about?"

"Five whole fucking years. Wha's that about?" Tammy sipped her tequila, spilling a stream down her chin and onto her rhinestone-studded T-shirt. Her head lolled back as she drained the dregs. She wiped her cheek with her wrist as she blinked. She puffed her cigarette before chucking it to the floor. I snatched it up, rescuing the linoleum from another singed hole. Tammy kneaded her eyes with her fists, then her palms, leaving soot-black circles and flakes of mascara around her eyes. She reminded me of a raccoon, and I laughed.

"What the fuck you laughing at?" Tammy reared up with her eyes blazing. Then she erupted with laughter.

After the guffaws dissolved, Tammy jabbed the rewind button once again. "The five years. What? I know I'm drunk.

Know it. No doubt. Know it."

Tammy giggled about her drunkenness. I'd exhausted enough of my buzz that I could no longer laugh at nothing. I checked the clock and devised a plan to wind down the evening, park her on the couch, grab her a sheet or blanket. I debated putting a bucket next to her in case she did throw up. Hell, she'd miss or knock it over.

Like a kid aching for another reason to stay up late, Tammy hankered for one more story before bedtime. Maybe it would pacify her so she would pass out sooner.

"It's been five years since I broke up with Steve," I said. Just mentioning his name once more made me wince.

"Steve? Now thas before me. I don't remember you yakking over no Steve."

"Yeah, it was over long before you and I met."

She nodded, her brow creased as she made a stab at concentrating. "Steve," she said, pronouncing his name correctly. "Sheve, Shteve ... bleve, heave, meev." Like some Dr. Seuss character, she tried to conjure up anything to rhyme with Steve. Then as if a light bulb snapped on in her skull, she hooted, "Did Steve leave your beave?" She chortled at her own vulgar nonsense.

I didn't laugh. "Well, we sort of mutually parted ways." I yawned as I stretched, not bothering to cover my mouth. Damn, I needed to hit the sack. "Five years ago. That was my last serious relationship."

Tammy's head jounced back and forth as if in acceptance. Her eyelids slid closer. Her lips twitched into a scowl. Thinking. Thinking. Trying to think.

"You was together five years?"

"No!" I yelped in frustration. She had sunk her teeth into my flippant comment, and she would not let go. "We were together for almost a year. Five years ago!"

She tried to whistle, sloppily pursing her moistened lips a few tries before giving up.

"Wow. Sheesh. That been like, you ...? You were so young. Just a babe. Eighteen? Nineteen? One whole year? Would have been like married almos'."

"Not hardly," I said.

"You're better without 'em." Tammy jerked her head in an attempt to nod and signify her approval of our breakup.

"Well, I guess. Like I'm saying, I loved him and everything. Thought I did anyway. I was young. We both needed to grow up I guess. But you know, if we'd stayed a couple, well then, where would I be now?"

Tammy burped and slouched in her chair. That sent us both cackling.

"Well, anyhow, he wasn't the right one. The right one, he's out there. Still waiting for me. So I guess I can sit tight for him." Mike's tempting grin sparkled before me.

She snorted. "Right one? Right one, shmun. You got it all wrong."

Oh shit. She wanted to bicker some more. I plunged my face into the pillow of my arms folded onto the kitchen table.

"Tam, let's go to bed. I'm beat. We gotta work early. Let's talk about this ..."

"Now wait minute, wade minute, just a minute. You are my friend, are you no?" She raised herself more upright from her chair and hoisted her eyelids as much as gravity allowed her.

I yawned long and loud.

"You are my friend. My very berry best friend right now." I smiled. I loved the way she qualified her statement. "And I shee, when I see very dear close friend of mine making big ass huge whale of mistake, well, is my duty, slolemly ..."

She stopped. She weaved sideways as she battled to right herself. She failed miserably and let herself sink as she slipped from the chair onto the floor with a thwack. Neither of us laughed. She jostled herself into a sitting position, propping herself against the wall, her shoulders rounded and her chin plummeting to her chest. Then she cocked her head toward me and continued, speaking slower and more steadily.

"So-lem-ly ... it is my solemn duty to keep my friend, my very good friend from making such awful mishtake."

I briefly considered her remarks and drew a blank, flinging up my arms hopelessly. "Tam, you're wasted! Let's hang it up for a night. We can talk about this ... we can talk tomorrow. Besides, I didn't marry him. We didn't get married. I didn't make no mistakes. Steve's a goner. Gone. Sayonara. Adios. Arreverderci. Whatever!"

Despite several pitchers of water and a fistful of Advils, I feared I would wake the next day damning everything in sight.

"No. That not what I'm saying! I'm saying ... now this what I'm saying ..." Tammy waved a crooked finger at me, the nail chewed raw. There we go, almost there. I only had to lead her to the couch. She was collapsing before my eyes. I stood and was socked with a head rush.

"Sit down, sit down. What I'm saying, there ain't no Mr. Right. No Mr. Right. Thas right. There's a Mr. Wrong. Mr. Maybe. Mis ... Mr. For Right Now, for the weekend for the ..."

Silly me, I took the bait. "Yeah, yeah. But you gotta believe. You can't go through life believing you're never gonna have nothing. That you're going nowhere. That no one special, no special someone's out there waiting for you, waiting for you to come along so they can scoop you up and out of this ..."

"BULLSHIT!"

Tammy's eyes, glazed by tequila and clouded by tobacco smoke, bolted open. She swayed, slammed her empty cup on the floor, and hurled the plastic tequila bottle bouncing across the kitchen, splattering what little remained. She stared into my eyes, and her sudden ability to focus made me blink.

"No way! Theresh no way. No man gonna rescue you. You on your own, girl. On your own!" She kicked her foot against the linoleum. "Don't go waiting on some man. There's no Mr. Nothing waiting on no one. No way, no how, no shit!"

I hate it when drunks get so damn plastered and fired up about something, usually something stupid or irrelevant, they mutate into maniacs. Tammy started smashing both fists against the floor. Her eyes, having lost their grip on mine, locked onto nothing. A nasty grimace swallowed her features.

"OK, OK, simmer down, calm yourself. Chill. No need to argue. You're right. No prince charming. I gotcha."

"No shit! He don't exist. You gotta stop this lying and bullshitting you been, I mean, we're ... we been hearing thish shit for ... since dressed up like brides and princesshes and shit ... Halloween, tricking and ... no fair. No right. No Mr. Rights. No!"

She swatted at the air and smacked her palms against the wall and the table legs within her reach. She was hollering and it was past one and we had to punch in at seven a.m. a half-hour from my house. Why'd I let Tammy sucker me into another drinking binge on a work night?

I told her to lighten up and quit swinging. She relaxed her fists and sat sullen and quiet. I tussled with her arms to lift her from the floor. She refused to budge.

"No fucking way no way no how." Her words tumbled into each other.

"Shut up, Tam. Time for bed," I said as gently as I could.

Tears leaked past her eyelids. I'd never seen her cry before about anything or anyone. I would have asked her about it later, but she wouldn't have remembered.

That night, damn her that Tammy, I had a wreck of a night's sleep. I tossed and slugged my pillows over Steve and Travis and even poor Harold and all the other men who had wandered in and out of my embrace. Then I dozed into a dream about Mike, that cute guy I kept running into. I woke the next morning with a terrific hangover and couldn't recall anything else about the dream.

13

After cruising south awhile, Johnny directed me east onto Route 19, so I made a left onto the two-lane. I steered along a faint yellow broken stripe dividing the asphalt. The road doglegged then veered south. We sped by mobile homes with fenced lagoons out back and vinyl-sided farmhouses with sun-bleached American flags hanging limp from their poles. Past gray wooden barns, some in use, others hopelessly abandoned to nature and her wicked ways. Miles and miles of barbed wire fence randomly adorned with the shredded remains of plastic grocery bags or smothered by cedar branches and clumps of fescue threatening to pull the rusted metal posts from their roots. The truck rumbled by at about thirty-five miles an hour, rising and falling with the sway of the surrounding landscape. We pounded pavement for another eternity before Johnny gestured me right onto a narrow road with no street sign.

Towering Johnson grass and multiflora rose bushes shrouded the crushed rock shoulders. The asphalt began switching between gravel and rock-sealed. I eased off the gas to maybe twenty or twenty-five at the most, jumpy about what I would find at each bend or every crest. Expecting a farmer hauling hay to round a blind turn or top the hill straying toward the center, his load listing toward my side of the unmarked lane barely wide enough for one vehicle, let alone two. I was so turned around and mixed up, I couldn't tell south from east, north, or west. It felt as if we had traveled thousands of miles since Willisburg.

Ellis started snoring. Son of a bitch couldn't shut up asleep even. A big-ass horsefly swooped in and landed on his cheek; its bite woke him with a jolt as he flailed at the pest. He slapped his thighs and the dashboard and the windows, anywhere the horsefly briefly touched down before the wind sucked the bug out the passenger window, leaving Ellis cussing to himself as he slumped in his seat.

The sun dipped behind the taller trees. We weaved past caved-in outbuildings and cows staring into space as they chewed and chewed and chewed with their mouths half-open. We had shared Route 19 with a smattering of cars after half an hour of driving. We didn't pass a single car on that country road, so I eventually quit worrying about colliding head-on with something other than a straggling cow or a stupid squirrel. No hint of life. No one followed us. I had no idea where Johnny was taking us.

A solid hush filled the truck cab, squeezing between the three of us jammed together on the truck's bench seat. If only the thick silence could have filtered through my dense skull and muzzled the jumbled voices screaming from my past, forever reminding me of memories that only stoked grief and rage.

I tried not to think about Steve. Whenever I did, it cranked that corkscrew in my gut a few more rounds. I just about swore off men after him, especially as he followed so close on Travis' heels.

Steve struck me as mature and sweet and unlike any of the boys I knew from high school. Charming, considerate. A gentleman. Pining after Travis and grieving over Momma, I clung to the first shoulder that sauntered by.

I met Steve just a handful of days after Momma's funeral at the Howell & Sons Mortuary in Cliff City. Using all my momma's savings, we buried her in a pink satin-lined oak coffin while a tape recorder piped in organ music. The funeral director promised to read a poem or some scripture, as we didn't have a preacher or anyone who could say anything special. We didn't belong to any church. Don't think for a second Father could have managed any of these depressing details. Father and I were her only family as far as I knew.

Throughout the service, a burning sensation doused my entire body. I couldn't say boo to the sparse assortment of mourners. I parked myself in the front row of folding chairs, all alone except for Shelly, who scampered in several minutes late to nab a seat next to me. A few rows behind me sat a couple women from the restaurant who had visited Momma in the hospital and an older guy I didn't recognize. Father paced the carpeted aisles, glaring at the flattened threads ahead of his feet. He wore a rumpled green collared shirt and beige corduroy pants with a pair of graying tennis shoes. I didn't own anything to wear to a funeral and had patched together a dreary outfit from my momma's closet. The only splash of color in the room glimmered from the flowered wreath of white lilies, yellow daisies, and purple irises we placed on Momma's casket.

I beat myself up over how I treated my momma before she died. During the months she faded away, I'd busied myself with Travis. Dashing off to rendezvous with him, scouring the streets for any chance encounter after his sudden rejection, or weeping behind my closed door once I finally surrendered to heartbreak.

Momma spent nights in the hospital a couple of times when the pain got too bad, but I'd waltzed through those hospital stays as Momma assured me, "Oh it's nothing, just a little stomach trouble."

Besides, the happiness that cocooned Travis and me blinded me from anyone or anything else. Love saturated my heart, my mind, my life. Not sickness. Not death. My bliss-filled world did not allow room for anything as disagreeable as that. Once our affair ended, I couldn't fathom anything else more meaningful than my own agony. The last time Momma checked into the hospital for good, it finally sunk in. She would not get better. This time, Momma would not come home.

During that last week, I swaddled her with all the love and affection I had previously wasted on Travis. I brought her hairbrush and hand creams and a framed family photo of her, me, and Father that she kept by her bedside. I baked her favorite meals and spooned small nibbles into her mouth, although she could barely swallow a bite. I tilted the cup for her to sip water. I brushed her hair and massaged her hands with lotion. I listened. I cried. While I chased around after that asshole, my momma had withered away. How would I ever forgive myself?

Two days after Momma's funeral, I clocked back in for work, glumly ringing up crap at a Cliff City ma & pa grocery.

I caught myself climbing up to the cookie jar on the top shelf of the kitchen cabinet where my momma stashed wads of dollar bills and loose change she collected in tips. I must have been about eight. I snagged a fistful. Not enough to notice, I'd hoped. She never mentioned anything. I spent it on a sack of Hostess Ding Dongs and Snickers bars from the Quikmart. She saved money in that jar until she racked up enough for a special outing, a pizza dinner, or a dumb kid movie she couldn't possibly have enjoyed. She set aside the larger notes where I couldn't reach for something more expensive, such as those curtains she special-ordered from JC Penney's.

I started crying silently, smearing the tears against the back of my hand and sniffling. I bent over to rummage underneath the counter for the box of Kleenex Dora had swiped off the shelves for me. I straightened, and an attractive man stood before me. I must have emerged a wreck, my nose dripping and my eyes wet and red.

"Oh. Sorry," I muttered. I directed my attention toward the register and the price tags as I punched the keys.

He couldn't miss the sympathy card Dora had taped to the board behind me – *Your Mother's in Heaven Now*. Maybe that's why none of the customers complained about my dull greetings and all my mistakes.

He smiled. A kind face. Clean-shaven and smooth except for a dimple on his chin. Blond, close-cropped hair razored short right above his ears. Pretty handsome.

I smoothed my hair and glanced at my loose-fitting T-shirt hanging over my jeans. I looked like shit.

"I'm sorry," he said with a sincere expression. "That must be awfully tough to lose your mother."

"Happens." I finished bagging his groceries before my gaze plummeted to my fingernails. The woman next in line cleared her throat. Her impatience hurried him away but not before I snuck one more peek. He was looking back at me with a queer smile.

Two days later, he waited in my line although Dora's was shorter. He set down a six-pack of Coronas and a handful of limes that skittered across my counter.

"Party time?" I purred as I captured the wayward limes before tossing them in a plastic bag with the receipt.

His straight white teeth flashed as he grinned. "Only when you're ... uh ready to join me. After work?" he said, his voice catching. He chuckled with a nervous energy, his eyes darting about before pleading his case with me.

Dora snickered. My next customer grunted as he smirked at

us both. My stomach somersaulted, and I shoved his bag at him, swiveling my face toward my cash register.

But the next day as I dressed for work, I curled my hair and mascaraed my lashes. I wore a dress with thin straps that cinched around my neck. My work apron covered most of my lower body, but nothing masked my naked shoulders and neckline.

He didn't show up. Why would he, you dunce, I snarled at myself. He'd put himself on the line, and I'd publicly rejected him. I brushed away my mild disappointment, knowing I needed more time to work through my emotions from Travis dumping me and Momma dying. I didn't even know his name. But I knew when I was ready, I'd discover plenty other guys springing up around me like mushrooms after a rainstorm on a warm, humid day.

I scuffed my sandals through the parking lot to my car after my shift ended, my head hanging as I scanned the broken asphalt before me.

"Good evening."

I jumped.

He leaned against a silver Mustang with black pinstripes, his hands resting against the sleek metal of the car's hood. He wore a dark blue button-down shirt with a starched collar tucked into gray chino pants. His friendly smile roped me in.

"I didn't mean to startle you. If you want me to go I will. I just figured that maybe yesterday wasn't a good day to ... I mean, I didn't intend to embarrass you at work."

After the initial shock from the sound of his voice, my breath quickly slowed, but my heart never quit racing.

For our first official date, Steve insisted on driving all the way to Willisburg to pick me up. I bolted from the front door as soon as his car rumbled up our street so I would not have to introduce him to Father. I returned home after eleven o'clock to find Father crouching in the darkened living room.

"Slut! Slut!" he growled as he lunged toward me, spewing vulgar references about "playing poker."

I spent the rest of that night attempting to sleep in the back seat of my momma's car, now mine. The next day while gassing up at Rory's, I ripped off the FOR RENT flyer pasted to the glass front door. I moved into my Willisburg rental that evening.

Steve and I started going out once or twice a week. Dating. Steve paid the tab for everything, including restaurants with china plates and linen napkins. We shared cotton candy on a stick at the county fair, buckets of buttered popcorn in dark movie theaters, banana splits from the Dairy Queen in the front seat of his car.

He worked at a copying center on the university campus. He dressed neatly: no cutoffs or stained T-shirts. He used aftershave but didn't drench himself with it. He said "Darn it!" instead of "Damn it!"

The perfect gentleman, Steve kept his hands in his pockets when he planted a goodnight peck on my cheek. At first, I wondered why he didn't try anything. I would have blocked him for sure. The snapshot of Travis still gave me heartburn.

Keeping your distance. Good. Let's watch where this leads.

Steve and I discussed everything and anything except sex. This amazed me, as I'd grown accustomed to boys asking, begging, trying, and even demanding at every opportunity. I began to regard Steve differently. Maybe this one was a man, not a boy. And that suited me fine. I needed time to learn to trust him. To trust period.

After Travis bailed on me, Momma's warning had finally hit home. For months before she died, she'd spent most of her days lying in bed. The shades shuttered against the late afternoon rays.

Momma knew she had little time left. She also knew I snuck off with Travis whenever possible. Once while I sat with her, slinking into a daydream about my picture-perfect future with Travis, she said her piece. She chose her path cautiously.

"Men will always be moving on you," she wheezed. "Coming and going." She paused. "One day here, the next day not."

She confided how Father only agreed to marry her after I was practically out of diapers, and she and I required health insurance through the university position he worked for a stint. I'd no clue that I was born before my parents married. It stunned me.

Then her eyelids slid together. She stopped speaking. She steadied her raspy breathing through pursed lips. "Could you get me a cup of water," she murmured.

After a sip, she continued. "Never forget they're only after ... they only want one thing. That's all they want from you." I assumed Momma's efforts to sit up and talk between her labored gasps caused the hurt marching across her features. She strained to corral my gaze. "You understand me, baby?"

I did not care to hear that same old "wait for the wedding ring" speech that up until then she only awkwardly circled. Her words grazed my window like tiny pebbles before falling unnoticed to the ground. A river couldn't dampen my thirst for Travis. Why just thinking about him melted my insides to mush.

"No matter what a man says or does, they only want from you. They don't care what's best. After they take that ..." her voice faded as she stared blankly at the crimping wallpaper. At the time, her advice confused me. Father never left her. After Travis ditched me, I finally caught on to what she so delicately revealed without spurring me to dislike my father more than I already did.

Then came Steve. I wanted to wake Momma from her grave and say, See? You're wrong. They're not all like that. They're not all like Travis. Not all like Father!

One awful Saturday a month after I'd moved away from my family home, Steve ushered me to the county morgue to identify Father's body after it was discovered floating in his favorite fishing pond near the house. Steve cradled me as I sobbed myself to sleep on the couch in his apartment that night. I woke the next morning fully dressed with a cotton sheet tucked under my chin.

Steve introduced me to his family at a picnic in his parents' fenced-in backyard on Labor Day. We ate barbecued chicken, watermelon, and coleslaw and drank iced tea and beer. Skittish at first, I stuck with the iced tea. Steve presented me to his father, a short and stocky man who grinned and laughed agreeably at everything. Steve's mother and sister, Abigail, conducted most of the conversations for Steve and his two elder brothers, their respective spouses, and assorted sons and daughters.

"Stevie's my baby," his mother said, her eyes glittering as she cocked her precisely curled hairdo at Steve.

They all cheerfully welcomed me into the fold. "Steve's told us so much about you!" his sister said as she shooed away her twins from the hot barbecue grill. A freak storm with hail the size of softballs could not have dented the smiles of any one of them. Steve's brother Karl drank one beer after another as his wife swatted him playfully and cautioned him he'd drink himself silly. The children chased after an ancient Irish Setter who finally dragged himself into a hiding spot underneath the porch.

"So, you two met this summer. That's so nice." His mother hiked her eyebrows as if expecting me to elaborate. I didn't, instead shyly offering an extra hand in the kitchen. "Now dear, you relax and enjoy yourself. Have another breast or a drumstick. Mr. Sappington must have barbecued the entire chicken coop," she said to a chorus of laughter.

Karl smirked, raised his bottle of beer to me as if in salute, and chugged another mouthful. The other brother and Abigail's husband soaked up the sun while lying on the chaise lounges. Steve checked in on me now and again, otherwise flinging Frisbees or wrestling with his slew of nieces and nephews.

"Come visit. Anytime! You don't need a special invitation," Steve's mother said, everyone gushing as we hugged our goodbyes to the whole family. By the time we left, my jaw ached from smiling. My heart flitted about ecstatically. I'd never had a family akin to Steve's. No one had ever accepted me into their clan this way. I'd finally found a home. Family.

My emotions blossomed into what I can only describe as love. We seemed so content in each other's company. We flipped over the same TV shows. I mastered his favorite shrimp stir-fry dish and served him dinner at my house. We hiked the river bluffs to view sunsets. I guess you could say I'd fallen for Steve. Except I viewed him differently than Travis. Not all slaphappy and lustful. Maybe this was more like the real thing. We were building our foundation. Our love would thrive and last. This time I was doing things the right way. A sophisticated, adult relationship. I was no longer the little girl lost in a pointless infatuation with that pathetic excuse of a man.

Steve hadn't made a single pass at me in four months. We hadn't discussed it either. I worried maybe he was one of those rare guys that believed men and women, especially women, should remain virgins until the wedding night. He didn't quote scripture or quiz me about my religion, although he said he attended church for Christmas and Easter with his family. I pictured Steve and me inside that white picket-fenced yard. I hoped my affair with Travis wouldn't tarnish this fairy tale for us.

We kissed, mostly quick pecks on the lips and hugs. We sometimes held hands when we strolled. I assumed he was a virgin. He was just afraid. How sweet! Yet I hadn't resigned myself to living the life of a nun. Maybe I would have to strike the match for this fire.

One Friday, I spent half the day showering, shaving, and primping. I stroked a satiny dress, untangling it from the hanger, and perfumed myself in all the right places. I curled my hair, spritzing it with mousse to create some extra bounce. I sailed through the grocery for steaks and a bottle of wine with my fake ID. I trotted over to Steve's unannounced to surprise him with a candle-lit dinner, projecting my arrival for an hour earlier than we arranged to meet.

I rang the doorbell to his apartment. After a quiet lull, I knocked.

Finally, a muffled voice hollered from within. "Who's that?"

"Steve? It's me." I cocked my face toward the peephole.

A few moments passed before he responded.

"What ... what are you doing here?" he asked breathlessly

from behind the closed door.

"Well, I'm ... I wanted to surprise you."

"Can you hold on a sec? I, uh. Hold on." His words drifted away from the door and moved deeper into his apartment.

I waited in the hallway toting a brown paper sack of food, waffling my weight from one foot to the other and back. Several minutes later, I heard the latch unlock and the door crept open. Steve poked his head through the narrow opening. Outfitted in red sweats and a wrinkled royal blue T-shirt emblazoned with crimson letters, he greeted me without his usual smile. His lips had frozen into a straight line.

"I thought I'd catch you before you left to meet me at Hong Kong's," I said as I timidly prodded the door open wider and crossed the threshold.

Then a voice rang out from the bedroom. A man's voice.

"Steve," the voice sang out, "I located the glitch in your electrical outlet. The wire wasn't properly grounded." His tone rose and fell like a buoy bobbing in the sea. "Shame, shame. Who did your wiring?" A slender man wearing a rib-knit tank top that showed off his tanned, sinewy arms strode out of the bedroom and into the main living area, a backpack slung over one shoulder. "Oh! You have a guest." He puckered his lips. "Well, at least you'll have all your electrical outlets at the ready, in case you require any ..." he paused as he looked me over, "... extra wattage." He smirked as he stuck his hand toward me. "Hi. I'm Greg. Greg the electrician."

Steve's facial muscles relaxed. "Yes, Greg helps me with ..."

Greg interrupted, his eyes riveted on me. "I assist Steve with his electrical needs. And with all his stereos and appliances and things, he has a great need. Always blowing circuits and such.

Well, job's done." He glided through the front doorway with a swift "bye now."

I set the bag on the kitchen counter. Steve glanced at me without meeting my gaze and cleared his throat. He ran his palms down his hair as he bounded over. "What's this?" He peeked into the grocery sack. "Dinner? Why how considerate!" he said in an unnaturally high pitch.

"I wanted to surprise you."

A month later, the timing clicked. And this time, Steve proposed. Well into a second bottle of wine, we snuggled on his couch while smooth jazz wafted from the turntable. Steve behaved a little tipsy and started slurring slightly. With his eyes shut, he timidly squeezed my fingers. "Come on."

We rolled around on his couch. Wet, clumsy kisses. I shed my blouse. He inspected my chest through squinting eyelids. He cupped my breasts, tracing the lacy edging of my bra with his fingertips gently before sliding both palms to my back, drawing me to him as he began nuzzling my neck. He kissed my chin and fondled my thighs, inflaming me more than ever before. Travis had never taken this long to get into my pants.

I maneuvered to unfasten his fly, but he nudged my hands away. Just as I became completely unglued, he suggested we move to his bed.

He led me into the near darkness of his bedroom and methodically pulled back the layers of bedspread and blanket and linen. I undressed, plopping my clothes in a pile on the floor. I hopped on the bed, splaying my limbs across the sheets, and watched him undo his jeans and pull off his shirt. He sat on the edge of the bed with his back to me as he shimmied out of his boxers. I crawled across the mattress toward him to flick my tongue along his spine.

"Don't ... that tickles," he said, his voice choking.

"Sorry." I caressed his back.

He turned and hesitantly embraced me with rigid, clammy arms. He breathed heavily. I tugged at his waist, guiding his body to lie next to me. I pressed my body against his, expecting something stiff to poke into my thigh. I felt nothing.

We snuggled under the covers. After more cuddling, I whispered an offer some might have viewed as obscene, yet most men would have jumped on. Steve sighed. "I'm sorry," he said before kicking the bedding away and swinging his legs off the bed to sit on the side. His shoulders sagged as his head dove into his hands.

I let Steve soldier through this himself, as he never discussed his problem with me. I didn't blame myself. Some men have ... trouble. I'd read the magazines. I hid my disappointment and pretended it didn't matter. Other times we'd come close, except when he retreated, I would let him slip from my fingers without protest.

The rest of our relationship clicked. He seemed so perfect for me. Our connection wasn't about sex, unlike my experience with Travis. Steve wanted me for me, not just a warm body to satisfy himself. Our romance would develop into something I believed would last. Something meaningful. True love. The real thing.

We celebrated Thanksgiving and Christmas with his family and ate cake at every birthday party for his numerous nephews and nieces. Everyone always welcomed me with hugs and kisses on my cheeks. His mother and Abigail simultaneously bubbled with delight whenever I visited. I smiled along with his parents, his siblings, and all those giggling and wriggling nieces and nephews. I'd found my place at their table. Finally ... Family.

After church on Easter, we all congregated as usual at his parents' house for Sunday brunch. The adults sat in the formal dining room while the youngsters streaked around the kitchen eating area knocking into cabinets and spilling fruit punch. The baby napped in a spare bedroom sandwiched between two pillows. Periodically Abigail and her mother would breeze in and out of the dining room carrying platefuls of baked ham, string bean casserole, and a Jell-O whipped cream concoction while refusing any and all offers of help from me or the brothers' wives. Karl's wife and the other sister-in-law would swish away to check on the baby or the other children. Steve's father laughed, his rooster neck quivering, as he shoveled forkful after forkful of potatoes, ham, and some pineapple dish prepared by one of Steve's sisters-in-law. I inhaled the deviled eggs, and his mother promised to write down her recipe for me.

Karl gulped one beer after another, smiling, laughing, and swiveling his head.

After we finished eating, Steve's mother and Abigail whisked away stacks of plates and bowls from the table. Steve's father leaned back in his chair and patted his full belly. His grin swung between Steve and me as he beamed at his youngest son and nodded his approval at me.

The nieces and nephews charged through the doorway, howling like banshees as they chased each other brandishing plastic forks and headless chocolate bunnies. Chaos reigned. The sisters-in-law shooed the children back to their table in the adjacent room at every opportunity.

Steve's mother and sister settled at the table for post-brunch chatter over coffee and slices of Key Lime pie. The adult voices hummed, lulling me into a mellow, satiated state.

Then Karl hoisted his beer bottle and presented a toast.

"To my little brother and his lovely lady friend!" Everyone cheered as they all raised their cups of coffee. Their praise jingled about my ears like softly chiming bells. Steve smiled weakly as his face flushed.

"To Cathy, the miracle worker!" Karl said before another hit off his beer. The bravos tapered.

"You've had too much to drink, Karl." His wife scolded him in an affectionate yet firm tone. "You're drinking yourself silly again."

"Now lay off me. I'm rejoicing. This is a grand day of jubilation! Why, this woman has delivered our baby brother back from the dead! She's saved him from eternal damnation." Karl guffawed, swigging his beer with a smirk. "Here's to the amazing woman who cured my little baby brother."

Karl's wife murmured to him as she struggled to snatch his beer.

"No!" Karl grimaced as he clutched the bottle, hugging it to his chest. "Mine!" He chortled, his chin jiggling. No one laughed with him.

The once gleeful faces surrounding me decayed into glum shells, no longer recognizable.

Shrill words from Steve's mother flew across the table. "Karl, we are having a nice family gathering. Now ..."

Karl ignored his mother. "But it's true. Didn't you know?" he asked as he studied me, captivated by my expression of total bewilderment. "Don't tell me she doesn't know about you, Steve?" He smacked his palm on the table, and now his entire frame shook with mirth. "Jesus H. Christ, Steve. Sweet little Stevie."

The other brother dropped his gaze to scrutinize the lace curlicues in the tablecloth.

"Shut up, Karl," his mother hissed. Tears plunged down her cheeks. "Shut up, please. Don't ruin this for everyone."

The rest of the family submerged into silence. Abigail zippered her mouth into a grim, unbending line.

"He's a fruitcake! You didn't know that, Cathy? Didn't you tell her, Steve? But now you're fixed. She's cured you, right? Isn't that right?"

Steve's father pushed himself away from the table and crossed his arms over his massive belly. "Ellen, I told you not to baby him. You just wouldn't let him grow up to be a man!" He glowered past the china sugar bowl at his sobbing wife.

Steve grasped for my arm, his eyes seared with hurt. "I'm sorry, Cathy. I thought it would work. I tried to change! I really want to!"

I left the house as the dining room erupted into more loud accusations and more tears.

Steve called me later that evening. I listened to him cry several minutes as my insides hardened to stone before I hung up.

14

I don't remember my dreams much anymore. Seems most mornings I wake up exhausted as if I've jogged hills all night. Where did my mind wander when it should have rested? Certainly does enough meandering during my waking hours as I'm folding laundry or washing dishes, or especially when I'm driving. I've usually pocketed something to pick at or fret about. The steady rumble of the engine, the tires whacking the ground in perfect rhythm, all soothed me into a reverie. Nothing else to do when you're staring at miles of road with hours to think. Think about Mike. What went wrong.

If only I could forget our last fight. It started like every other, except that one ended especially bad, and the recollection burns me like acid. Damn! Peeling away the layers of that raw onion stung my eyes. But I couldn't stop. I had to find the threads tying my past to my present. I had to understand why the hell I ended up driving through the Ozarks to God knows where with two strangers and that fricking freezer in the back of my truck. Guess I'm still trying to figure everything out. Guess I'll never truly understand what went wrong.

We had our last fight on the fourth of April, a Wednesday night. Just laid off, downsized, cut back, or fired from my last job. I had wasted another afternoon at the Rallis County welfare office in Cliff City. Pretty deserted, but they still made me stand until my legs throbbed. The men and women glued to their chairs behind their fake walls moved like molasses in January. Maybe not enough coffee, some of them nursing hangovers, I'm sure. By the time the gray-haired lady bothered to peer at me through her glasses as if I were bird shit splattered on her car windshield, I scuffled with the urge to spit on her.

After another afternoon blown in some bureaucrat's version of hell, I trudged home spoiling for a fight. Maybe Mike would bop in for a change so I could lay into him and unleash my frustration. I did my best not to vent at my Mitchell, although I'm not peaches and cream with my baby every minute of the day.

I'd stormed into Velva's on my way home from the welfare office and picked up three cans of the cheapest beer I could buy with quarters and dimes I'd scrounged out of the bottom of my purse and off the floorboard of my pickup. I guzzled all of them, the last two after I put Mitchell to bed. I was full of juice and on fire.

And lucky me, Mike barged in, swearing at the screen door after he stumbled through. I'd tucked Mitchell in hours before.

"What the fuck's going on here? No beer in the fridge. Nothin' to eat but ... what's that shit? Don't look like food. You slopping that to the brat or what?"

"Shut the fuck up!" I slammed the refrigerator door, ripping the handle out of his fingers. He staggered backward, swinging his head and leaving it at a slant, rapidly blinking as he grimaced in my direction.

He swayed as he wagged his finger at me. He was hammered. He smelled of cheap whiskey, flat warm beer, and rotting garbage. He hadn't swapped out his clothes in days; I caught a whiff of that too. I pummeled the air to clear the fumes he spewed with each breath.

"Now, now, now, little lady, that's no way for a lady to talk."

"How dare you show up stinking like shit. I need money for rent! I need money for food! I need money for the goddamn electricity to keep this refrigerator going. I need money for medicine. Don't you come here complaining! You don't pitch in here at all. You don't bring in any money to pay for shit. You pop by and fuck everything up whenever you're around. Don't come in my house for anything unless you plan to help out. I'm sick of you and your shit." I had battled to lower my voice, yet I began yelling out of control in record time.

Mike shuffled to the counter to rest against, grabbing the surface for support, and then slumped into a chair with a bent leg. He leaned too far back, so the chair legs slid from underneath, and he tumbled to the floor. It took him a few minutes to muscle himself up off the linoleum. The fall sobered him a bit. He straightened his legs, standing cautiously before pitching backward against the wall. With one hand, he buffed his eyes and swiped thick wads of greasy hair off his face. He strained to focus, his eyes flickering; the effort was wearing on him.

"I don't need to hear crap from you. I've had a bad day myself."

"You've had a bad day? You've had a fuckin' bad day? What, working? Were you working today? Maybe bothering to nail down a job? Bullshit! Busy bumming cash, hustling somebody for liquor, maybe. You worm! My checks are bouncing. Mitchell is growing out of everything. He's got holes in the one pair of shoes he can still force onto his feet. Damn you!"

I was broke with a pile of unpaid past due bills, despairing over my future, and worrying about how to feed Mitchell through the summer without the school's free breakfast and lunch program. He must have hit a growth spurt because he ate everything in sight.

"Now, no. None of your lip. None of that shit," he said. He wore washed-out jeans too long for his legs, the bell bottoms tattered and dirty. A T-shirt riddled with holes celebrating the 1982 White Trash Bash on the Gastein River stretched across his belly.

"Where have you been slumming? Haven't seen that ugly mug for, how long has it been now? I stopped counting. You piece of shit! You working on anything other than fucking up whatever's left of your liver?"

He was so pathetically drunk. So barely able to stand. What the hell had ever attracted me to him?

"Now you listen here," he said as he tried to step away from the wall but failed and slouched back against it. Unable to target his scowl on me, he shook a limp finger at the wall as if he were lecturing the buckling wallpaper. "You, you need to ... Why don't you try to be little nicer. Little nicer maybe."

I righted the vinyl chair that unseated him, shoving it next to the kitchen table. He'd bent the one crooked leg even more, making it list awkwardly. I cussed as I wrangled with it, finally giving up and chucking the chair out the door. It hit the garage with a thwack.

"Now, now you're the one throwing and breaking stuff."

"Oh, shut up! Shut up you goddamn pig. You make me sick!"

Mike's body weaved and twitched to maintain balance. He raked the wall with his open palm as he jockeyed for his bearings, shuddering and blinking, then staring at nothing. I sneered, yet he didn't notice. I suppose I appeared to him as little more than a loud, blurry blob. What was I thinking? In his condition, he couldn't understand a word I said. None of this would soak in. Why did I bother? I was pissed. Pissed at him, pissed at everything.

He nodded as if agreeing with me.

“Guess I’ll go,” he said. He tottered toward my bedroom. My bedroom! Mine! I stomped across the floor and planted myself in front of him.

“No! Get the hell out of here! You are not crashing here tonight. No way! I’m done. I’m through. I’m tired of tripping over your mess. You’re out of here! No more of this shit. Get out!”

He wavered midair then flung himself against the wall for support. Smothered with several months’ worth of whiskers, his face scrunched with confusion.

“What, not ... what do you want me to go? I ...”

I’d never seen him that plastered, that wretched. So completely revolting and despicable. The cracked rubber on his left sneaker had split, and his sockless toes stuck out. He could have passed for a homeless bum. Then it punched me in my gut. He was a homeless bum! A mangy dog seeking a corner where no one would run him off. Steam gushed through my veins.

“Stupid fuck! You’re not welcome here anymore! I need help raising Mitchell. He’s your son too. It shouldn’t all fall on me. It shouldn’t be up to me alone to feed and clothe him. Damn you for drinking your life away to nothing!”

Mike chewed on that. His eyelids fluttered. He scratched himself with his free hand. He almost lost his balance and then righted himself again.

“Fine, fine. Shitfire! I’m outta here. I’m done with this shithole.”

“Fine! We’re done with you too!”

He teetered, stumbled sideways, and banged into the kitchen table, aiming to knock it over to aggravate me even more. His hands flailed at the edges in a botched attempt to find purchase, and he fell backward onto the floor again.

I marched toward his hunched frame and roared at him. "Get out! Get out! Get the fuck out now! And don't come back! I'm done with you and your piece of shit self. Don't ever show your face here again unless you have rent money! You hear? Rent!" He couldn't or wouldn't lift his gaze to meet mine.

Mike reached for the table lip to pull himself up, but he couldn't sustain his grasp and collapsed to the floor, sprawled on his back. He closed his eyes.

"No, you don't pass out here! Get up! Get up and get out!"

I clenched his wrist and dragged him to the door, cursing and hissing venom every inch of the way. Mike's head lolled, and he twisted around trying to figure out what locked onto his arm. Then he came to and nabbed my ankle. I wrenched my leg out of his grip and shouted at him. He mumbled and swung a fist at me. I towed him within a foot of the door. I yanked open the door, then thrust the screen door ajar as I grabbed Mike again. I was ready to haul him out and heave him off my porch. As I started to lug him through the door, he roused again with a strength that surprised me for his inebriated state of weakness. He wrestled his arm from me and scrambled into a sitting position.

"What you doing, bitch? What the hell you doing to me? Let go! Let go of me or I'll teach you a thing or two." His smoldering eyes bore into me for a couple seconds of clarity before dissolving back into disorder.

I boiled over. I seized Mitchell's school backpack from its hook by the door and struck Mike with it, smacking his head, his shoulders, his back, his legs. He sat cross-legged on the floor with both limbs shielding himself, cussing as he labored to push himself up between blows. The backpack contained paperback comics from the library, no hefty books or such, though the plastic buckles and their straps would have stung if they whipped across his face.

We both hollered and bellowed unintelligible stuff. Loud. Loud enough to wake Mitchell.

How long had he watched me swatting at his daddy as if he were a mosquito? His stoned, slobbering father struggling to protect his body, incapable of rising from the ground or defending himself. Tears streamed down Mitchell's face, so he'd watched long enough. How much he must have heard from his tiny bedroom, I could only guess.

I dropped the backpack. A cheap vinyl number decorated with a silly grinning Disney character.

Silence.

Mike's gaze followed mine. He widened and narrowed his eyes a bunch before he could focus on Mitchell. My poor, precious baby Mitchell sniffling and crying as he gaped at Mike in horror. Mitchell's torn T-shirt barely covered his stomach, and a drawstring held up an old pair of oversized gym shorts above his scrawny hips.

During every other brawl, Mitchell hid in his room or buried himself in the sofa cushions. If I managed to control the volume and shut his bedroom door, he usually slept through everything. That night he woke to a bad dream instead.

I glared at Mike. I addressed him in the most hateful tone I could muster. "You happy now? You see what you're doing here? We don't need you. We don't want you. Get out. Don't come back." I would have clobbered him in a parting shot, but I couldn't with Mitchell there.

Mike kneaded his chin as his head flopped. He blinked as if adjusting his vision, but his eyes simply floated aimlessly. Using his hands, he launched himself to his knees before boosting himself onto his feet by pulling up on the kitchen counter. He didn't utter a syllable. One misstep, then a palm pawing the counter for balance. He lurched toward the door.

Mitchell suddenly let out an unearthly howl.

He sprinted to Mike, ramming into him and nearly knocking him over. Mike bore the blow with a shudder, then fumbled for the counter with his other hand as he slumped back against the sink. He tilted his head toward Mitchell, who had flung his arms around Mike and bawled into his jeans.

A puzzled look shadowed Mike's features. He wobbled, his fingers clawing the pitted countertop for a secure handhold. He almost fell, then somehow he steadied himself, even with the hysterical Mitchell clinging to him. Mike's bleary eyes drifted across the cabinets and the sink before fixing on the shaking and whimpering boy latched to his body. He dragged one hand off the counter and laid it on Mitchell's head, petting him as if Mitchell were a puppy, then smoothing his hair over and over. Mike tried to speak. His speech slurred, and I couldn't comprehend a word. Mitchell burrowed his face into Mike's hip and moaned. Mike braced his back against the counter as he put both hands on Mitchell, rubbing Mitchell's shoulders. Mike stared far off, like something no longer in the room cornered his attention. He muttered, his head slowly bobbing as if in conversation.

I was stunned. Dumbfounded. Speechless. Mitchell had never touched his father, let alone run to him like that. Eyes downcast, scurrying out of a room when a drunk or foul-tempered Mike lumbered in. Mitchell crept under his covers when I couldn't stop Mike from barreling into his bedroom to bark about this or that. Mitchell avoided making any noise or laughing too loud at early morning cartoons when Mike was sleeping one off. Diving out of his way, dodging his sights.

I reacted. Some of it was the beer. No, No, Cathy. Don't blame it on the liquor. I wasn't intoxicated, only juiced. Sort of buzzed.

I reacted badly. Very badly.

"Get your hands off him!"

Mike's mouth dangled open. His glassy eyes strayed.

"Get your filthy mitts off my son! You just crawled out of a gutter, don't you touch him!"

Mike didn't appear to have heard me. His palms cupped Mitchell's head. Mitchell, my angel. His sobbing ebbed to an occasional hiccup or a sniffle. He pressed himself into Mike's grimy jeans, his arms coiling Mike's waist, holding tight like he would never let go.

"Don't even! You leave him be. You leave him out of this. How dare you come here and ... Let go of my boy! Get your disgusting, filthy hands off my son! Now! Do it, you scum bucket asswipe!"

I'd never witnessed anything similar to this in all my days as the mother to these two little boys. Mike, the older brother, hollered at Mitchell or ignored him whenever provided the chance. Mike would throw a towel at him, ordering him to his room when Mike coveted the television and the couch all to himself, swearing at Mitchell for pouring all the milk into his cereal bowl and not finishing it. Mitchell lowered his head when Mike appeared and generally disappeared as any little brother would when the bullying other entered the room.

Once I scolded Mike into apologizing for smashing a Lego contraption Mitchell had built and left where Mike intended to sit.

"Can't you two get along?" I pleaded with Mike during another ruckus.

The two of them huddled against the kitchen counter. Mike stared into space. Mitchell, now silent with his puffy eyelids sealed, his fingers tangled in the belt loops of Mike's fraying jeans.

I'd stomached enough. I lunged for Mitchell, glued my hands to his shoulders, and jerked him toward me. He began wailing again, limbs flailing as he escaped from me and bolted for his father. Astonishment mingled with my fury. I'd never seen anything so amazing or so infuriating.

How? When could this have happened? When did Mitchell learn to want Mike? Mike rarely hung around, and when he did ... well, he certainly wasn't a father. He never spoke kindly to Mitchell. Never anything other than a gruff command or a crass remark if he even acknowledged Mitchell was alive. When the hell did Mitchell grow to care about him?

My brain ricocheted off the walls of my skull in complete chaos. My anger mixed with shock and erupted in a toxic reaction. I seized Mitchell, my hands clamping onto his narrow hip bones to rip him away from his father.

"No! Let me go!" Mitchell tussled with me as I separated him from Mike.

"He's no daddy for you. You deserve better. I should have found you a better daddy. Not some lush ..."

"No! Don't leave. Stay. Don't make him leave, Mommy. Don't

make him go! Daddy! Daddy stay!" Sobs clogged his voice.

He yanked and wriggled out of my arms and ran to Mike again. I blew up. I grabbed Mitchell and tugged with all my might. Mitchell lost his grip and turned on me, slapping and kicking. I shoved him as hard as I could, slamming him against the wall. He collided with a thud and tumbled onto the linoleum. He started to cry a soundless cry. His shoulders shook. His tears wetted his T-shirt.

Mike squinted at me as he tried to target his eyes on my face. His gaze sagged before plunging to my feet. He drooped his head toward Mitchell.

It suddenly hit me what I'd done. I wanted to die.

"Mitchell, Mitch-Mitch, baby, sweetie, I'm sorry, I'm so, so sorry. Mommy didn't mean to hurt you, Mommy didn't mean to. Oh baby, baby, baby."

The tears splashed down my cheeks and into his hair. I hugged him, molding him to my chest. We both cried and cried and cried. After an eternity, he quit shaking. He had sobbed himself to sleep. I sat there on the kitchen floor rocking him in my lap and whispering into his hair, again and again, how sorry I was, so, so sorry. Sorry about everything.

How could I have done that to my darling Mitchell! What the hell possessed me? Was I no different than that woman who buckled her babies into their car seats and released the brake so the car coasted into a lake, drowning them? Or maybe the one who threw her kids over the freeway guardrail before joining them to crash through the windshield of an oncoming vehicle.

I had no idea before that I was capable of such evil. Of harming my own child. What was wrong with me? What had I done?

I couldn't say how much time had passed while I cradled Mitchell. When I finally looked up, Mike was gone.

15

Well damn. This is just as much your fault as mine. You can bean me with an old shoe if I wander again like a stick moseying on a creek, bogging down in every eddy and logjam. I know you're more interested in where we were going. Where Johnny was taking us. Us and that big freezer, no longer plugged in and beginning to thaw.

The road we traveled narrowed to the point where a car coming the opposite direction rounding a bend would bulldoze right into my bumper. None came. The once graveled surface had disintegrated into hard-packed dirt. The pastures with scattered clusters of cedar and locust had merged into dense timber of pine, oak, and dogwood. The trees bordering the road stretched their leafy and needle-encrusted branches across, entangling each other and forming an arch overhead, protecting us from the prying rays of the sun. Leaves from years past littered the lane. My tires tossed them, but from my rearview mirror, I spied their copper-colored remains lying behind us as if never disturbed. Clumps of grass spread outward, spilling into the threadbare tire tracks here and there.

Rusted barbed wire fences sandwiched the road, straining against the fescue that choked through. Weeds wrangled the strung wire and rotting cedar posts to the ground. Decades ago, some farmer wrapped the barbed wire around live oak trees rather than bothering with sinking a post. With age the trunks fattened, bursting through the girdle of metal strands. Nothing stops Mother Nature. She always wins. She takes her sweet time, but she'll get the best of us yet. Ashes to ashes, dust to dust.

A rabbit skittered in front of us, darting helter-skelter before dashing through the busted fence and into the woods.

The sun peeked through a gap in the leaves now and again. We soldiered on, bisecting shadows mostly. A granddaddy black snake spanning the width of the road glided across and into the undergrowth as we approached. I'd quit worrying about bashing head-on into a car for some time as we puttered along at five to ten miles an hour with the engine sputtering like a worn-out lawnmower.

Johnny signaled me to stop, so I jammed my foot against the brake pedal and halted the truck. He motioned for Ellis to open the door and scoot out. Johnny bounded out of the cab, both feet landing at the same time. He paused at each tire and squatted, flipping the lever on the hubcaps to engage the vehicle's four-wheel drive. I switched the truck into four-wheel mode also. Ellis strode back and forth in a short, neat line outside. After messing with the locks, Johnny hoisted himself in and slid next to me. Ellis crawled in before slamming the door. I eased off the brake, and we advanced at a lazy pace.

The roadbed of leaves and twisted thorny stalks with only a trace of a route straightened then appeared to go on forever. The trees crowding us grew thick, strangled by Virginia creeper, kudzu, and poison ivy.

Barbed wire no longer separated the road from the woods, allowing us to dive deeper into the dim maze of dull greens and browns. I couldn't determine anywhere to turn, but Johnny piloted me toward a slight breach between two cedars, each about as tall as a house. I angled the Ford, and we rolled up the windows so the stiff branches wouldn't scratch us. The engine roared as I nudged the gas pedal. The tire tread shredded through the soil and weeds. They spun before they finally grabbed hold, and we lurched over a hump and through a shallow ditch. The spiky vines snagged the axles as the tires crunched hollow logs and snapped the crushed saplings. Stumpy shrubs grappled with the pickup. After we mowed over the bushes, they swung to and fro wildly for a few seconds. A fallen branch clutched the rear axle, thumping the underbelly of the vehicle with each cycle until it finally broke into chunks, and we left it behind.

With Johnny guiding, we edged through the forest following something of an abandoned farm road. I didn't ask where we were going. Ellis clammed up. Only his eyes flitted here and there, his hands clinging to the dashboard as the cab jolted with every dip in the terrain, every log we clambered over. I thanked my lucky stars for purchasing a cheap truck that could master this trek.

We must have trampled a couple hundred yards or more, creeping through the swarming underbrush and rambling tree branches. The woods never relented. Sunlight did not reach this patch of earth. The rustic backcountry seeped through our closed windows like a stew on a low simmer: dirt, cedar, mulching leaves, a faint hours-old musk from a startled skunk. A spider web the size of a car flared before us. We tore through it, the shorn fragments encasing the windshield wipers and the mirrors in a silky gauze.

We weaved through a stand where the boughs rose higher. The bushes and coarse grasses thinned out and shrank to waist-high. You could almost see more than five feet in front of the windshield. The truck scaled a toppled tree, and we bounced down hard on the other side. Ellis let out a wisp of protest and cussed. We seesawed several more yards before Johnny pointed out a chink between the fat tree trunks. He navigated through the trees, communicating with his hands to direct each route change. He flagged me to halt then reverse a tad. Branches blocked the passenger door, so we all climbed out on my side. A pulsating chorus of locusts and chirping insects greeted us.

The sun no longer beat down on us, only the suffocating heat and humidity still smothered us. The air was lifeless, so we lacked any natural airconditioning. I started to miss even the hot stuff that had blown through the cab as we sped along the highway. I must have looked like a farmhand, with those large damp blotches under my pits and between my shoulder blades, tangled strands of hair stuck to my neck.

Ellis scampered around, collected a handful of stones, and flung them, aiming at tree trunks and branches. Johnny surveyed, his head rotating gradually left to right. Ellis threw another pebble, but instead of hitting a tree, it splashed into water.

"Well I'll be. It's a regular little pond! Maybe good fishing. Anybody ready for a cool dip?" Ellis chortled, not expecting an answer.

Neither Johnny nor I laughed along with him. Foamy olive-green scum and dead leaves camouflaged the pond. Waterlogged limbs stripped of their bark, and dying trees poked through the surface. The pebble Ellis tossed hatched ripples that ended in silent armies of tiny waves crashing against the leaf-strewn banks and tree bark. Now you could identify the pond; in the gloom of this shrouded woodland, the once still water could have passed for solid ground. It was bigger than the public pool in Cliff City. I wouldn't have swum in it if you paid me: the mud squishing between your toes, the slimy algae hitching onto your arms, whatever lived in that nasty, brackish water swishing around your legs. Leeches.

Johnny scanned the timber surrounding the pond. A feeble trail uncluttered by hefty rocks and tree trunks led toward the water's edge. I figured he was planning to haul the freezer into the water and allow it to sink to the bottom. Johnny didn't bother asking Ellis to pitch in. He'd take care of this on his own.

After he dragged the freezer the two or three yards to the pond's spongy waterline, he undid the knot he had tied so taut and loosened the ropes a bit. My heart pounded. My muscles screeched and twitched. Otherwise, I stood still as if staked to the ground, unable to help, unable to budge, barely able to breathe.

Ellis had meandered off to duck any more tasks. He inspected the moss blanketing a massive boulder, scraping it with a stick as he faked an unshakeable interest.

Then Johnny unlatched the lid. The metal pieces grated against each other as he pried them apart. He was smart, that Johnny. He knew the seal on the freezer lid would have kept it floating, preventing the water from trickling in to swamp the box and force it to descend. Stooping to gather four or five slender branches, he wedged them under the lid. He cinched the ropes again and tightened the knot to secure the shims. Then he heaved and pushed until the freezer started to slip into the murky water lapping the tongue of his boots. Something underwater snared the freezer, but Johnny freed it. The freezer still cleared the water by at least two feet. Johnny treaded farther into the pond as he thrust the freezer away from the bank. The dark scum clung to his faded jeans right below his knees.

Johnny guided the appliance out to deeper water, generating a wake momentarily clear of pond scum and decaying leaves. The water was up to his crotch. Johnny tilted the freezer by grabbing the lid and reaching underwater for the bottom of the freezer to ease it on its back. The mucky water began pouring in past the branch shims through the slim opening of the freezer. The freezer was partially submerged. The water sloshed against his belt buckle. He shoved the drifting hulk, and as it strayed further out into the lake, the freezer filled with water and slid out of sight. I watched the bubbles, big ones and little ones, as they surged, rested for an instant on the surface, then exploded into nothing. After they died, the water flattened.

Johnny slogged out of the pond. Fibrous streaks of algae stuck to his jeans, and water streamed out of his boots as he strode back to the pickup. He stared straight ahead with his head high and his gaze targeting the space in front of him.

Ellis kept his trap shut. He slunk from behind a towering hickory tree then skittered to the truck. His eyes sprinted between Johnny and me. He obviously hankered to grill me about the freezer or hurl a smart crack about dumping it in this remote waterhole hidden in this vacant countryside. Something from Johnny told him to quit.

I couldn't have cared less. I wanted to die. My man, my love had just sunk to the bottom of a forgotten farm pond. The man I pictured sitting next to on the gymnasium bleachers clapping and tearing up as our son received his high school diploma. The man I needed to mow the lawn or fix a torn screen. The man I longed to grow old with. If I'd had the strength and if Johnny would of let me, I would of thrown myself in after him. I couldn't even cry. My chest burned as if I'd swallowed a jagged hunk of ice. I couldn't move, like a husk of an ancient tree, waiting for lightning to strike and torch me to nothing.

16

No, Mike had not been his standard self that final night. Not stumbling drunk. Not mean, sarcastic, kicking things. He apologized. Told me he was sincerely sorry. A Mike I'd never seen before materialized on my porch. Arms hanging limp, ready to stomach anything I could dish up, or so he believed. I guess he expected me to start yelling in my usual style.

Mike's face gleamed in the light cast from the kitchen. "I never meant to be such a terrible person to you, to you both. I let the liquor control me. I let the anger control me. I blamed you for a lot of things that weren't your fault. I blamed ... I blamed little Mitchell. And I am thanking God on a daily basis for forgiving me for all I have done. For all I have not done. I pray you can someday ... both of you can someday forgive me as well. I have renewed my life with Christ. I am finally prepared to be Mitchell's father – to raise him and provide him the advice my own daddy offered me that I ignored. I know it's not too late. With the Lord's guidance, I will be the father my son needs. And deserves."

Struck dumb, I gaped through the screen door mesh at a man I could only dream about before. God? So that's what it took to straighten him out. I could handle that. I'm not the churchgoing sort. Momma tried, and Father just mocked her for it. I could take religion or leave it on a shelf. Weddings, funerals, Christmas. The religious zealots annoyed me with their self-righteous squawking. But at times, I can tune in and some of it actually makes sense.

I'd prepared for a fight, not for this. Amazed, I suddenly accelerated from Reverse to Full Throttle. My heart soared.

Our family man is back! And this time, maybe no more beer bottles shattering across my yard.

No more smashed windows or busted furniture. No more screaming matches between Mike and me while our darling Mitchell cowers under his sheets. That would all change! Mike and Mitchell pitching a baseball outside while I cook supper. Sunday matinees in Cliff City for the three of us. Evening strolls through the neighborhood to catch fireflies in June. Saturday morning cartoons on the couch. Mike holding me, holding me so close, and not ever letting me go. Mike, my darling angel, Michael.

My drop-jaw dazed expression curved into a smile. Tears sprung and ran tracks down my skin. I'd always craved this. I would have a real family! A whole family! Mike would reunite with us as Mitchell's father. He had returned to me! As my husband maybe? Chunky layers of caked-on hurt from years of heartache melted in seconds. Of course it would be hard work. Mike and Mitchell and I would make up the squandered time. Years upon wasted years. We had neglected so much of our lives, of each other. So much fallow ground, except we would plow through this as a family!

Pure joy blazed through me, same as when I discovered I was pregnant with Mitchell. I reached for the screen doorknob to allow Mike in the house. We could begin right that very minute. Mike and I had so much to talk about!

Before I could open the door, he resumed speaking in an odd fashion that did not invite a response. It echoed more like a carefully written speech he'd rehearsed for days.

"Yes, the Lord has blessed me so. And I have rejected his blessings. Now I finally realize how wrong I was. The drinking and the hatefulness almost destroyed everything God has given me. Sara ... it was Sara who showed me."

He looked at me, yet he did not see me. He looked through me. "Sara is a wonderful woman. A strong, caring woman at our Church. The Praise Be Church of Worship in Cliff City. The Church took me in and ... Sara helped me accept Jesus as my personal savior. She has the faith and strength of ten of me. She lived a nightmare as the wife of a gambler and an alcoholic," he paused, "an alcoholic, a drunk like myself. He spent all his paycheck, all her savings, on alcohol and gambling. When he arrived home, he would beat her." Mike's eyes flashed with a hint of the rage he had tucked away in a pocket. "He hit her with his fists. He stole from his boss. He and Sara had to declare bankruptcy. Sara lost her home, her job. Then he deserted her. She joined the Church years ago not only for herself but for sinners like me. To help others. She counseled me, prayed with me, and finally helped me overcome my evil obsession with alcohol. Sara showed me how Jesus can save my soul. She is an angel."

My perspiration turned into a sweat.

"I have been sober for five weeks. One of the church members found work for me at his business. I am living in the home of another church member until ..." He blinked as he paused. "More than two months have passed since ... that night. There is so much to say. 'Sorry' is all I can offer. I am sorry. I do not expect your forgiveness. I hope you will listen. Please accept my apology. I have asked Jesus for forgiveness, and he has responded by granting me salvation. And although the Lord's forgiveness and love are all I can hope and pray for, your forgiveness is, well, it is important to me too. I will make it up to you, I don't know how. Sara says we can send some of my paycheck every month.

And of course Mitchell ... well, Mitchell will have his own room at our home when Sara and I find a house of our own. Sara and I want him with us as much as ... well as much and as often as possible."

My fingers froze on the screen door handle. My gut churned and left me queasy, like I'd smelled rotting meat. My lips sealed tight, yet the venom leaked out.

"Who the hell is Sara?" I flung each word with the momentum of a baseball flying over home plate.

Mike carried on as if he were conversing with a stranger. "Sara is ... She and I have been through so many trials these last two months. She is so strong." Mike closed his eyes. "And she is a loving woman. She knows she will never be a mother to Mitchell, but she will help me be a better father, I can promise you that." He resonated like a preacher slathering it on thick so his followers would top off the basket in exchange for one hell of a hereafter.

"Who the fuck is Sara? And why is she going to be around my Mitchell? Wh-what the hell are you telling me?"

Mike blinked, cleared his throat, and rose taller as if he found a solid beam to shore him up. Not a stiff shot of booze, not tonight. Something more potent.

"Sara and I are to be married. Next month. At our Church."

I sucked in a lungful of air and mouthed a soundless "bullshit."

A shadow cloaked Mike's face. He dipped his head, his eyes scanning his clean shoes before facing me again.

"Bullshit! Don't give me this shit, Mike. Haven't I been through enough? Don't feed me this crap now. Don't ... if this is your idea of a game or a joke, is it ... April Fools! Damn you, asshole!"

He watched me with an unnatural calmness stapled to a steel resolve as if to brace himself for the tornado about to touch down.

"For thirteen years we've been playing house! Is that it? Just fucking playing house? We had a kid together! You couldn't hold down a goddamn job and I've been caring for our son ..." I struggled to restrain my voice, afraid we would wake Mitchell again. "That beautiful little boy of ours whom you have neglected, terrorized and pissed on since before he was born. And now, you are going to 'settle down' with some goddamn church lady and she's going to help you raise him? Bullshit, man! I'll take all your paycheck. The whole goddamn thing. Goddamn son of a bitch."

I hammered away, trying to rile him. That's what had worked in the past. Not long ago when I still considered him my man, he'd lumber into the house, fuming after getting sacked, losing another lottery scratch-off game, hungering for another drink, kicking and hollering, and I would lay into him. We'd yell back and forth. Then he'd break a plate or slam a cabinet door off its hinges. Something would snap, and we'd both quit. Survey each other, then call a truce. End up in bed if not loving each other, at least giving our best effort. Fight and fuck. That served us for a spell, more or less.

He wouldn't even nibble at the bait. His starched collar dug into his freshly shaved neck. His thin brown shoelaces were knotted in precise bows, the two pairs of loops each exactly the same length. Moths and some tiny insects fluttered around the porch light bulb. He sighed as sorrow crept across his features, then he clenched his jaw before he resumed.

"Sara warned me this would be hard. Harder than sobriety.

Nothing could be harder than admitting responsibility for my sins. And after I welcomed his love, after I followed him to the path of salvation, nothing could mean more than giving my life to Jesus, even though dear Jesus, I am not worthy of your forgiveness," he gulped "or yours, Cathy. And I promise you, from the bottom of my heart, I will make this up to you. I used you. Horribly. I took advantage of you. I hurt you, I ... and now, here you are, a single mother, and ..." his arms spread to his sides, his gaze digesting the essence of my cheap-rental-house-minimum-wage existence.

Fuck you!

I didn't have to say it out loud. I said it with my entire body. My bloodshot eyes. The curse shrieked from every pore of my skin. He couldn't hear my words, but he must have felt them socking his chest. He understood me. Yet he rolled on.

"I have kept you from finding the man who would love you and cherish you, a man who would provide for you and protect you. I could take the easy way out. I could blame it on the liquor. Blame it on the bartenders, the school teachers who never believed in me, my parents who weren't firm enough to discipline me, the media and all its lustful, sinful ..."

"Oh shut up, will you shut up with all that nonsense! I'm not going to suffer through any more of your sermons. You're not drinking for now. Great! That'll last about another month. Maybe. So Jesus hauled you into the wagon. You'll fall off. You'll fall off and hit hard. I know you, Michael Matthew Nicholson. You are not that tough to figure out. None of you drunks are. Such goddamn idiots! So now, instead of crawling onto a barstool, you're kneeling in some building holding hands with this shit Sara ..."

He lifted his hand and gently interrupted me. "I have put you through an ordeal and you have every right to be upset. I understand your anger and frustration. I am the cause. Direct your anger at me. Direct your frustration at me." He recited the phrases he'd obviously practiced. "This is all my fault. Do not criticize Sara, please. She is a good woman and prays for you and Mitchell."

"Fuck her! Fuck her and her goddamn prayers. She can shove 'em where the sun don't shine."

Mike continued displaying his palm to shush me, yet it did no good. No one could stop me now. I wasn't simply mad. I seethed with fury. I was hissing and spitting rage.

If he brings up that bitch one more time ...

But as soon as my anger vomited forth, a sadness swamped me.

I'd learned to hate him over the years. We would simmer and stew over each other's slights for a while until we boiled over into a screaming contest. But with every bout, the pain inside me swelled. Oh how I hated him. Hated him for abandoning our precious child who would grow up without a loving father, maybe growing up to consider himself worthless as well. Hated him for abandoning me. Hated how much I ached for him to lie beside me in our bed and reach for me, cling to me, croon my name into my hair. The smile he occasionally surrendered, years and years ago, when he enveloped me in his arms and gazed into my face with a tenderness that dissolved all doubt.

I lowered my voice. "I have waited for you. I have waited for years! I have waited for you to come to your senses and help me raise this boy of ours! I have waited patiently for you to be my ... partner, husband, maybe. You're damn right you used me. I hoped one day, someday, you would wake up and realize ... that you would see what we have.

"I took care of you in the mornings when you felt like a ping pong ball on a tennis court. I tiptoed around, letting you sleep in, while I had to get dressed for some dead-end job while you got your act together. Waiting for you to pull your head out of your ass! For thirteen fucking years!" My words swelled louder. "When you were out of work, which was every other week of your goddamn life, I paid the bills! I listened to you groan about this lousy job or that lousy interview. I let you back in, again and again, no matter how loaded you were, no matter how nasty you smelled, no matter how shitty you looked. You think your Sara would put up with that crap? I went through all that grief. And what we had, what we have had ... we've been a couple too long, Mike, too many years for you to pull this shit, and you know this bitch, this stupid fucking cunt bitch for less than what, two months?" My voice quavered, "And you're going to marry her!"

I started sobbing. Loud, drawn-out agonizing sobs. I could barely catch my breath, but I had to dump this load. Every other time he had been so mindlessly plastered he wouldn't have comprehended a word. In the past, we would argue about who had to pick up the garbage he'd knocked over, when would he replace that busted cabinet from his last midnight ruckus, why there was no ice in the freezer. Trivial stuff that didn't mean shit. We never talked about why he always drank, why we always fought. Why I needed him to help with Mitchell when he woke up frightened by a nightmare or hobbled home after a beating by that snot-nosed bully at school. Never explained how much I yearned for him by my side, drunk or sober, to care for our child together, to make me his wife. To make me ... something.

I sputtered and squalled all at once. "... having a baby, all by myself. No family, no man. You left me! You left me and you only came home when you were broke or wanting a roof overhead and a warm body to keep you from freezing to death in the winter. Fuck you! I don't want to hear about your problems and how you have been through hell and back to stay sober. I don't want any of your damn religious jabber. I don't want your prayers. I don't want your apologies or your sorry, so, so sorrys."

"What do you want?"

His question clipped me in mid-flight. I'd expected him to soothe my blubbering with a few shallow phrases he learned in his church. I shuddered. Could I say it out loud? All those hours cursing him, wondering when he would stumble home next. Hating him for shirking us and crying alone in my bed, our bed, with a pillow smothering my weeping so I wouldn't disturb Mitchell. Wishing he would return, full of remorse and ready to muscle through life with us. On our team. Drying out or crocked, I didn't care. I just wanted him back.

"I want you! Mike, I want you and me and Mitchell. I want my family!"

Now's the time, girl! Say it now!

I never summoned the courage to say it before. Afraid of the rejection I'd lived with from men since ... since I was a little girl. I don't believe I ever told him I loved him. I'm sure I'd mumbled it across his cheek a half-dozen times or less. Maybe purred "love you" into his ear before we nodded off for the night or to his back as he walked away. Maybe it wasn't until right then I finally understood how badly I loved him. Loved him for who he was, for what he was, with all his faults. No questions. No conditions. No apologies necessary.

"I love you!" My words boxed my ears, and I lowered my voice. "I have always, always, through all of it, I have always loved you. I love you, Mike. Please ..."

More than a regular paycheck or a handyman, I wanted Mike. I wanted him forever – even Mike the drunk. I loved him and wanted him any way I could have him. I'd never confessed that. I never harnessed the strength, or the stupidity, to tell him I loved him. I would have married him on the spot, even in his latest rendition as a bible-thumping bore. If only he would hug me and whisper into my hair he wanted me too.

"Don't you get it? Nobody else but me cares. Nobody cares about you or me or Mitchell but us! Not your church, or your Jesus, or your dumb fucking Sara. She can't give you what I can! She doesn't want a washed-out lush. She won't let you in after you're drinking again next week or next month. Damn it! Listen to me! Look at me! We are a family. A family! Good or bad, for better or for worse, we're all we've got. No one but me gives a shit about you. The real you. No one else but me will tend to you, keep taking you back no matter how wasted, how poor, how terrible you stink. I love you! I love you and I ... I've given up everything for you. You and Mitchell. Can't you see what we've been doing here for the last thirteen years? You can't wash that away! You can't sprinkle yourself with holy water and everything changes. Nothing's different. I love you! Mitchell, only God knows why, he loves you too. You're his daddy. His daddy! He needs you every day. Here with us! Not just every other weekend. I need you! You need us! Jesus don't need you. Sara doesn't know who the fuck you are. I know you. I know who you are. I want you back. It's not too late. It's not too late for us. For all of us."

Mike blanched. His face scrunched in concentration.

I was panting and sobbing all at once. My head throbbed, yet for once, the blood pumping through my veins did not muddle my thoughts or cause pain or exhaustion. It awakened me. It enlightened and inspired me as if filling me with a brilliant light. This is why I'm here. This is my purpose in life! To love this man, to be his woman, to raise our son. A swift wind blew away all the hurts and anger and confusion I'd collected over the years, sucked them out the door, and flung them far beyond the cow pastures and up to the stars.

"I will take you back now, and I will take you back next week and I will take you back when your church boots you out because you've quit saying their prayers." I was empty. Spent. No words left.

Mike's lips pursed as he studied the itty-bitty wire squares of the screen door.

Only one thing raced through my brain.

Now's my chance!

Time to wipe the memory of dishwater Sara out of his skull, gather him in my arms, and remind him how much he loved me. How much he hungered to cradle me in his arms. I just had to steamroll over my pride and throw myself at his feet. He would remember. Everything would come back to him. How we belonged to each other. The smiles, the laughter. The love. We had our share. It hadn't all been ugly.

I did it without thinking, almost an animal instinct. I shoved the screen door open and lunged for him. I couldn't control myself. I was trembling and choking on sobs while tears slid down my cheeks. Mike's eyes locked onto mine, and he stepped backward to dodge the screen door swinging into him. My hands grasped for him as he retreated.

I didn't push him, at least I don't believe I did. When he backed up, his footing fumbled. As I shot toward him, he thrust his arms in front of him. Maybe he was trying to protect himself and ward me off, afraid I was going to smack him or cause him harm. I doubt he was preparing to return my embrace.

I wasn't aiming to hit him. I just had this crushing desire to swaddle him in my arms. To touch him. To cocoon with him the way we used to. That would fix everything.

He jockeyed to catch his balance, except as he struggled, he stepped onto the edge of the stoop, and he toppled backward. I latched onto his wrists and held on for dear life. Then I lost my balance too. We both fell down the porch to the concrete walk. I had a death grip on Mike's hands, so he could not break his fall. I landed on top of him. The back of his head striking the concrete made a muffled thud, like a baseball bat whacking a sofa cushion.

"Oh my God." I laughed and cried all at once. "I'm such a klutz."

We would giggle about this later, I told myself, as we rocked each other to dreamland that night. I let go of his wrists and rolled off him. He didn't say anything. He just kept staring skyward.

"Mike. Hey, I ..."

He was no longer breathing. The blood leaking from his skull slithered across the concrete and swamped the cracks.

In one single, intensely awful instant, it struck me how much my life had changed.

Forever.

17

Johnny picked his way through the weeds and thorn bushes toward me and placed both palms on my shoulders. He led me to the driver's side of the truck and helped me into the cab, then gently scooted me to the passenger's seat next to the window.

Spasms of pain stabbed me. I gaped blindly through the glass, unable to focus on a thing. I must have blacked out because I don't have any memory of the drive through the woods and the roughened countryside, the tattered plastic grocery bags draping the barbed wire, the collapsing barns, the shallow ponds with their brownish-beige stalks of cattails. The sun had died, leaving behind the hot, stagnant air and the sickly sweet stink of summer: rotting watermelon rinds and hay drying in the barn. Twilight had strolled past before dwindling as well, inviting scattered stars to glint and wink. I could only see pitch-darkness by the time we pulled out onto something resembling a traveled roadway, with nothing but the pickup's headlights cutting us a path through the night.

Ellis sat between us, relatively calm and noiseless. I hardly would have noticed if he'd performed a handstand on the dashboard. My thoughts skittered about elsewhere, rambling along forgotten trails overgrown with thorny vines and littered with splintered tree limbs. Johnny drove as we all sat in silence. It didn't matter how many more hours we trekked. Didn't matter where we headed or what happened. I rested my temple against the metal of the car door.

Miles and miles later, we crested a slight hill, and Johnny

veered onto the turnoff for Milesdale. He swung into the gas station. He refueled my tank. He must have paid with his own money, as I was cash poor by then. As a final goodbye and good riddance, Ellis clamped his mouth shut as he slammed the door and stomped off, wringing his hands as if washing himself of me and my troubles. I watched his flapping backpack jiggle away until it disappeared into black shadows.

After refueling, Johnny bound into the driver's seat, keyed the ignition, and gunned the engine. He pulled the lever to Drive and slowly steered my truck into a parking spot underneath a blinding light shining next to the building, its brightness scarcely dimmed by hundreds of moths and other flying insects.

Johnny, his pants still damp up to his thighs and streaked with bits of pond scum, walked to the passenger window and asked if I could drive. I said yes. I said thank you as I searched his eyes for answers and explanations I would never find, not on this green earth. Hot fudge sundae stared back. A lifetime passed between us.

"Let go," he said finally. He spoke calmly and evenly without emotion.

The energy drained out of every muscle in my body and went slack. I couldn't sense my limbs as if I'd left them somewhere else. I sank into my seat. A lifeless lump of emptiness. Then I shattered like a glass vase as tears spilled down my cheeks. "I didn't mean it! I didn't mean to kill him! It was an accident! I don't want him dead!" I howled it out loud.

Johnny lifted his chin as if a creak or a murmur attracted his attention, his gaze zooming in on something far in the distance. His coffee-colored skin captured the gleam of the outdoor lamp. His eyes registered blank when they met my tearful glance. Only his lips moved.

"Let go," he said again.

I relaxed my fists to release him. Was I really holding onto Johnny? Clinging to him like a clump of driftwood floating by? Anything to keep from drowning. He seemed so close. His firm, low voice in my ear. His soft breath tickling my chin. I shook my head in confusion. My tears temporarily blinded me before their flow slowed to a trickle.

I took one last eyeful of Johnny. The window opening framed his face, his chest, his immense biceps, chopping him off right below the elbows. I couldn't see his hands. How could I still have them in mine?

He nodded. A slight smile. He was telling me to let go of his hands. Of the past. To let go of Mike. I felt my fingers clasping something. Yet when I looked at my curled fists in my lap, I found nothing there.

Then he slipped out of reach, gliding beyond the light's glow into the simmering summer evening. I would never see him again.

I sat in my pickup for God knows how long. Gnats flitted in and out of the open windows, landing here and there for a second or two. I swatted at one that kept attempting to dock on my eyelashes. The slap startled me, even though it came from my own palm and left my face stinging amidst the itching from all the dried tear tracks. I didn't bother to wipe off its guts.

I finally mustered the effort to drag myself to the driver's seat, twist the key, jam the pedal, and thrust the lever into Reverse so I could back out of the parking area. Then I shifted forward into Drive and barreled ahead into the night.

The whole trip home, I wept as I prayed over Mike. A memorial service. Not a proper one, with flowers and a preacher.

Kind tributes from friends and neighbors and loved ones. But love. Lots of love, Michael.

I flipped through memories about my Michael until tears clogged my eyes and forced me to pull over as if a summer rainstorm dumped gallons across my windshield, blocking my vision.

Then I thought about Johnny and what he said. What he meant. His words filled my emptiness with a mild hope and kept me from crashing through the guardrail and plunging head-on into a dried-up creek bed on my way home.

You nailed that right, Johnny. It is time. Let go. Time to let go of all the pain. All the disappointment. All the ugliness. If I could only wash it all clean as I did that night before. Untangling the garden hose and spraying the broken concrete by my porch between the steps and the garage door, rinsing away all the blood with all the tears and all the hurt. Except hosing down the concrete doesn't make everything go away. How will I ever scrub away that stain?

I retraced my footprints a thousand times as my four tires spun around that gloomy ride home. I asked myself what I could have changed and when. Could I have altered how anything went down? Not just that night I lost Mike, but could I have changed anything about my entire goddamn life?

Have you ever watched the snow falling, falling, falling as it plummets from heaven above? And suddenly, it switches directions on you, just a slight tack to the left or right. You can barely tell, although if you're paying attention, you can't miss the exact moment the wind shifts.

Usually, we only notice major changes. Like you absentmindedly walk into the street in front of a speeding car. Or the doctor informs you it's cancer, or you arrive home to a deserted house, or the boss says, "You're fired!" More often, change occurs gradually. A marriage that dies out like the embers in the fireplace. Losing your mind one puzzle piece at a time. Best friends leaving messages for each other on their answering machines for weeks until they just hang up when the recording starts. Nothing that jumps out at you or shoves you against a wall. No screaming or smashing shards of glass. Then little by little, step by step, one day or one instant your life drifts off course. And there's no going back.

When did that wind shift on me? Where did I make a wrong turn? Should I have said "No"? Did I stay too long? Should I have tried that? Would Mike be alive if I'd done one single thing differently?

I tweaked this, fiddled with that. Lifted a dusty sheet or pried open a painted-shut drawer.

What's under there? How'd that crop up? Why? Why? Why?

If I'd only let go of Mike that night, maybe he would have thrown his arms back and caught himself, protecting his skull from bashing against the concrete. Maybe he would of suffered just a busted wrist or wrenched back. Instead, I'd held on too long and too tight.

I cradled his mangled head in my lap, drenching my cutoff shorts and T-shirt with his blood. I moaned into his hair, kissing his forehead, his nose, his lips. I begged him to come back.

After grieving for what seemed a lifetime, I clicked into gear. I had to hide Mike before someone stumbled upon him. Somehow I rallied the unearthly strength to drag his body into the freezer. Peel off my clothes and soak them in the cold wash cycle to fend off stains. Hose off all the blood that pooled onto the concrete slab.

Tell no one.

That is one decision I will never second-guess, never regret. That was a horrible accident. Yet I knew how it would look. What everyone would think. I followed my survival instincts.

If I'd called the police, they would have taken Mitchell. Even if I could have justified everything, even if they would have listened, which I'm sure they wouldn't have, not to an unemployed, single mother with bad checks outstanding.

Hide his body. Now!

They would have brought in reinforcements. Harold and his twenty-two-year-old assistant deputy would not have had the resources, the experience, nor Harold the stomach to manage this crime scene on their own. The county emergency vehicles would have parked in my driveway, spilled out into pockmarked Judge Weaver, and blockaded our dead-end road. Red, white and blue lights circling and splashing bucketloads of color across the neighbors' houses and the clusters of cedar trees. Uniformed officers, an ambulance, a body bag. A police photographer snapping pictures one frame after another. Reporters squawking, locals gawking. We would have made the front page of the Cliff City Gazette.

I would have cried. Mitchell would have woken, rubbing his eyes and probably sucking his thumb as an officer blocked him from running to me. From seeing Mike. The blood. Mitchell would have awoken to a nightmare.

I would have tried to describe what transpired. First to one cop, then to a gang of them with their pads of paper and their handcuffs clipped to their belts. Between sobs, or would I have composed myself by then? Numb, my shoulders shaking, teeth chattering in the stillness of the heat, I would have babbled. About the stairs. About the screen door flying open and knocking him off balance. About me fighting to hold onto Mike, to embrace him, to wrap myself around him as if I would never let go.

I would have told them how much I loved him. How I needed him. How I wanted him. How I grabbed for him, but he was already gone. How I couldn't stop him from leaving. How sorry, so, so sorry I was. And would be forever.

No, they would never have listened. They would not have cared. They would have scribbled notes. They would have stared. One cop would have motioned to another. They would have barked into their patrol car radios. They would have led me to a marked car, the flashers lighting up the pre-dawn sky. Harold, his drooping puppy dog face, watching as they hauled me away.

And who all would have testified against me? The neighbors who overheard me and Mike hollering at each other in a rage night after drunken night or Mr. Coble recalling the frequent thunder of angry shouts, crashing objects, and slamming doors? A gas station attendant or two who eavesdropped on us arguing? Or maybe Harold and just about anyone else who'd caught an earful about how I'd had it with Mike and his bullshit. The regulars at Larry's Tavern who laughed as Mike and I cursed and threatened each other up and down?

"Damn," one would scratch his whiskered chin, "I'd never figured she really meant it. I would have ... err ... said somethin' to y'all before all this if I'd any notion she'd go and ... you know ..."

Who would I have called from jail? Sadie? Tammy? They didn't have any money for a lawyer or a bondsman. They couldn't have bailed me out. The state would have tended to me. Shoot! They would have hired me a burned-out birdbrained lawyer in a rumpled suit, hey, maybe the same one they scrounged up for me through the welfare office! What a hoot!

And what would have happened to Mitchell, my adorable, precious best thing that ever happened to me Mitchell, best thing to ever happen to Mike as well? They would have chucked him from one foster home to the next. Would they have let me talk to him? To explain? And what would he have said? What would Mitchell have thought about this mess? What would I have said to him? How could I tell him his daddy died. How I had killed him. How could I ever confess to Mitchell what I'd done? How could I gaze into that beautiful face and those trusting green-gray eyes and tell him? How could I ask him for forgiveness? I ached for forgiveness.

Forgive me, sweet Mitchell, for taking away a father who finally realized all he wanted to do was love you.

How could he understand? He's just a little boy. A smart little boy, except he never would of understood. And then he would have to drag that with him for the rest of his life, knowing his mother, his own momma killed his daddy. He never would have understood. No one would have understood. Do you?

Rolling waves of despair washed over me, and my palms slipped from the wheel. I slumped forward, crushed by the misery and the loss. Then a voice broke through and tossed me a rope.

I'll see you tomorrow.

And an image of him emerged, as clear as if he stood before me. Mitchell smiling at me, giggling, grasping my hand, begging me to push him on the swing some more. Skipping. Pouting when I said no. Shoveling mouthful after mouthful of macaroni and cheese until his cheeks bulged and yellow-tinged drool spurted from the corners of his lips. Kissing his forehead as he slept.

I mustered all the energy I could and thrust aside all the fears, all the guilt, all the hurt.

"Get out of my way!" I shouted. I turned the key and fired up the engine, swerving away from the shoulder into the right-hand lane. My fingers tightened around the wheel as my eyes targeted the road ahead of me.

My foot flattened the gas pedal as the moon began its nighttime tour. It soared in the eastern sky above the horizon. It brightened the heavens and erased many of the stars, permitting only the brilliant ones that sparkled beyond the treetops to the west. The lights of Cliff City flooded the darkness more powerfully than the egg-shaped moon, accenting the skyline with a foggy haze. As I pointed north, the moon kept pace with me, sailing steadily to the right of my truck. I raced it all the way back up the highway. Back home.

18

Today I'm enjoying the heat, if you can believe it, sitting here on my porch steeping in it. Poor man's sauna. That's mid-August at my house. It's hot. Killer hot, according to the radio guy. Another scorcher. The humidity adds weight to the air, blanketing you in a wet towel. You don't want to move much. Slight gusts of wind waft by, but they're good for nothing. The dog days of summer. I'm lazing on my back stoop, sucking in each lungful as if I'm breathing through a damp kitchen rag. Taking a hit from my Marlboro. Mitchell's at Sadie's, so I can sneak one outside without him busting me. I'm trying not to smoke in front of him, as I'm struggling twenty-four-seven at being the best mom possible for my Mitchell.

Sweat runs down my skin as if it has someplace better to go. Even if the air conditioner worked right, I'd still be out here, outside. The bugs flitting about in the bristly foxtail and spotted knapweed are buzzing over this or that, yet it almost seems quiet now that all the cicadas are dead and gone. They shot up from the ground early with the hotter than hot June we just rode out. They had their fun, and now you can't even find their dried-up shells anymore. Not long ago you couldn't cross from here to the mailbox without crunching at least a couple of their corpses under your sneakers. Maybe some varmint's eaten them all. Johnny could probably find some. Johnny is a good finder, a finder of things and loose ends. I'm a finder too. A finder and a keeper. I just find most of it's useless. Usually.

Like the past. Johnny says to let go. Get rid of it. Look out your front windshield, not your rearview mirror. I made that up. Johnny never said anything like that, though he said something to that effect before he walked away from me forever. Johnny's parting advice still caresses my cheek same as a spring breeze.

Why did Johnny show up that day? That one day when I couldn't have coped without him. To move that freezer out of my garage. Once it was too late for any explaining. Too late for apologies. Too late for Mike and me.

Johnny knew. He knew where to dump it. He knew everything. About Mike. About me. He didn't question me. He didn't accuse me of anything. He didn't speak until he came across the right thing to say. He didn't hate me for what I'd done. He didn't judge in the manner anyone else would. He just helped me ferry my burden, and as far as I can tell, he's still sharing the load. Thank God, because I can't bear this on my own.

What happened to Johnny that forced him to learn how to let go?

Maybe Mike brought Johnny into our lives. My guardian angel, my Michael. He saw me drowning, and he called for help. He knew how hopeless my situation had become. He understood what they would do to us, to our Mitchell, if the police barreled in with guns cocked and found Michael dead, lying in a pool of his own blood, his eyes glazed, frozen stiff for eternity. He knew what the police would suspect as they observed me stammering and muttering excuses and explanations. Mike knew. I'm sure it sounds weird, but I get this sense that Mike, sitting on a cloud somewhere, understands what occurred. He knows it was an accident. He knows I love him. And maybe he's sorry he couldn't love me back. He told me as much before he died.

Maybe on his way up to Heaven, he glided by a group of angels, tapped one on the shoulder above his wing, and asked politely. Maybe he had to persuade them. Maybe he had to insist.

"See, I got this problem, yeah, back there, I just can't brush it off. Is there anything we can do?" Maybe that accounts for Johnny.

Momma always said, "God only gives you what you can handle." Maybe God figured me for someone who could only handle so much. Or maybe He realized I'd handled my fair share already.

Yet, I waited for them to come for me. After moving the freezer and dropping off Johnny and Ellis, I nosed my Ford into my driveway as the dawn rose. I threw myself on my bed, lying in the clothes I'd worn since the morning before. I slept until the afternoon, waking when Mitchell bounded into the house with Sadie not far behind cradling a pan of warm brownies, her chunky face knitted into worry lines. All that day and for many days since, I have listened for those sirens and watched for those glaring lights to blast up my driveway and drag me to prison. Sometimes I hear something coming, except it's not for me.

The police sirens did wake us last week. They came for the old man across the street, or at least that's what I assumed. According to Marita, the checkout girl at Velva's, Mr. Coble's personal assistant, not the one with the rhinestone nose stud but the latest one with the tattoos circling her wrists, well, she got hopped up on some bad shit and collapsed on his kitchen floor. So Mr. Coble telephones the ambulance for her. However, the social service people started poking around and decided he needed professional care unavailable from personal assistants who OD on something stolen from a medicine cabinet. Lord knows how long he'll rot in a nursing home, yelling about everything and nothing. Someone stuck a realtor's FOR SALE sign in his yard yesterday.

I scratch my neck at the sweat crawling across my skin like an insect. They say the heatwave will let up soon. They always say that. And funny thing, they're always right. Temperatures will eventually fall as autumn blows in with cooler evenings and refreshing, drenching rains. A tall glass of cold apple juice would be nice, but I'm too lazy to get up and pour myself one. Too busy with memories I can't swallow easily.

Yeah, I bet you're saying, "Shut up already! Enough! Stop reliving the past." Like Johnny tried to tell me. It is time. Let go. Time to move on.

A line of ants troops by me on the concrete walkway, diving temporarily into a crack before popping up and rejoining the parade.

Shit, is that the phone again? A bitch from a collection agency called earlier. I'm expecting to hear from Tammy. I've left two messages on her machine this week already. She'd finally bought herself a cell phone, so maybe she's ignoring her home phone. I can't afford a cell phone yet, just that noisy thing in the kitchen. Might as well answer it. I can always hang up. I plant my cigarette in the grass so it'll die out and I can finish it later.

"'ello," I exhale into the receiver after the screen door smacks behind me.

"Move your lazy ass. Took you five rings."

Speak of the devil. "Your ugly voice is music to my ears."

"Hell with you. Hey, gotta make this short. I'm on company time." Tammy's words barged into each other. "What's up?"

I don't have more to report about our pending move. "Not much. School here starts in a few weeks. When's it start in your area?"

"Fuck if I know. I don't have a brat in school. Anyway, gotta get your butt here first before we fuss with that. You still aiming west?"

"Uh-huh. Gotta hustle up some dough. I'm talking to the unemployment office to see if they'll mail my checks there until I get a job. They've got a shitload of paperwork for me. If I knew I had a job lined up, I wouldn't bother with those assholes. Tough walking away from easy money, though. My checks keep rolling in if I stay." I trace a tomato sauce splatter on the wallpaper that resembles a spider.

"Hmmm. Well, let me know. I'm sure we can dig up work here for you. The Springs is a boomtown nowadays. It's way bigger than Shit City. If you can't get a job where I'm working you'll find something else," Tammy says between hits. What a great gig: she can chat on the company telephone long-distance while smoking!

"Yeah? I need cash to move."

"Got any grand ideas?"

"A yard sale, but I don't know if this junk is worth the hassle." I sandwich the phone between my ear and my shoulder as I scrape at a tiny splinter burrowing into my ring finger.

"How about that fat-ass friend of yours? She could probably spare a few bills."

I wince at Tammy's snide remark. I love Tammy dearly, except I hate how she knocks my Sadie. And I'm ashamed I've considered that already but I'm afraid to ask. "Well I'm working on a plan. Working on it."

I listen to Tammy breathing. We've both run out of things to say. "Well, I better skedaddle before they tan my ass," she says.

"Yeah. Well, anyway. I just wanted to say 'hey.' Catch up and all."

"I miss you too, girlfriend. Nobody here knows how to have a good time the way we do," Tammy says without a lick of sarcasm.

I smile. "Me too."

"I even miss that rugrat of yours. Tell my buddy Auntie Tammy's got a surprise for him when you show up." She chuckles wickedly.

My eyes well up as I laugh along with her. "And what would that be? He ain't legal to drink."

"No, no, you'll love this. It's a fairy tale book I scored at a swap meet. Got drawings. It's about a horny Cinderella who has to fuck every dude in the kingdom to find her prince charming, the one who can make her moan until midnight."

"Damn, girl. You are disgusting. I'm not letting my child around you ever again." We both erupt into thigh-slapping guffaws.

"Hey, it'd make a great porno movie! What do you think? Should we write a screenplay and sell it and make a million bucks? No, no, I'm serious here, quit laughing."

I laugh and laugh and laugh until I practically double over and the tears flow. I'm leaning against my kitchen counter, gabbing on the telephone, staring out my dirty kitchen window. But I taste tequila as I spin side to side on my barstool, clutching at the bar to keep from toppling as we giggle. For a second, I'm running with my reckless younger self, living in the present without a worry for the future or a hoot for the past. I remember who I was before Mike careened into my heart. Before so much changed forever.

"No, listen to me. We could go into business as porno movie

producers. Or the internet maybe. I met this guy here who does websites or ... well, he spends hours on a computer ... oh fuck! I gotta go." The phone clicks before I have a chance to say goodbye.

"Bye, Tam. Love ya," I say into the muted mouthpiece.

I step outside, back into the blazing sun. It's as hot inside as out, even with the window AC rattling. I fish my cigarette out of the grass and relight the end. Four more puffs and it's toast. I stub it into the concrete as I let the last lungful trickle through my lips and float away. Another black mark on this shack. No one will notice one more. Just in time too, as Mitchell skips up the driveway cradling something in his hands.

"Whatcha got, bunny?"

He turns his head, still watching his cupped palms. "A frog. I hope this one don't escape."

"Well, you can't keep him! We don't have no room for a pet in this house."

He shrugs as his gaze remains glued to the frog.

"Be careful with him." As a toddler, Mitchell would capture frogs and accidentally squash the life out of each and every one. Snot running from his nose and his face twisted in confusion, he would cry, "No jump! No jump!" while shoving the limp creatures at me, their glassy eyes bulging after dying a silent death from massive internal injuries.

"I am! I'm holding him the way you showed me. By the legs." Mitchell demonstrates his skill by allowing the frog to pull itself along with only its front legs from one of his scooped hands to the next as Mitchell gently clasps the frog's back legs between his thumb and index finger.

"Be easy on him." It's just a frog, yet my gut twinged every time I found their bloated little bodies after Mitchell abandoned them to the flies and the heat.

He gasps as the frog attempts a getaway. Mitchell maintains a grip on one of the legs as he regains control of the other. He hasn't taken his eyes off the animal. He probably walked the entire stretch from Sadie's with his eyeballs locked onto the frog, stubbing his toes on hunks of loose asphalt and almost tripping over the tall clumps of grass in the ditch beside the road. I chuckle while picturing his journey from Sadie's with his tiny prisoner. Then I complain about the heat.

Mitchell scrunches his face without looking up. "Why aren't you in the house with a fan?"

I don't respond since he won't heed my answer. His captive has him entranced.

"Why don't you let that slimy thing go and let's get us some ice cream or maybe apple juice." I swat at a flying insect scheming to land on my arm.

Mitchell lets the frog squirm from one rounded palm to the next. No doubt he'll tire of it soon enough, so I say nothing. I sit there soaking up the heat like a sponge, the harsh afternoon rays stinging my eyes.

I lift my arm to block the sun so I can size up Mitchell. He turned seven this spring. The buttons on his sleeveless plaid shirt are mismatched, but he's tucked the tails into his cutoffs, so it's hard to tell. His denim cutoffs squish his thighs as they ride high above his spindly knees. Did he sprout another few inches while at Sadie's? His cheeks are pink from the sun and the heat. The tops of his shoulders sport shiny flaming patches, and I'm spoiling to shoo him inside or to a shady spot, yet I leave him in peace. His sun-bleached hair, wild and long as a rock star's, hangs in his eyes. He needs a haircut as soon as I can snag some extra dollars. I certainly won't trim his hair myself like last time. He has a skinned knee, from what I have no idea. He loves to climb trees and chase critters in the woods surrounding our house, although he trots home itching from chigger bites and crawling with ticks. He's learning to read better, though he still follows the words with his fingertip and mouths every syllable. He'll start second grade soon. He stands motionless except for his treadmilling hands.

"You didn't bring me any cookies, did ya'?"

He jiggles the frog. "He peed on me!" Mitchell squeals, his eyes unwavering from his treasure.

"What y'all do this morning?" I half expect him to ignore my question.

"I don't know," he mumbles as he shuffles the frog between his fingers.

I'd go and kiss him, smooth his hair, and smooch his forehead, but I'm too lazy to get up. I love the musky scent of his fresh sweat, the gap left by a lost baby tooth his tongue squeezes through, his velvety skin. I want to hold on to everything about these younger years forever.

"Come here and sit on my lap. Let me hug you. Come here and let me hug my sweet little baby."

He smirks. He doesn't care to be treated like a baby, he regularly informs me. Or he gives me that smirk.

Probably just as well, I sigh to myself. He'll sniff tobacco smoke on my breath, flash that scared grimace and worry about me dying from lung cancer or talking out of my throat, same as the cowboys in those TV ads.

"How's Sadie?"

He parts his lips to speak, then he pauses. His nose wrinkles as he tracks his frog on its endless race. "She's ... OK."

I quiz him about her again, curious why he has muzzled himself. He's too genuine to lie or even hide anything from me.

He blinks as he purses his lips. "She's fine."

You can't fool me, little man.

"Mitchell!" I draw out his name steadily as if unthreading a strand from a spool. He quickly scans my features before veering his eyes to the frog, which is battling more and more frantically for freedom.

"She's ... uh ... kind of sad," he says, retreating from my stare.

I jerk my head in slight exasperation at my boy.

"You didn't tell her, did you," I say without much anger.

He focuses on the frog as it wriggles. "I ... well ... She asked me about school and ... I sort of ..."

"You told her we're moving to Colorado, didn't you?"

The shadow of guilt on his face keeps me from overheating.

"Mitchell, you know I wanted to tell her about that. You knew she'd be upset. I wanted to tell her myself, someway, somehow so she wouldn't get hurt. You know we're her only friends. Her only family. Now what am I going to do?" I cannot raise my voice to him, not these days. I don't dare scold him for his petty mistakes, not after what I've done. Especially not after what I've done to him. To the only daddy he ever knew.

Mitchell frowns, and I immediately regret snapping at him.

"Don't worry," I say, wrestling to appear cheerful. "Besides, who knows. Maybe Sadie will come with us. I'm sure Tammy can make room enough for her until we get a pad of our own."

We both giggle as we picture the four of us sharing a matchbox-sized apartment. Sadie crowding by us to pop a potpie in the toaster oven on a small square of countertop in a kitchen tiny and congested as a closet. Mitchell sticks out his tongue as he quakes with boyish laughter, his attention momentarily wandering. The frog seizes its opportunity by hopping out of Mitchell's prison and plunging into the grass.

"Damn!" Mitchell gasps before peering at me fearfully.

"Young man, watch your mouth or I'll wash it with soap."

"Sorry, Mom."

We embrace each other's gazes for a second before Mitchell darts after the fleeing frog.

Damn. He has Mike's smile. I have my constant reminder of my past, my piece of Mike, my precious little package. He resembles Mike more and more. Or maybe it's my mind toying with me again.

And then I fetch him out of the back of the closet, pull him from his hanger, wrap him around my shoulders and relive the warmth and tenderness before things went so wrong.

I am sorry, Mike. Sorry things ended this way. I will always love you, always miss you. Forever you will be with me. I know you forgive me. And I forgive you. And I'm going to do whatever it takes to be the best mother for him. To love him and remind him daily that he is loved. I owe this to you, Mike. I promise you, Michael, I will repay you. On your watery grave, I swear I will do our son right. I will fill his life with love and hope, not bitterness and disappointment. And I swear to God and all the angels and saints as my witnesses, I will never raise a hand to him again.

My eyes mist. I wipe at a lone teardrop, praying Mitchell chases his frog awhile longer so he won't see me like this. So he won't see my expression and instantly know who floats before me.

I can't help myself. Memories of Mike walk up, and I can't shoo them away. Memories I'll never let go of. Never want to let go. Mike tickling me until I would almost pee in my pants. His Willie Nelson impersonation. Watching him sleep. The Sunday we made love in the shower. That time he collapsed after lugging a wooden coffee table I nabbed at an estate auction, shouting he'd busted his back and him lying on the floor all afternoon insisting I feed him by hand, spooning beer through his lips with most spilling down his cheeks and into his hair until I threatened to call an ambulance. The way I would catch him staring at me in awe as if I were a delicate red rose in full bloom.

And then the screaming matches and the broken things, although I'm trying to shake all that ugly stuff. The loneliness. The aching. The emptiness. The nothingness. I'm afraid I will carry those around with me for a long time until I can find somewhere to dump them as well.

The End.

Book Club Discussion Questions

1. Do you have sympathy for the narrator, Cathy? If yes, why? No, why not? If yes and no, explain.

2. Does your opinion of the narrator, Cathy, change during the book?

3. At the end of Moving Men, the narrator addresses the reader directly. How would you respond to her? What would you say to her at different points in the book if you could speak to her?

4. Moving Men portrays men in different negative roles including: absentee father, seducer, bully. Which character representing some or all these roles did you react to the most?

5. Moving Men portrays men in different positive roles including: Good Samaritan, friend, penitent. Which character representing some or all these roles did you react to the most?

6. What were the various roles played by the character Mike and how did that change throughout the book?

7. How would you describe the friendships between the narrator, Cathy, and Tammy? Between Cathy and her neighbor Sadie or her high school friends?

8. How did Cathy's family history influence her decisions while single? While living with Mike? While a mother?

9. Who is Johnny? And why did he help Cathy, no questions asked?

10. What do you think is going to happen to Cathy after the book ends?

thank you thank you thank you

to everyone who has helped me in my quest to tell this story, but thanks above all

JOAN ASBEE

ANN ROBINSON

KELLY MERRITT

KYLE K. MANN

CHARLES R. DONALDSON

MY AMAZING CHILDREN NICK & MAGGIE

MY EVER-PATIENT & LOVING MOM & DAD

and FLYING TREES PUBLISHING

ABOUT THE AUTHOR

Karene Horst

As a fourth-grader, Karene Horst decided she wanted to be a writer when she grew up, and it's been downhill ever since.

Karene is a contributing editor for GonzoToday.com, an online magazine on culture, politics and music. Her debut novel Moving Men is a 2023 Wishing Shelf Book Award winner.

A Californian by birth and by choice, Karene grew up in Santa Monica. She moved to the Midwest to finish college and wound up in the Ozarks for three decades. When not traveling in her van to the beach and around North America or wandering out of the country, Karene now lives and plays in the mountains of Southern California snowboarding, skiing, hiking, kayaking and mountain biking while dodging rattlesnakes and wildfires.

Read more from Karene or contact her via:
flyingtreespublishing.com/karene-horst
flyingtreespublishing@gmail.com
facebook @authorkarenehorst

www.ingramcontent.com/pod-product-compliance
Lightning Source LLC
LaVergne TN
LVHW091119080826
845145LV00008B/1972

* 9 7 8 1 9 5 5 5 5 2 0 1 1 *